Praise for The Chrysalis

"Lawyer Terrell's first novel is a gem of suspense. . . . An entertaining read."

—*Library Journal*

"[*The Chrysalis*] builds in intensity to an exciting climax. Rich details about the art-auction business and case law are woven throughout this fascinating debut."

—*Booklist*

"Quick, sure images, tight storytelling, solid suspense."

—STEVE BERRY, author of *The Charlemagne Pursuit*

"Lawyer turned author Heather Terrell employs her vast legal experience in this engrossing debut thriller. . . . The result is a compelling, fast-paced mystery filled with twists."

—*Romantic Times*

"Think *The Da Vinci Code* meets *Girl With a Pearl Earring*. . . . [An] accessible, fast-paced romp through the upper crust of the collecting world."

—*Pittsburgh* magazine

"Flemish art, Nazi skulduggery, and American money—in *The Chrysalis*, Heather Terrell follows the path of a famous painting through an important period of history that must not be forgotten, and interweaves the stories of three centuries into a dark cocoon of intrigue and suspense."

—KATHERINE NEVILLE, author of *The Fire*

"A tale that's not only 'ripped from the headlines' but captures some of that *Da Vinci Code* cachet."
—*Pittsburgh Post-Gazette*

"Part mystery and part legal drama, *The Chrysalis* is a noteworthy, dramatic debut from an impressive author."
—Bookreporter.com

"One of those rare thrillers that both entertain and intrigue."
—TESS GERRITSEN, author of *The Keepsake*

"Heather Terrell has taken a legal thriller and turned it into a masterpiece of art, history, and the amazing deception born in the face of love and money. A fabulous debut from a talented new author."
—Curled Up With a Good Book

"This story of deception, intrigue, greed and dishonor holds the reader's attention from the first page to the last. . . . The next in the series can't arrive too soon."
—BookLoons

"Strong and realistic characters . . . [Terrell] has richly detailed these widely differing historical times and has produced a thriller that is also a romance."
—ReviewingtheEvidence.com

"The author educates as well as entertains her audience at a level anyone who is not a lawyer or an art student can understand. . . . Extremely well done."
—The Mystery Reader

Praise for THE MAP THIEF

"Terrell's fascinating mystery spans centuries and takes readers on a tour of ancient cities and archeological digs and through the hearts of emperors and kingmakers. . . . A thrilling ride from the boardrooms of New York to an ancient burial site in China."
—*Romantic Times*

"Heather Terrell's new thriller moves effortlessly through time as she maps out a suspenseful novel that's as smart and well-written as it is inventive, original, and surprising. *The Map Thief* cements Terrell's position as one of the genre's up-and-coming stars."
—M. J. ROSE, author of *The Reincarnationist*

"A rip-roaring read . . . In a richly detailed fashion, [Terrell] weaves truth with fiction and paints a vivid picture. . . . This is one exciting and informative read."
—Fredericksburg *Free-Lance Star*

"Provocative, well-documented, and evocative."
—JAVIER SIERRA, author of *The Secret Supper*

"The premise, quite plausible, is that the Chinese did much more exploration than historians know about . . . Clever plot, well told tale."
—*Crimespree Magazine*

"Terrell has transformed her series into something much more than that of a legal thriller. . . . The combination of actual historical fact and her distinctive new direction for the series make this a captivating thriller."
—BookBitch

"Artfully arranged . . . accurate in the smallest detail . . . Deception, intrigue, and treachery at every turn keep the main characters high stepping throughout this adventure. . . . This is a must read and one that will keep you thoroughly entertained."
—*Midwest Book Review*

ALSO BY HEATHER TERRELL

The Chrysalis
Brigid of Kildare

THE
MAP THIEF

A Novel

HEATHER
TERRELL

BALLANTINE BOOKS • NEW YORK

The Map Thief is a work of historical fiction. Apart from the well-known actual people, events, and locales that figure in the narrative, all names, characters, places, and incidents are the products of the author's imagination or are used fictitiously. Any resemblance to current events or locales, or to living persons, is entirely coincidental.

2009 Ballantine Books Mass Market Edition

Published in the United States by Ballantine Books, an imprint of The Random House Publishing Group, a division of Random House, Inc., New York.

BALLANTINE and colophon are registered trademarks of Random House, Inc.

Originally published in hardcover in the United States by Ballantine Books, an imprint of The Random House Publishing Group, a division of Random House, Inc., in 2008.

This book contains an excerpt from the forthcoming hardcover edition of *Brigid of Kildare* by Heather Terrell. This excerpt has been set for this edition only and may not reflect the final content of the forthcoming edition.

ISBN 978-0-345-49469-6

Printed in the United States of America

www.ballantinebooks.com

For Jim and Jack

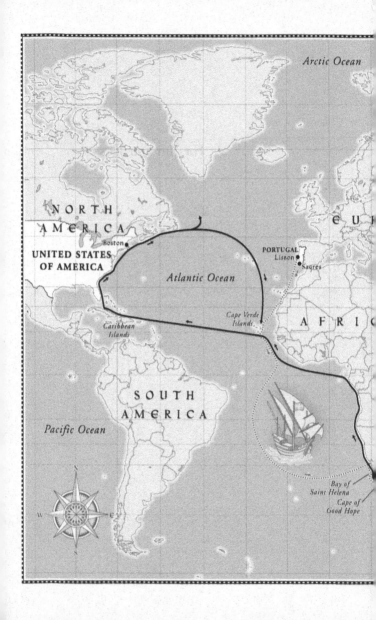

Arctic Ocean

NORTH
AMERICA

Boston

UNITED STATES
OF AMERICA

Atlantic Ocean

PORTUGAL
Lisbon
Sagres

EU

Caribbean
Islands

Cape Verde
Islands

AFRIC

SOUTH
AMERICA

Pacific Ocean

Bay of
Saint Helena
Cape of
Good Hope

N
W   E
S

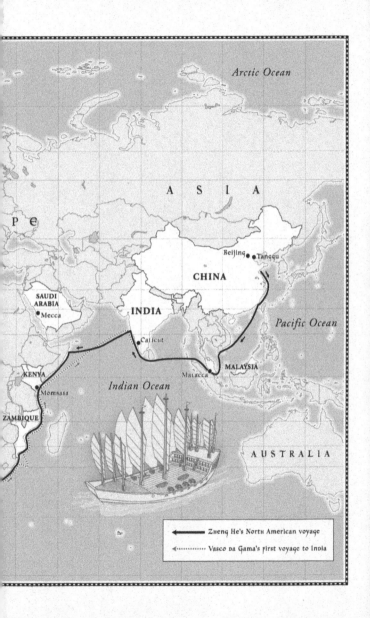

Arctic Ocean

A S I A

P e

CHINA

Beijing Tanggu

SAUDI
ARABIA
Mecca

INDIA

Pacific Ocean

Calicut

KENYA
Mombasa

MALAYSIA
Malacca

Indian Ocean

ZAMBIQUE

AUSTRALIA

Zheng He's North American voyage

Vasco da Gama's first voyage to India

The Mongolian steppes thunder as three hundred thousand horses charge across the plains. The ground vibrates from the unison marching of the nearly one million foot soldiers that follow in the cavalry's wake. The arid soil of the steppes cracks under the army's weight, and opens into countless new chasms.

Without warning, the air grows silent, and the multitudes part. A towering figure on horseback cloaked in vibrant yellow gallops to the front of the ranks. It is Emperor Yongle, His Imperial Majesty of China, heir to the Dragon Throne and the Son of Heaven.

The emperor knows that he should not ride unprotected across the steppes. He knows that he should ride shielded from sight, as mere mortals are forbidden to look upon the Son of Heaven. But he loves the fight, and he understands this battle against the rebel Mongol leader may be his last.

Yet the emperor cannot help but believe that the gods will favor him with one more victory, as they have done so often in the past. And he must triumph against the insurgent Mongol forces outside on the battlefield in order to triumph against his political adversaries, the mandarins, inside his own kingdom.

For the mandarins have been whispering that the rebellion is a sign that the gods have forsaken the emperor and his grand plans. The emperor must vanquish the rebels and prove the mandarins wrong before his pliable son and chosen successor, Zhu Gaozhi, starts listening to their whispers and abandons the emperor's projects when he ascends the Dragon Throne.

The aging emperor cannot allow this to happen. He must protect his beloved monuments, the Forbidden City and Great Wall among them, which declare China's might to the world. He must keep intact the vast empire of tribute and trade he so carefully reconstructed after centuries of neglect. Most of all, he must safeguard his beloved navy, the largest and most advanced the world has ever known, and its plans for far-reaching voyages.

The gods know that he has only ever wanted to make his people have faith in their own rule after so many years of foreign Mongol domination. He must make the Mongol rebels kowtow to him, so that his glorious legacy will not be lost to the mandarins' self-serving schemings when Zhu Gaozhi becomes the Son of Heaven.

The battle horns cry out, and the air reverberates with their sound. The emperor places his hand on the hilt of his sword, ready to fight alongside the soldiers as if he were a mere mortal. He longs for victory, but if he is to die, he will die on these steppes and not caged within the Forbidden City like some rarefied bird.

The fast clap of a horse interrupts the herald of the horns. The emperor wonders who dares to disrupt this moment, *his* moment. He turns to see his general dismounting and kneeling at his side.

"Your Imperial Majesty, it is not fitting that you should head the troops. I beg that you allow me to lead the charge against the rebel Mongols."

Staring down at the general, the emperor's legendary black eyes flash in anger. "Never forget that *I* am the Son of Heaven. I will ride out among the men." He watches until the general backs away.

The emperor looks out onto the battlefield. He regrets only that his trusted adviser, Admiral Zheng He, cannot ride alongside him in what could well be his last moments. But Zheng cannot. The emperor has other plans for him.

Emperor Yongle smiles as he unsheathes his sword, spurs on his horse, and roars to the army to follow his lead. He is a dreamer and a gambler, and he will die as he has lived. He leaves it to the gods to decide his fate and his legacy to China.

Mara marched across the conference room. She let the door slam behind her like an exclamation point. She needed to make sure that her clients, the Republic of Cyprus and the famed Mallory Museum, understood her last proposal to be exactly that, her last.

She had delivered her ultimatum with bravado, after tossing the incriminating photographs across the table. But now, as she walked down the long hallway to her office, the boldness slipped off her. Mara wondered whether she had chosen the right negotiating tactic. She had bandied about the prospect of a lawsuit against the museum if the parties could not agree to terms, but she really wanted the parties to reach a resolution without litigation. She no longer trusted the court system to render justice for either client. For any client.

Mara waved off her assistant, Peggy, and walked into her office, shutting the door behind her. She sat at her desk, took note of the time, and told herself that she would wait exactly thirty minutes before returning to the conference room. That should give the ambassador of Cyprus, the head of the Cypriot Church, and the director of the Mallory Museum time enough to consider her proposition. And time for her to formulate a next step should they decline it.

Joe's distinctive knock sounded on her door. Mara

would have been angered by anyone else's interruption. She didn't like anyone to see the apprehension beneath her self-confident veneer. But Joe knew that he needn't worry; he had seen all sides of her.

The former FBI director lumbered in, his paunchy stomach protruding from the open jacket of his rumpled gray suit. "How's it goin' in there?" From his shambling appearance and nonthreatening demeanor, an onlooker would never guess the nature of his prior profession. And that was exactly Joe's intention. He fostered this misperception, using it to lull his subjects to complacency while circling in for the kill.

"As you'd suspect," Mara answered.

"Gave 'em that last proposal we came up with last night, huh?" he asked, his speech thick with a New York accent—Brooklyn, as he was quick to point out.

"Yes. You should've seen the shell-shocked looks on their faces. I had to get out of there to let them stew."

"Ah, they'll bite. You think that fancy museum wants the public to think it's no better than some grave robber? Nah." He chuckled, no doubt thinking of the august Mallory Museum smeared with a damaging suit.

Mara didn't answer. Instead, she raked her hand through her newly shorn hair as she mulled over their strategy. Out of habit, her fingers continued on past her shoulder, as if the missing hair still lay there.

Joe heaved himself off the chair. "You'll do great," he said, closing the door behind him.

Mara spun her desk chair around so that she faced toward the window with its breathtaking view of Central Park. She needed to turn away from the distracting files of other clients—auction houses, dealers, collectors, and governments all wanting Mara to resolve their conflicts—to focus on the matter at hand. The Republic of Cyprus and the Mallory Museum needed to secretly settle a dispute over certain fourteenth-century Cypriot icons that had wormed their way into the museum's collection from an art dealer that Cyprus now held in custody. Both parties believed they could achieve the most advantageous settlement if they negotiated quietly and creatively; hence, they'd decided to hire Mara Coyne and her unorthodox firm.

Mara heard another, fainter knock at the door. She assumed Joe had one last piece of advice to offer; he usually did. "Come on in," she said, without turning back toward the door.

"Mara, you have a call."

Mara swung around, not bothering to mask her irritation at Peggy's uncharacteristic interruption. "You know I'm in the middle of a settlement negotiation. I can't take a call."

"And *you* know I wouldn't disrupt you unless I had to." Peggy could give as good as she could get, one of the qualities Mara loved about her. Usually. "It's Richard Tobias."

"Richard Tobias?" With her mind focused on the Cyprus case, the name meant nothing to Mara. She was about to tell Peggy to take a message when the caller's identity dawned on her—it was the legendary conservative kingmaker.

She grabbed for the phone. "Good afternoon, Mr. Tobias. This is Mara Coyne. What can I do for you?"

"I am in need of your services."

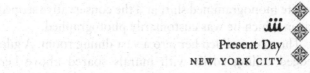

iii

Present Day

NEW YORK CITY

Of course Richard Tobias wanted to meet at "his usual haunt," the hallowed Metropolitan Club, Mara thought to herself. Richard was not one to let his privileged toes touch any unsavory public aspect of New York. She'd once read an interview in which he called Manhattan a "heathen" city and had envisioned him shuddering at the thought of people actually living amid its perceived squalor.

Richard had extended an invitation for Mara to join him for dinner. She had called back to accept only after the Cypriots and the Mallory Museum had tentatively agreed to her proposal. Her cab pulled up to the bustling, tourist-laden corner of Fifth Avenue and Sixtieth Street, a surprising location for the ultraprivate club. When it was built in 1894, however, enormous mansions had populated Fifth Avenue, rather than destinations for sightseers and the nouveau riche.

Mara let a formally dressed doorman take her elbow as she got out of the cab. She then walked through the open courtyard to the entrance. A concierge welcomed her, asked for the name of her dinner date, and helped her off with her lightweight overcoat. Underneath, Mara had dressed to fit the expected part, in a traditional, black bouclé dinner suit that she knew accentuated her blue-green eyes. She assumed that Richard would be kitted out in the expertly tailored charcoal suit with a white monogrammed shirt and the conservative striped tie in which he was customarily photographed.

The maître d' led her into a vast dining room. A gilt-edged ceiling adrift with murals soared above her. Heavy velvet tapestries framed the twelve-foot-high windows, keeping the outside world at bay. An ornate marble fireplace so tall she could nearly step into it dominated one wall, while cameo-like medallions decorated the other. And sconces, expertly lit with the flicker of candlelight, were everywhere. Yet for all its beauty, the decor was a touch musty, almost intentionally so. As if the patrons found flawless furnishing to be the upstart trappings of an arriviste.

The maître d' gestured to a desirable center table. There sat the silver-haired Richard Tobias. He looked precisely as she had imagined him.

Until he stood up. All five foot six of him. Mara was shocked, having expected Richard Tobias's height to match his stature. She thought how he must love the trimmings of wealth and power; they added the illusion of height to his tiny frame.

He stretched out his hand to shake hers in welcome. "Miss Coyne. So good of you to come."

"Mr. Tobias. It's an honor."

"Please, Miss Coyne, call me Richard."

The name Richard Tobias brought back a flood of memories from Mara's childhood. Mara's father—a first-generation Irish immigrant turned Republican—had become involved with a behind-the-scenes alliance to back a cadre of local Boston political candidates with a slate of conservative positions. Her father had mentioned Richard's name at that time, and Mara associated it with the secretive planning sessions that launched her father into the political arena, albeit as a contributor and minor player. Richard operated on a far grander scale than her father, more as a national puppeteer. At least that's what the scant articles about and interviews with the reserved figure suggested, as well as her father's innuendos.

He gestured for her to sit, and as she did she felt his steely eyes on her tall, slim form and lightly freckled cheeks. "You're younger than I thought you'd be. Given your reputation."

Resisting the temptation to retort that he was shorter than she thought he'd be, she smiled instead. "I guess I'll take that as a compliment."

She and Richard spent the first minutes perusing the menu and savoring the impeccable service, nearly invisible yet intuitively attentive. Their exchange of pleasantries, which curiously contained no mention of her father, seemed interminable to Mara, who was usually too rushed to engage in social niceties. Yet she knew better than to reveal her impatience, as she sensed that Richard expected her to play the role of deferential daughter figure. She knew how to perform it well, as she used to do so regularly with her father, before he became irritated by her walking away from the path of law firm partner.

Mara waited for Richard to broach the cause for their meeting, though she had already guessed at the reason. Legend had it that the wealthy patrician possessed an art collection rivaling some of the nation's top museums, so she deduced that he had inadvertently acquired a piece with a controversial past. And hoped she might broker a quiet resolution. After all, her firm had garnered a reputation for precisely such work, in certain hushed circles. "I mentioned that I am in need of your services."

"Yes." She kept her eyes down and stirred her tea, wondering whether a Nazi past tainted his Renoir, or a church-desecration charge plagued his sixteenth-century Netherlandish religious triptych. Mara heard the curlicued rococo clock on the fireplace mantel tick as she waited for what seemed like a confession.

"I will require your firm's most circumspect services."

"We pride ourselves on our discretion."

He nodded once in confirmation. "Excellent. I understood that privacy was your calling card."

"How can we help you?"

Richard lowered his voice as he answered: "I hope I am not being presumptuous in assuming that you are aware of the political work I do."

"Of course not, Mr.—" Mara stumbled on his first name. "Richard." Even if Mara did not have a childhood familiarity with Richard Tobias, as an average follower of the nation's political scene, she would have read his name in news articles covering national elections. Or she might have seen him in the background of a group picture with the president or a dinner with a senator. Never the foreground.

"You may not be as familiar with my other vocation. As I grow closer and closer to meeting my Maker, my conscience has reared up. It has demanded that I use part of my assets to start a foundation funding certain archaeological digs and historical research. One of these digs is located in China on the famed Silk Road.

"I received two urgent calls over the past two days. In the first, I learned that the chief archaeologist at the site had unearthed a map memorializing the voyage of a fifteenth-century Ming dynasty admiral, Zheng He. The map was allegedly created sometime in the 1420s and depicts the world then known to the Chinese—Asia, parts of the Arabic world and Africa, and a rough outline of other regions. If this is true, the map would be one of the earliest even partial world maps in history."

In her shock, Mara forgot her expected role and interjected, "Such a map would be priceless." She remembered that she was no cartographical expert and backtracked: "I would guess."

"One would think," he said dryly. "In the second phone call, I was told that the map was stolen from the site the very evening I learned of its discovery: last evening. I would like to hire you to locate the map—if it indeed exists—and return it to me. Cost is not to be spared. I am not concerned with your methods, but publicity is not an option. In particular, I would like to keep the robbery from the Chinese government. A major theft might jeopardize my foundation's right to dig at the site."

Mara withdrew into her chair. How had someone like Richard learned of the other side of her work? Her firm's main function was to dispense swift, fair, and private dispute resolution for clients engaged in some of the thorniest battles over plundered art and artifa For other clients, it lobbied for legislation tha roughen the passage of purloined pieces into legitimate markets, a brisk business with the stolen-art trade bustling at $6 billion per year. Yet these two types of assignments represented only part of the firm's work—the aboveboard part. When required, to return art to those clients Mara believed were its true owners, her firm operated in a gray netherworld—neither on the side of the law nor on the side of the criminals. Mara dealt with thieves, fences, and the collectors who commissioned crimes to track down pieces; the art criminals talked to Mara because they knew that her work might stave off a more official investigation and that she would keep their secrets. Her goal was not their prosecution—her experience with the life-altering *Chrysalis* case had left her too jaded for that—but the satisfaction of placing a stolen piece back into its owner's hands.

Since Richard comprehended the full scope of her work, Mara dropped the reverent role-playing. If he was hiring her to dive deep into murky waters, then he must appreciate her ability to withstand the pressure and the dim visibility.

"Publicity is never an option for my clients. You must know that. That's one reason they choose my firm. Among many." She watched as Richard's eyes narrowed in assessment of her.

When Richard answered, his paternal tone was gone, replaced by a brusque, somber one. "Good. We understand each other."

Mara paused before stating her nonnegotiable condition to the engagement. "You also understand, I assume, that I handle matters only for clients who I believe will rightfully own or return the stolen item?"

"Of course," he answered without hesitation. "I need

you to leave for China tomorrow to meet with the archaeologist and begin your investigation. Are you able to do so?"

"Yes." For a prominent client like Richard, who could beget other like clients, Mara could manage a hasty departure.

"Then we have an agreement."

His brush freezes in mid-stroke as he hears the call to prayer. The muezzin's cry swoops like a hawk up and over the sloping roofs gleaming with the imperial yellow tiles, and around the protective roar of the dragons and phoenixes guarding every roof corner. It comes through the red-lacquered pillars lining the corridors to the studio, and beckons him to stop his calligraphy practice, retire to the worship room, face Mecca, and pray.

He knows he should rise and join the others, yet he continues. The eye of the calligraphy tutor will see any defect in the creation of the character, any hesitation in his stroke, even if the resulting character appears flawless. His calligraphy must be perfect if he is to be chosen for Admiral Zheng He's upcoming voyage. And he must be chosen if he is to restore honor to his family.

He lowers his brush back down to the silk scroll, flicks his wrist, and finishes the character. He then runs his brush across the inkstone, pulls back the sleeve of his robe with his left hand, and places his right wrist on the rest. He places his brush higher up on the scroll and pushes off, onto the next character. With a few careful but fluid strokes, he completes his practice of "Peach Blossom Spring." After quickly returning his tools to their rightful place in the studio, he inspects his work. He hopes the tutor will find that it meets the standards of the Official Style.

With little time left before prayer begins, he darts down the corridor in such haste that he forgets to walk with the mandated pigeon step. Craning his neck to see if his gaffe has been observed, he sees that he is alone, a rarity in the immense, bustling complex where every move of every inhabitant is weighed and judged according to a centuries-old code of conduct.

He adopts the pigeon step and moves with a small, hesitant, soundless tread. As fast as it will permit, he hurries through the maze of hallways. He passes the hordes of artisans and laborers rushing to finish their tasks before the emissaries of foreign countries arrive in a few months' time to celebrate the unveiling of the Forbidden City on New Year's Day, 2 February 1421.

He slides into the room reserved for worship, drops down to his knees onto an empty mat in the back, and touches his forehead to the ground. His supplications include a plea that no one has witnessed his late arrival. He cannot afford any ill reports to tarnish his name. Peering out from beneath the black, winglike flaps of his official headwear, he scans the room. Prayer seems to absorb the other Muslim eunuchs.

He hears his name whispered as he readies to leave the prayer room: "Ma Zhi."

It is Ma Liang, his friend and fellow Yunnan kinsman of Muslim, or Hui, descent. Islam had come to Zhi and Liang's home village of Kunyang when Genghis Khan and his Mongol forces swept across Yunnan. Yet only Emperor Yongle's policy of religious tolerance—allowing the practice of Buddhism, Lamaism, Confucianism, Taoism, and Islam—permits them to worship within the walls of the Forbidden City.

Liang is one of the few Zhi trusts among the eunuch ranks, so rife with all forms of conspiracies, from the petty, clucking rivalries of the old-womanly eunuchs to the militaristic maneuverings of the younger ones, who still cling to the vestiges of masculinity before time turns them soft.

"So late to prayer?" Liang asks.

" 'Peach Blossom Spring' practice."

"Ah, the Tao path poem." Liang nods in understanding and forgiveness. The studies necessary to become a mapmaker—calligraphy, navigation, geography, cartography, and astronomy—have been a form of worship for Zhi for the nearly five years of his imperial service. He needs to dedicate all the time he can manage in between his official duties to his master. Especially now that Admiral Zheng's selection of officers for the sixth imperial expedition is imminent.

"Did anyone else see?"

"No. Only me."

Relief courses through Zhi; he knows that a single slip could mean disqualification from the admiral's consideration process. "Allah be praised. Come, we must hurry to the afternoon meal." The friends accelerate their pace, never lifting their eyes above the flagstone walkways of the walled Imperial City, which encloses the Forbidden City. Still, the young men manage to wind their way expertly through the labyrinth of seemingly identical red doorways to reach their assigned courtyard.

They enter their square, just southwest of the Beian Gate. The open space sits adjacent to the building housing the Silijian, or Imperial Ceremonial Directorate, the prestigious eunuch agency in charge of all imperial policies, where Zhi and Liang work.

They scurry by the directorate and approach the substantial teak dining and sleeping buildings designated for them. Each time he passes the newly erected structures, Zhi thinks of his good fortune: as a young eunuch, he could have been allotted to the kitchens or gardens, or allocated to a junior concubine and have to live in a makeshift hut, like that of his family at home. Instead, he was assigned to serve the only agency offering the promising opportunity to study with Hanlin Academy scholars.

The clink of gambling tiles grows louder as they near the dining house. The sound stops as a somber sea of rough-hewn navy robes are set in motion and the menial eunuchs who serve the meals rise from their game of Ma Diao Pai. They bow low to acknowledge Zhi and Liang, in the constant recognition of rank the Imperial and Forbidden Cities mandate.

The friends' eyes meet with the same thought: if the kitchen eunuchs await completion of the meal outside, then it has already been served inside. The bamboo rod has punished lesser offenses than late arrival to mealtime. With reluctant steps, the two pass through the doorway.

The young men are ordered to kowtow to the agency director. They rush to prostrate themselves and knock their foreheads on the flagstones in the direction of a red robe embroidered with a fierce python. Director

Tang waves the bamboo rod before them, but then nods to signal his appeasement. It is an unprecedented act of leniency.

The men retreat into seats in the farthest corner of the room. A glorious, unusual aroma wafts down the table. It smells vaguely familiar to Zhi, like the roast mutton with scallions from the emperor's own kitchens they once had the fortune to try. The bowl passes to Zhi and Liang. It is indeed a mutton dish, a castoff from the imperial table. Of the hundreds of dishes that parade by His Imperial Majesty at every meal, he selects only a few. The emperor leaves the remainder to his wives and concubines, then to the court officials, and finally to the senior eunuchs if all others reject them.

The young men dip their chopsticks into the bowl. As they begin to share in the emperor's delicacies, Zhi stops and thinks of his parents and brothers. In his grandparents' days—when the Mongols reigned and Islamic families held positions of prominence in the Yunnan region—the Ma family had dined on meat regularly. During Zhi's youth, however, when the Ma family fell in standing, they subsisted on rice and seasonal vegetables and ate meat only for special celebrations. He hopes that the taels his family receives from his imperial service allow them the luxury more frequently. For his family and their betterment, he thinks, the sacrifice of his manhood was insignificant.

A gong sounds. The shrill chatter of their fellow diners quiets to rice-papery whisperings. Then a hush descends on the group as Director Tang readies for an announcement.

"Our Emperor Yongle, the Son of Heaven, has given us back the splendor of China. His honored father,

Emperor Hongwu, drove the barbarian Mongols from our country, but it is His Imperial Majesty who restored to us our magnificent Great Wall, enlarged the Grand Canal uniting all of China, and built this Imperial City, with the Forbidden City at its heart center. The emperor also brought back honor to his loyal servants the eunuchs."

Zhi watches from beneath the rim of his headgear as his fellow eunuchs nod in proud agreement. Emperor Hongwu had relegated eunuchs to the lowest of positions, placing mandarins in the senior governmental roles. Only under Emperor Yongle have the eunuchs resumed power, controlling foreign policy and advocating its importance. Since then, they have taken full advantage of the fact that, as genderless males unable to threaten the imperial primogeniture, they alone may reside and work in close proximity to the emperor inside the palace complex enclosing the Forbidden City.

"The emperor sees fit to honor this directorate further. As His Imperial Majesty readies the Forbidden City for its unveiling, he also prepares a new fleet of ships for an unprecedented journey under the command of Admiral Zheng. After returning the honored ambassadors here for the Forbidden City celebrations to their home countries, the fleet will survey the entire world and bring all worthy subjects into the Emperor's glorious tribute system. Our agency is privileged that His Imperial Majesty will consider certain lowly servants from our ranks for this expedition."

Director Tang extends his hand, and one of the lesser eunuchs places a scroll into his palm. The room grows silent, and the director unrolls the scroll slowly—so slowly that Zhi is certain the other eunuchs can hear his heart pounding. "Yang Lian, Wei Zhongxian, Wang Yanzhi, Zuo Qiuming, Liu Zhong, Wang Ruoyu . . ."

Zhi waits and waits as the director recites the long list of candidates. With each name, he becomes more anxious and silently beseeches Allah that his name be spoken.

". . . finally, among them will be Ma Zhi. If any of these unworthy candidates pass the examination, they will be considered for the position of assistant to a fleet mapmaker on the voyage of Admiral Zheng."

"Is this really the best plan we can come up with?" Mara looked around the conference room. Dawn had crested over the roofs of the nearby buildings, sending a dim haze of sunlight over the boardroom table strewn with coffee cups and papers.

It was the morning after her dinner with Richard. Mara had been holed up with her team in the conference room since she'd left him at the Metropolitan Club. They had only a rough strategy to show for their efforts, and Mara was tired and increasingly apprehensive as her flight time neared.

As soon as she blurted out the sarcastic question, she regretted it. Mara knew that no one could undertake the complicated, sensitive work that she demanded of her colleagues every day, with every new matter. She required that they step outside the parameters of their varied talents—art history, criminology, and the law—and pool their knowledge to answer the key question: who had the motivation to steal the artwork?

For Mara believed that they could find the art thief if they understood the artwork's history, meaning, and marketplace: its creator's intentions, its potential patrons and collectors, its past and current historical and political impact, even its symbolism. Only then could they track it down, negotiate for its recovery, and return it to its true owners. And they did all this under intense time pressure.

Before she could apologize, Joe answered her with a gruff tone just as annoyed as her own. "You know better than to ask a stupid question like that. *Mister* Tobias gave you zilch to go on, so we can't do a damn thing but hand you the basics." He met Mara's stare with his hazel eyes, though fatigue and irritation robbed them of their usual bright twinkle.

"You're right, Joe." She gave him an appeasing look, though she knew he'd forgive her. They had known each other for only three years—since the fallout of the *Chrysalis* case, which had derailed her career as an attorney and placed her on this new path—but they had forged a strong, almost familial bond during that time, as each had been essentially alone. When they first met, Joe was the director of the FBI Art Crime Unit, heading up the investigation into the fraud perpetrated by Mara's former client, the esteemed art auction house Beazley's. During the proceedings, Mara found an unlikely, sympathetic ally in Joe, and when he told her of his plans to retire at the case's conclusion, she conceived of the idea of her firm. To her surprise, he agreed—with the caveat that Mara would serve as the front person, with Joe in the background schooling her in the art underworld and networking her with his contacts. Joe was too well known a figure to be the face of the firm himself. And to her further surprise, she loved the work, even though it was a departure from the safe world of law-firm practice. Or maybe because of it.

"I'm sorry, guys. I'm just exhausted, but that's no excuse. We're all beat." They had worked side by side through the night to form the best strategy possible in the circumstances. While Mara was able to assume whatever role worked best with clients, her eagerness to restore the artwork often made it hard for her to control her impatience with her own team.

"No need to apologize, Mara," Bruce said. His eyes looked less bloodshot than Joe's, though as a former FBI Art Crime Unit prosecutor who worked under Joe's direction, he was probably more accustomed to all-nighters. When Mara had expressed a desire to relinquish the complicated legal research that arose in the negotiations and lobbying work, Joe had suggested that they hire Bruce.

The conference room door opened, and Catherine walked in with the final reports in her hands. Mara was thankful for this distraction by the team's art historian, a quiet, thoughtful woman who worked like a demon behind the closed doors of her office. She could assemble a flawless provenance for any object, from any time, along with painstaking explanations of the object's iconography and historical meaning, as well as lists of possible collectors. Mara thanked her team for their understanding and redirected everyone's attention to the initial plans to recover the map.

The group reviewed the itinerary and dossiers on the antique-map business and major players in the map-theft underworld. The documents contained a list of contacts for Mara: touch points—art thieves who might have handled the map on its way to its final, unknown destination—as well as fences, dealers, and collectors with a possible interest in a rare fifteenth-century map. The list was short: the marketplace for an antique map, even an invaluable one, was tiny. Catherine had included a brief history on cartography so Mara could understand where this map—the little they knew of it—fit into the overall chronicle of mapmaking. If the archaeologist's description of the map was accurate, the chart would indeed be a singular find.

On her way to Xi'an, China, the closest airport to the remote excavation, Mara would have a brief layover in Hong Kong. She planned on using the stop to reach out to some additional contacts. Beyond these first insubstantial plans, she would have to remain fluid, ready to change her course with whatever current she encountered. She felt the excitement build, and some anxiety too.

They rose and ambled out of the room. Bruce and Catherine wished Mara luck as they headed home for a quick rest and shower before returning to the office to cope with the clients Mara had to leave behind. Joe motioned for Mara to join him in his office before she left to pack.

"You seem pretty antsy," he said.

"I am, Joe. Although I'd only admit it to you."

"Why so worried?"

"I can't put a finger on why, but the case has me a little unsettled."

"Don't let it shake you." He paused. "I sure hope it's not because you'll be answering to this notorious Tobias character," he said with a roll of his eyes. Joe's liberal political leanings made working for the conservative Tobias hard for him to take.

"No, no," she assured him. "We've had other high-profile clients before."

"You're gonna do great, Mara. And I've got your back."

Mara took one last look at the clothes laid out on her bed before packing them into her indestructible bag. The sea of black pants, sweaters, and skirts had served her well on previous trips. Her travel took her to places and settings she could not always anticipate on departure, and the assortment of lightweight and heavy attire—with the odd dressy piece—covered nearly every venue.

Mara slid into the inky twill pants and cashmere sweater in which she usually traveled. Then she pulled on her black knee-high boots. Topped off by a leather jacket with a removable lining, she felt ready.

For once, she had a few minutes to spare before her car arrived. She took a quick turn around her much-neglected apartment, checking to see if anything needed tending, not that she expected any loose ends. She never knew how long she'd be gone, so she did not crowd the place with items requiring care or attention, like houseplants or groceries.

The dust on some picture frames gleamed in the waning daylight. As Mara reached up to wipe off the photograph of her grandmother, the painting over her fireplace caught her eye—a legacy from Lillian Joyce, the late grand dame of provenance from Beazley's. Mara and Lillian had become close in the days leading up to the *Chrysalis* case as they conducted a clandestine investigation into Beazley's wrongdoing. Still, their improbable friendship had not prepared Mara for Lillian's generous bequest of the painting and a trust.

Given that Mara spent most of her limited time at the apartment sleeping, she really hadn't looked at the

seventeenth-century Johannes Miereveld portrait for
some time. She stepped back to assess it. An ornately
clad older woman, draped in ropes of shining, marble-
sized pearls, stared back at Mara. With her hands
planted on her hips, the woman's unusual stance chal-
lenged the viewer. Her carriage, as well as the curling
maps on the table behind her, signaled the vast scope of
her authority. Miereveld had captured a most extraordinary woman for his day—a woman of power.

The portrait reminded Mara of Lillian and her final
encouragement to rise to a greater destiny than that of
cog in the wheel of a behemoth commercial law firm.
Though Mara was proud, she wondered how Lillian
would perceive the team she'd formed and the restitu-
tion work they did. To be sure, her work was altruistic
in nature now, and she had fulfilled Lillian's deathbed
wish to return the cache of Nazi-looted artwork they'd
uncovered in Beazley's coffers to its rightful owners. Yet
in some ways, Mara's life was no different than it had
been at Severin, Oliver & Means—hours and hours
spent at the office and on the road—before the *Chrysalis*
case forced her off course from the blind pursuit of partnership.

Mara knew her father wished that she had ignored
the moral quandary the *Chrysalis* case presented and
pursued Severin's golden ring instead. Such an achievement would have helped legitimize his own somewhat
shady rise from an Irish immigrant background to successful Boston businessman and politician.

The house phone rang, announcing the arrival of her
town car. Mara tore herself away from the Miereveld
painting and her own musings. She gathered her bags,
walked out the door, and locked it tightly behind her.

The iron fish swings about wildly in its box of water. A bead of sweat forms on Zhi's forehead, travels down the length of his brow, and dangles before splashing into the fish's domain. He prays to Allah that the black-robed examiners from Hanlin Academy do not see the droplet fall.

Zhi knows that he must control the compass and make it find true south. When clouds hide the stars at night and obscure the sun by day, he must be able to assist the chief navigator and mapmaker on board by using the iron fish to calculate south and the other sixteen wind directions that derive from it. He must then be able to depict the bearings on maps and charts.

He reviews again the steps he had undertaken for the compass's proper construction and operation. The fish, while still molten, was cooled with the tail facing the north to magnetize it. He had created a watertight box by nailing hardwood to a teak frame, then sealing it with coconut fiber and a mixture of boiled tung oil and lime. He had painted on its visible base a diagram of the sixteen wind directions. Then he had placed the fish in the box on the water's surface away from the wind, so that it would float freely.

When he places one hand on each side of the box, he realizes the error. The air seems still, but in fact, it stirs.

Zhi makes the necessary adjustment, and the fish's tail stabilizes. To his relief, it reveals true south.

After Zhi performs this exercise in various locations around the new capital and on waterways, the examiners permit him to prove his competence in astronomy and latitude calculations. By night, he uses a specially notched and perforated jade disk to identify critical constellations, most important the polestar, the star around which all the stars rotate. Much like the entire world circles around their glorious emperor, the Son of Heaven, Zhi thinks to himself. From the location of the polestar and the measurement of its height above the horizon, Zhi calculates latitude. Again and again.

Though still nervous, Zhi draws comfort from the fact that the examiners allow him to advance while many have been dropped. At dawn on the sixth day of testing, the examiners leave him alone in the studio with a single silk scroll, his writing brush, inkstone, color pigments, and a guard to ensure the map's authorship. Zhi is to create a map of China.

With care, he unrolls the scroll, noting the tiny imperfections in the weave, as they will affect his brushstrokes. Once his brush touches the scroll, he cannot alter the marking. He readies his paints and begins.

His brush quivers as it hovers over the scroll. Zhi tells himself there is no need to be so anxious. He has already completed a copy of a sailing chart of the Strait of Malacca to the examiners' satisfaction. And in many ways, that narrow chart, nearly the length of a grown man with its snakelike, variable perspective of coastal features along the route, and its reams of accompanying calligraphy detailing star positions, latitudes, and bearings, is far more difficult than the map he now undertakes.

Closing his eyes and inhaling deeply, Zhi outlines the coast of China from memory. All along its eastern border he depicts the sea with threatening black waves. He dots the interior landscape with symbols of mountains, coloring them in deep blue, emerald green, or brown, depending on vegetation density, and emblems of towns. He dissects the countryside with sinuous lines of yellow or slate blue, representations of rivers that vary in color depending on the amount of silt in their waters. He fashions a swath of dusty blue at the top to denote the vast desert region. After painting calligraphy-filled squares along the edges of the scroll to denote the bordering barbarian countries, he zigzags an imposing jet-black Great Wall across the whole of the land.

He takes special care with the lower right corner, the location of his home village of Kunyang in Yunnan. He selects a verdant green for Moon Mountain and a brilliant blue for its lake, where he and his brothers played and swam when the stifling heat of summer made their work in the fields impossible. He draws with pride the civic buildings, where the Ma family once governed, before the Ming emperors overthrew the Mongols and the Ma men and women became rice farmers. With a bittersweet smile of recollection, he emphasizes the town square where he and Shu, the Yunnanese girl he left behind when he chose the eunuch path, had sought each other out during market days and festivals. Though their meetings were few, he had been drawn to her quiet, strong manner, and believed she shared his feelings and intentions.

Only then does he address the blank space at the

scroll's center. He mixes a rare amethyst-colored paint and dips in his brush. The Forbidden City, purple with joy and happiness, emerges.

As the daylight wanes, Zhi nods to the guard to indicate the map's completion. The guard leads him to a room crowded with a high, rectangular table and curved chairs to await the examiners' return. Zhi keeps his head bowed, his gaze fixed on his hands. He thinks how his long, nimble fingers, so mocked by his burly farming brothers, serve him well in this role.

The examiners enter. Zhi drops down, with the left knee before the right and his back straight as a broom handle. After they give him leave to rise, he presents the map to them.

The passport control line snaked through the customs area of the Hong Kong airport. Mara rubbed her eyes, trying to wipe away some of the sleepiness left over from the fourteen-hour flight. She wanted to be sharp for her meeting with Paul Wong.

As Mara wound her way to the front of the line, she looked around the airport terminal, the world's largest. The soaring glass-and-steel structure opened for business on a momentous date: July 6, 1998, when the Chinese took Hong Kong back from the British. Mara appreciated the crisp modernity of its appearance and layout, but she missed the rush of the roller-coaster-like approach pattern of the old airport. Its single landing strip had required arriving planes to fly toward a mountainside, then buzz over Kowloon rooftops before taking a last-minute turn to dive down for landing.

She collected her luggage in baggage claim and then exited to the receiving area. Long queues of waiting families thronged the ropes. Away from the fray, in a black uniform, inscribed cap, and white gloves, stood her driver. He took her bags, and together they strode through the airport and out into the cool, damp night.

The Peninsula Hotel's signature green Rolls-Royce Phantom awaited them. Mara settled into the voluminous backseat, stretched out her legs, and watched the street scenes. They passed ultramodern office buildings crowded up against the ramshackle Night Market, with its stalls chockablock with traditional Chinese silk and jade, cheap merchandise, and steaming food served from steel carts. Hong Kong had such a curious mix of cutting-edge commercialism and traditional customs.

The Phantom rounded the Peninsula Hotel's semicircular drive. Though it was located on the Kowloon side of Hong Kong, a bit of a distance from the city's commercial center, Mara couldn't resist staying at the lavish 1928 hotel. She loved its decor, with its nod to the British colonialist past, and the stunning views of Victoria Harbour. Though she could afford many extravagances due to Lillian's bequest, Mara dipped into her coffers primarily when it came to hotels. She loved hotels capable of transporting her to a different place and time.

Mara stepped out of the car, hearing the splash of the Peninsula's dramatic fountain in the background. A formally dressed attendant guided her into the opulent, marble-pillared lobby. Intimate dining areas, decorated with bamboo chairs, arching palms, and gently rotating ceiling fans, flanked each side of the check-in desk. A string quartet played on a balcony overlooking the lobby. She had entered Hong Kong of the early twentieth century.

A bellboy in a white suit and cap led her to the harbor-view room. Rich pewter silk, shot with blue, adorned the walls and upholstery, and heavy damask ivory linens covered the bed. Mara was thinking how the sumptuous room could have been located in nearly any world-class city until the bellboy drew back the drapes and revealed the unparalleled vista of the Hong Kong skyline. Even though years in New York had jaded Mara, this display of neon skyscrapers never failed in its competition to impress.

Mara entered Spring Moon a few minutes early. The Peninsula's Cantonese restaurant glowed ruby red, like the inside of a lacquer box. Dark teak floors and furniture enhanced the traditional feel. Somber-looking businessmen in dark suits populated most of the tables.

The maître d' seated Mara at her table, and she reviewed the dossiers while sipping green tea. Within moments, her unmistakably tall dining companion approached the table. Upon the death of his father, Paul Wong, a Harvard-educated, Wall Street–trained financier, had returned to Hong Kong to run the family antiquities conglomerate.

Mara stood up. She and Paul nodded in greeting, an abbreviated version of a bow. Then they shook hands in the Western manner.

"Paul, so good to see you."

"Mara, always a pleasure. When I'm not the focus of your investigation, that is." The first time Mara had encountered Paul, she'd been searching for a marble lion carved during the Tang dynasty that might or might not have passed through Paul's establishment during his father's tenure. Because it hadn't furthered her investigation, Mara had turned a blind eye toward the vast Wong Antiquities empire, a fact much appreciated by Paul. Since then, he'd pitched in to help her when her work took her to Asia, as long as it didn't threaten his family's livelihood. The often shady nature of the business—rife with pilfered pieces and fakes—didn't sit well with Paul.

As they talked of the recent political developments, Mara slipped intuitively into the role most advantageous for garnering information: softening her aggressive edges and keeping her demeanor appealingly demure. Though Paul's education and work experience made him very Western in some ways, she understood that he responded better to a reserved bearing.

Paul updated her on the current governmental players and the truth behind the propaganda campaigns. Still Communist in theory, the once-hermetic China had flung open its doors in recent years. The increasingly mercantile country embraced any and all means of becoming a major player on the world stage—rushing headlong toward a market economy, modernizing industry and infrastructure, hunting down international investors, stimulating its billion citizens to crave material goods, and revitalizing old symbols of its universal prowess. And creating new ones.

"I take it you didn't travel all this way for a political update you could read in *The New York Times,* Mara. What brings you to Hong Kong?"

"I'm wondering if you've heard any rumblings about a stolen map."

Paul chuckled. "I'm always hearing 'rumblings' about a stolen map. Among other items."

Mara laughed at the ridiculousness of her question. "Sorry, I should be more specific. I'm looking for a map created by the Chinese in the early 1400s of the world as they knew it at that time—you know, Asia and parts of Africa."

"And you think that map is here in China?"

"I think it *was* here quite recently. I'm not certain of its location now."

He shot her a quizzical look. "That's an odd request."

"Why?"

"I can think of many reasons."

"Like what?" Mara thirsted for more details about the history of mapmaking and the map-theft world, and she knew that jack-of-all-trades Paul would have some interesting tidbits. Her own dossier, quickly compiled by Catherine, gave her only the broadest of overviews, though Mara knew Catherine was trying to fill in the blanks back in New York.

"Well, to start, I'm pretty sure that there weren't any world maps—as we'd conceive of them—made in the early 1400s."

"Really?" Mara had read this in the dossier, but she wanted to hear Paul's take.

"Really. I'm fairly certain that, other than some inaccurate world maps made in classical times and a simple Arabic chart made by al-Idrisi in the twelfth century, world maps as we think of them didn't come into existence until the mid-1400s."

"Why is that?"

"Very early world maps—from anytime in the 1400s—were created only once the European countries began their famous discoveries. So the idea of a world map produced by the *Chinese* in the early 1400s is quite unlikely."

"Why?"

"I can think of at least two reasons. First, while early Chinese maps have been discovered—some from as early as 300 B.C.—those maps all focus on China or on countries nearby. The only exceptions are some navigational charts that served as guides for sailors entering adjacent seas.

"Second, in the 1420s, the very xenophobic Emperor Zhu Gaozhi, usually known by his dynastic title, Hongxi, inherited the throne. Though Zhu Gaozhi died within a year of assuming it, his son Zhu Zhanji succeeded him, taking the name Xuande, and he reinforced his father's policies. Naval exploration—and mapping of any such discoveries, whether by the Chinese or anyone else—was prohibited. From that point forward, China became inward-looking. Until quite recently, in some ways."

"Would mapmaking of the known world have been permitted before Emperor Hongxi assumed the throne?"

Paul paused, processing his impressive command of Chinese medieval history. "In the very early 1400s? In theory, I guess so. Emperor Zhu Di, who's typically known as Yongle, sat on the throne from about 1402 to around 1424, and he pursued ambitious building projects within China and an elaborate foreign policy plan without. He did have a fleet commanded by Admiral Zheng He . . ." Paul trailed off, then laughed before continuing: "But there's no evidence of any large-scale expeditions beyond the Indian Ocean that would yield information for a world map, just some crazy speculations. And even if a world map had been created in the early 1400s, I doubt it would have survived the purging by Emperors Hongxi and Xuande."

This was the second time Mara had heard Admiral Zheng He's name, but she didn't want to explain why she was familiar with a fifteenth-century admiral known to few outside of China. Instead, she gave Paul a sheepish smile. "I guess my client was wrong about the origin and date of this map."

Mara allowed the conversation to settle into silence.

With great deliberation and even greater restraint, she spooned tea leaves into a strainer, lifted the teapot to pour steaming water over them into a cup, and sat quietly while it steeped. She then handed the cup to Paul. Keeping her eyes fixed downward on the cup, she asked, "Still, I must pursue my client's matter. Perhaps you can help me in another way?"

"Of course, Mara."

Mara knew Paul liked to play the chivalrous role. She described the location of the archaeological dig from which the map had been stolen and inquired, "Are you aware of any local"—she paused, prudent in her choice of the next word—"groups who might be able to shed light on what happened at the site?"

He hesitated, as if he was assessing whether to part with his precious information even in the name of gallantry. "I do know the name of an important businessman in that region."

"I'd very much appreciate an introduction."

With reluctance, he said, "I don't know, Mara. His people trade in much worse things than stolen art."

"I can take care of myself, Paul."

"I know you think you can handle yourself in most situations, but his guys are pretty rough."

"Do you think his people are involved in the map theft?"

"I don't think anything happens in his region without his stamp of approval."

"Then I need to meet with him."

Paul scanned her, as if assessing her willingness to take the risk. He pulled a leatherbound notepad and silver pen from his inner jacket pocket and, after consulting his BlackBerry, scribbled down a few words.

"His name is Li Wen. I will contact him to let him know you're coming. And that you're a friend. But I must insist that you let a trustworthy man I know in that area accompany you to the meeting." He ripped a small sheet of paper from the pad and handed it to her.

She nodded. "Of course, Paul. I'd be grateful to have your protection."

After dinner, Mara crawled into the vast marble tub in her hotel bathroom. The nearly scalding water seeped into her skin, soaking away the long hours of cramped travel. She stared out the window at the glorious view of Hong Kong at midnight, but she couldn't focus on it. Her cell phone, perched on the tub's ledge, kept creeping into her consciousness, urging her to pick it up. Her hand hovered over the phone as she waged an internal battle to quash the impulse. The resistant part of her lost, and she placed the call.

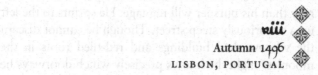
Antonio hears the slam of the tavern door over the din of the prostitutes and gamblers and drunks at the bar. Yet the dice are hot in his hand and the ale warm in his belly, so he pays it no heed. Until he hears the roar of his name.

Merda, he thinks. He knows the voice and knows the reason. Antonio has spent one afternoon too many in the company of the particularly delectable wife of a local fishmonger. If he were a gentleman, he would stand and take his beating like one. But he isn't a gentleman.

So Antonio drops the dice and hits the wood-plank floor. Crawling through the discarded mussel shells and olive pits, he scuttles like a crab behind the bar. Lucinda, a prostitute turned barmaid he now regrets scorning, tries to block him. He pushes her work-hardened calves aside.

His pathway cleared, he gets up, runs to the back door, and kicks it open. He climbs the rat-infested stone steps out of the cellarlike tavern. Pausing briefly at the top of the stairs, he closes his eyes and charts the best route through the rabbit warren of the Alfama neighborhood alleyways that coil around the fortified base of Castelo de São Jorge like a maze.

Antonio begins running, thinking that his mapmaker's mind will guide him better in the pitch black than his straining eyes ever could. And certainly with more accuracy than his pursuer will manage. He sprints to the left up a notoriously steep street. Though he cannot discern the whitewashed buildings and red-tiled roofs in the moonless night, he knows precisely which doorways he passes from previous nocturnal visits.

Yet to his surprise, Antonio hears the steady thud of footsteps in his wake. Has he overestimated his advantage? Or has he underestimated the driving anger of his cuckolded follower?

His hunter grows near enough that he can hear labored breath reverberate in the narrow alley, so tight he can touch both sides of the street at the same time. "Antonio, I'll kill you!"

Antonio knows he must change course, and he knows where he must go. He tears right onto a lane that constricts like a snake. Ducking under ropes heavy with wash left out to dry, he squeezes out and onto the steps of the Sedes Episcopalis.

He dreads passing through the cathedral's main door, with its vainglorious height of nearly four men, and under the two castellated bell towers. They remind him of the platform for the hanging noose. But this is the last place anyone would expect him, so Antonio enters.

Controlling his panting, he walks into the gloomy, hushed interior. Belatedly, he realizes he has intruded upon a midnight vigil. The abundant candlelight disappoints him; he had counted on near-complete darkness. He cannot turn back, so he leaves the illumination of the nave and seeks the shadows of the ambulatory chapels.

Antonio pushes open the gilded ironwork of the Capela de Santo Ildefonso, which he picks for its close

proximity to a side door. Kneeling before the sarcophagus of the companion in arms to King Afonso IV, he
assumes the position of a penitent. In a sort of vigil different from that of the other churchgoers, he keeps a
surreptitious yet constant watch for his pursuer. Yet no
one comes for him.

In time, his prayerful posture slackens, and he thinks
he may be safe. He is struck by the similarity between
the rose window and his trusted navigational instrument, the compass rose. The rush of the chase wears
off, the ale takes hold again, and Antonio drifts off.

Then the slice of a blade on his ribs startles him awake.

Mara walked past the tables crowded with an ebullient mix of successful young locals and expats. An almost celebratory mood filled the hip restaurant, Felix, where the late-night diners seemed to toast to China's abundant wealth and shining future. In the presence of China's heady mixture of a surging, newly open economy and expanding global influence, one could almost forget about the news reports claiming human rights violations and tainted food and toys.

She searched for a hostess to accommodate her in the small, metallic bar at the back of the restaurant. Finding someone wasn't easy amid the bustle and pulsating music, so Mara seated herself at a tiny steel table near the window. She looked around. Though she'd stayed at the Peninsula many times, she'd never visited Felix, on the twenty-eighth floor, so utterly different from Spring Moon. With its steel walls rippling with waves and its harbor view, she almost felt as though she were bobbing on the picturesque waterfront.

After giving the waitress her drink order, she waited for her date to arrive. The time gave her more opportunities to second-guess her phone call. She had told herself that meeting him would yield an inside look into the political regime—and whether or not the Chinese government had heard any murmurings about this map. Yet if she were honest with herself, that was only an excuse.

Mara saw him approach from across the restaurant—not hard, given his height. She felt her heart leap, though it'd been over five years. Maybe this wasn't such a good idea after all.

He was "Black Irish" as some called it, complete with the gift of gab. His jet-black hair was now tinged with premature gray. Yet time had not dulled the ruddiness of his cheeks or the gleam in his eyes. He seemed thinner, more sinewy than before.

"Sam McIlrath." Mara stood and began to nod, as she'd done with Paul. But he cut her off and squeezed her tight.

"What's with the Chinese bowing? Give me a hug!"

Mara returned the embrace, though it felt strange after so long, and then backed into her chair. He settled into the one facing hers. Now that he was sitting across from her, she didn't know what to say.

Sam spoke first. "I almost fell onto my office floor when I heard your voice tonight."

She laughed. "It's good to see that some things never change—like you working until midnight."

"Old habits die hard," he said, staring at her. "You look amazing. I like the shorter hair."

She reached up to touch it; she'd recently cut her auburn hair to a chin-length bob. No more crutches, she'd told herself. Without her long hair to hide behind, Mara felt curiously naked. Especially with Sam. They had dated at Georgetown, through her time at Columbia Law School, and into her first years at Severin. Passionate and ambitious about politics, when he'd received the State Department posting of his dreams in China, he'd left without a second thought. America, and her.

The initial awkwardness past, they barraged each other with questions. Even though years and pain separated them, they reconnected. They spoke in a shorthand Mara had nearly forgotten and finished each other's sentences. To her surprise, she felt comfortable, as though she'd slipped back into her own skin for a change. It was a relief to be herself, with someone who knew her well. She no longer missed him, but she mourned for the innocent, trusting self she'd been when they were together.

They asked each other about their families, their work, and their once-mutual friends. They talked about everything but their personal lives. Mara told herself she just didn't want to know, though mostly she didn't want him to ask about her own. She couldn't bear to reveal the humiliation of Michael Roarke's betrayal—to Sam, of all people. If he didn't already know.

"I've been following this new career of yours," he said.

"You have?" Her entire body tensed, waiting to hear what he knew.

"It made the newspapers at one point, even out here. Well, I should say that the *Chrysalis* case made the papers."

Oh no, she groaned inwardly. What did he know? Though the intervening years had softened the blow and she now viewed the experience as a gift, an entrée to a preferable life, she preferred not to discuss the particulars with Sam.

Yet Sam didn't ask her for details, sparing her the embarrassment of reliving them. Instead, he said, "So, that *Chrysalis* case seems to have led you to this new venture. I'd love to hear about it."

Mara was relieved by the chance to talk about her work. She told Sam about the members of her group and their moral agenda, careful to discuss only her dispute-resolution and lobbying efforts.

Sam smiled at her. "You just light up when you describe your firm. It's really wonderful to see. I never saw that spark in your eyes when you worked for Severin."

"The matters we handle are so different than any case I managed at Severin. So rewarding."

"You certainly won some fans out here when you lobbied the U.S. government to restrict imports of archaeological goods under the Convention on Cultural Property Implementation Act."

"Really?" Mara was surprised; she'd assumed that her efforts to recover stolen artifacts might make her unpopular in certain Chinese circles. She hadn't thought through the larger perception of her lobbying work.

"Really. My contacts were thrilled; they hoped that if the United States backed the request and cut off one of the markets for stolen Chinese antiquities, then it might stop some of the archaeological looting."

Mara used his reference to the Chinese government as an opportunity to steer the conversation to his career. She had heard rumors about his rise in America's political machine with the new Asian powerhouse, and she knew that he'd love the opportunity to brag.

As the conversation dwindled, Mara began to lay the groundwork for her favor. After the natural exchange, the manipulative compliment she'd been planning felt false. Then she reminded herself how he'd hurt her. How he'd ended their almost eight-year relationship with an abrupt phone call. And she didn't feel so bad. She leaned forward with a conspiratorial grin and asked, "You probably know all sorts of behind-the-scenes happenings with the Chinese government?"

Sam gave her one of his self-satisfied smirks. She knew he'd respond to flattery, though it saddened her a bit. "I don't think any outsider can know everything. But, yeah, I guess I know as much as any foreigner."

Mara took a sip of her drink and gave him a coy glance. "Do you think you could find something out for me?"

"Sure, why not," he said, stretching his arms out magnanimously.

Mara told him a little bit about the map, and asked him to use his network to find out whether the Chinese regime had caught wind of it.

Sam leaned back in his chair, his first withdrawal since he'd arrived. "You know the Chinese government is determined to buy back its past, Mara. They just spent millions at an auction reacquiring treasure looted from Beijing's Summer Palace by British and French troops a hundred and forty years ago—bronze animal heads that once decorated a zodiac fountain there. They'll stop at nothing to recover their cultural heritage, to find symbolic artifacts connecting their historical supremacy with their current power."

She persisted. "I'm not asking you to keep the map from the Chinese. Just to let me know if they've heard about its discovery. And its theft. Will you do that for me?"

His voice dropped to a whisper. "Mara, do you realize

what you're asking? You want me to spy on an authoritarian regime that's hell-bent on reassembling its past, so you can find out whether they know that your client kept secret a priceless antique map? A map they'd love to get their hands on?"

She could do nothing but give him her most winning smile and say, "Yes."

He hesitated, knocked back the rest of his whiskey, and shook his head in disbelief. Then he said, "I guess I owe you that."

Zhi returns to his sleeping quarters with a heavy step. The other eunuchs have long since retired. Except for Liang, who lies awake, waiting for him.

As he undresses and slides into the simple, low couch-bed adjacent to Liang's, he hears his friend whisper, "What did the examiners say about your work?"

Zhi pauses before answering. He does not want to utter his suspicions aloud, tempting fate to make them true. "They were quiet after I showed them my map."

"Quiet?"

"Yes, quiet."

"They said nothing at all?"

"I think I heard one examiner say the map was 'not traditional.' "

Liang gasps in his falsetto voice, so common to eunuchs. Somehow Zhi has maintained his low tones and natural gait.

Silence descends on the friends. They both know that in the imperial regime, "not traditional" is tantamount to heretical. Though not formally announced, it seems as though the examiners' verdict has already been rendered.

Zhi waits until he hears Liang's light snore. Then, in the low light of the moon, he reaches under his bed and slides out a rectangular teak box. Careful not to rattle the lock as he opens it, he works his hand under the silken sack on top, which contains his *pao,* his precious, severed parts, which must remain with him always if he is to ascend to heaven as a whole man. He pulls out a slender scroll.

Shielding it from the eyes of any awakening—or spying—eunuch, he unrolls it. A painting of a lotus blossom materializes. Raindrops weigh down its ivory petals, like the tears of a beautiful woman forsaken by her love. The lotus blossom is Shu. He thinks about their last encounter, several years ago at the Kunyang New Year's festival.

He had just acquiesced to his family's request that he enter the imperial eunuch service, one that offered betterment for the Ma family. His parents and brothers had gathered on one end of the town square, sharing the good news with other villagers, when he broke from them. He wanted to be alone, to be a normal young man for one last New Year's celebration, not a half man in the making. As he wandered around the market stalls bursting with spices and silks, he saw Shu.

With the slow, graceful step that had entranced him from the beginning, she walked toward him. He watched the swing of her black hair as she moved, and silently formed the words to tell her of his decision. When she grew close, he saw that her dark eyes brimmed with tears. He realized that he need not say anything. The news had already reached her.

He dared to say her given name and take her face in his hands—for the first time and the last. Brushing away the tears as they fell down her cheek, he started to speak, to apologize for leaving her before they had the chance to begin. She placed a single finger on his lips and spoke the words of forgiveness for which he so longed. "I understand," she said.

Zhi looks again at the lotus painting he created on a lonesome night when he risked the bamboo rod and stole away to the studio. He prays to Allah that he is wrong about the examiners' reaction. For only with his advancement and its attendant elevation of his family and honor for his ancestors will his sacrifice of Shu, and his surrender of a normal life, be worthwhile. Only then will he be worthy of Shu's forgiveness.

The next morning, Zhi serves tea to Master Shen, one of eight managing directors of the Imperial Ceremonial Directorate. He holds the teacup with joined palms and raises it to chest height. He approaches the master and kneels at his feet with head bowed in a sign of deference. He then holds the teacup out to him.

Zhi has heard the master tell others that he performs the tea presentation without flaw. Once, this was a source of pride, since it drew the master's special favor. Now, with his presumed examination failure, Zhi fears this will be the zenith of his life's work.

As the master reaches for the cup, the guard announces a messenger at the entryway. Zhi rises from his knees to greet the courier and take the missive from him. He walks to the master's worktable to register the communiqué in the official record books.

Zhi spreads the scroll out on the table so that he can review it before discussing its contents with the master. More and more, as Zhi's education progresses, the master relies on Zhi to help process the countless communications delivered to the agency and coordinate policies between the capital and the provinces. Zhi screens the documents received for imperial inspection, assesses them, and makes preliminary recommendations to the master. He does much more than serve tea.

To his surprise, Zhi sees that his own name appears throughout the text. Though he can guess at its contents, he knows it would be impermissible to continue reviewing the scroll, so he hands it to the master and waits. Though Zhi has grown used to standing by, the master's careful perusal of the scroll seems interminable. Finally, he speaks.

"Ma Zhi, the decision regarding Admiral Zheng's crew has been made. You are to report to Director Tang."

Zhi keeps his face static and respectful as he bows in thanks. Yet his heart leaps in joy at the possibility that he might be selected, that his sacrifice is bearing fruit. As he walks down the long corridors to the director's chamber, however, his elation begins to abate, and anxiety over the specter of rejection mounts.

He distracts himself by studying the few eunuchs standing outside the chamber. All candidates for the roles on the expedition, Zhi assumes. He scrutinizes the face of each eunuch exiting the chamber for hints of the outcome, but he finds their countenances unreadable. As he reaches the front of the queue, Zhi hears his name being called. He pauses to say a silent prayer and then passes under the red archway flanked by ruby-lacquered pillars into the crowded room. Zhi kneels before the director.

The conversations continue as if he were not present. He overhears excited exchanges about the voyage's gigantic, nine-masted treasure ships and the nearly thirty thousand sailors who will man them. Zhi is tall, so even though his eyes and head are lowered as etiquette demands, he can see the room quite well from under the wings of his cap. He recognizes the director's staff of fussing assistants, but not the others in naval dress.

One of the assistants orders him to rise.

"Ma Zhi," Director Tang says, without lifting his eyes from the scroll that lies before him on the table. "We have the report of your examination here. The Hanlin Academy teachers found your knowledge of astronomy, navigation, geography, and calligraphy adequate for the role of assistant to an expedition mapmaker. However, they have reservations about your ability to render maps in the traditional fashion, which would be your primary function."

The director continues, keeping his eyes on the parchment spread before him. "Still, despite this, Heaven shines upon you. Admiral Zheng himself happened to cast his eyes upon your map and found your depiction of the purple Forbidden City to his liking. You have been accepted as assistant to the mapmaker and navigator on one of the fleet's grain ships."

Zhi swells with pride, even though his place will not be on one of the famed treasure ships. To be selected for the journey at all honors the Ma family, helping return them to the high status they held in his grandparents' time, before a change in politics brought them low.

"That is not correct, Director." A voice sounds from the shadowy back of the chamber. A booming, deep voice uncharacteristic in the eunuch community.

The voice could only belong to Admiral Zheng. Even if he is denied a place on the voyage, Zhi thinks, Allah has blessed him by allowing him to be in the presence of the legendary soldier and naval explorer. From his boyhood days, Zhi has worshipped his distant relative, who was called Ma He before Emperor Yongle selected him from the eunuch ranks, made him his closest adviser, and changed his family name. Zheng, the most successful son from Zhi's hometown, had become commander in chief of the largest fleet ever built and leader of five expeditions around the known world. The chance to follow in Zheng's footsteps was one of the main reasons Zhi had complied with his family's request to volunteer for the openings in the imperial eunuch service. Even though it had meant abandoning Shu.

Admiral Zheng strides like a tiger to the front of the room, near to the director and Zhi. Though still not raising his eyes, Zhi can see the swath of a long red robe, a color only someone of Admiral Zheng's stature may wear. Zhi chastises himself; he never should have permitted himself to feel a momentary flash of conceit. He knows that he is not worthy of the director's decision. Or Admiral Zheng's notice.

The voice sounds again. "Ma Zhi will be on one of the treasure ships under the command of my admiral Zhou Wen, the *Ch'ing Ho, Pure Harmony.* Ma Zhi will assist the chief mapmaker of the *Ch'ing Ho* in the charting of the voyage that Admiral Zhou's fleet will undertake."

zai

Present Day

XI'AN, CHINA

Mara elbowed her way through the crowds of tourists. Seniors in jogging suits, frayed-jean backpackers, and pashmina-wrapped culture warriors jammed the Xi'an airport. Located in central China between the Wei River to the north and the Qinling Mountains to the south, Xi'an had become a must-see city for most travelers through China. Though the ancient city was once the gateway to the Silk Road and the capital of the ancient Tang dynasty, this wasn't what drew the tourists. No, they arrived in droves to see the Terra-Cotta Warriors.

Legend had it that in 1974, a group of peasants stumbled across some distinctive pottery while digging for a well near a royal burial site. Mara knew that it was more likely that the peasants were grave robbers, but this was beside the point. Archaeologists descended upon the site when the pottery reached the marketplace, and they unearthed a tomb filled with over seven thousand life-size clay soldiers, horses, and chariots arranged in battle formation, each modeled after a real-life counterpart. Some thought this to be the tomb of the first emperor of all China in the second century B.C., and UNESCO listed it as a world heritage site in 1987. The entire region became a destination not just for tourists but for archaeologists determined to find the next Terra-Cotta Warriors tomb.

Passing the groups in line for the tour buses, Mara exited the terminal. As soon as she stepped outside, the stench of burning chemicals from the factories of industrial Xi'an assaulted her, like the smoke of a forest fire. She coughed and reached for a scarf to protect herself against the offensive smell. Looking around for her ride, she realized for the first time that many of the locals wore surgical masks. If the tourists were expecting a Disney version of ancient China, they were about to be disappointed.

Cloth to her mouth, she weaved in and out of the parked cars and buses, hunting for the driver engaged to take her to the site. Finding no one and exhausted from the effort and travel, she plunked down on a bench. She was just in time to watch a beat-up Toyota Land Cruiser in an indeterminate shade of rust screech to a halt at the curbside. A bespectacled Chinese man scurried out from the vehicle. He carried a hastily written paper with him, bearing a single word: COYNE. Her car had arrived.

Mara grabbed her bags and walked toward him. She pointed to the sign. "I'm Coyne."

"So sorry," the driver apologized and took her bags. "I'm Bernard Huang, assistant director of the site. Please call me Huang. I'm here to take you to Mr. Coleman."

Mara climbed into the backseat, squeezing in amid the messy array of papers and specimen boxes. The car took off, heading southwest to the rural site. After her efforts to engage Huang in conversation failed, she just focused on the view from the window.

Even in the closed car, she smelled the industrial waste that Xi'an's burgeoning economy chugged out into the air. And she could see it. Though it was early afternoon,

Huang turned on the headlights to better navigate through the gritty smog.

Tying her scarf around her nose and mouth, Mara closed her eyes. The lightest noise used to waken her, but unremitting exhaustion had turned Mara into a deep sleeper. When the Land Cruiser hit a mountainous bump she awakened, only to drift back into sleep as though the jarring road were nothing but a rocking chair.

She woke up for good to the sound of her name, whispered at first, then crescendoed to a near yell. She guessed they'd arrived. Not sure how many hours they'd been driving, she stumbled out of the car and nearly into the dig itself.

Mara stood on the periphery of a vast trench. It was much deeper and longer than the standard pits she'd seen, though scored by the standard stratigraphical markings. Huang stood even nearer to the edge, precipitously so. He leaned over, searching for someone or something.

"Ben, she's here!" He yelled and waved. Mara looked down into the pit. It was crowded with workers, indistinguishable from the back in their white shirts and broad-brimmed hats. One of the masses lifted his head, squinted up into the dying daylight, and then ambled over toward the ladder.

A lanky man emerged stratum by stratum from the pit as if born from the earth. His curly hair, his clothes, the premature creases in his skin, even his thick glasses were coated with a fine layer of dirt.

He squinted as he walked toward her, his height— maybe six foot four—revealed as he grew close. Once his eyes adjusted, he examined her slowly, as if she were a just-unearthed artifact he couldn't quite make out until he had brushed away the grime with great delicacy.

The disheveled, dusty man before her appeared in stark contrast to the academic rigor evident from his résumé. Ben Coleman, she recalled from her dog-eared dossier, was an academic born to academics. Schooled exclusively at the Ivy Leagues, Harvard and then the University of Pennsylvania, he had an impeccable scholarly pedigree. Penn had granted him an honorary interdisciplinary professorship, but he never taught, never published papers, and, for that matter, rarely appeared on campus. A renowned expert in the obscure ancient Tocharian people—whoever they were—he did the sort of work that demanded his presence in remote areas of China.

The dossier listed no wife, no children, not even a home address. He could be reached only by e-mail, cell phone, or through a post office box on the Penn campus.

As he approached, Mara reached out her hand to shake his in greeting. Ben wiped his hands on a cloth and extended his own. His scrubbing was in vain. When he withdrew his hand from Mara's, earth clung to her fingers.

After they made their introductions, Ben took her on a tour of the site. Workers crammed the numerous pits, a near village of tents had been erected in the distance, and scientific staff shuttled back and forth between the two in a well-orchestrated dance. Expensive, pristine equipment populated the pits and perimeters, though Mara spotted handmade wheelbarrows with wooden wheels as well as piles of pickaxes, buckets, and trowels.

The flurry surprised Mara. In the course of her work she had visited plenty of digs, but they seemed sleepy compared to this. After all, the history they sought had rested in the ground for centuries, if not millennia. What were a few more days? Not for Ben Coleman's dig the usual drowsiness, she thought, then corrected herself: Richard Tobias's dig. Maybe the deep pockets of the excavation's patron quickened the pace.

As Ben ushered Mara around, neither one mentioned Richard Tobias, but his august presence loomed between them. Though Ben played the part of willing tour guide, Mara wasn't surprised that his manner bristled just a bit. She guessed that Ben perceived her visit to be an investigation into the theft, even though she didn't know what Tobias and his people had told Ben about her.

Mara resolved to placate any suspicions he might have that her visit was an investigation into *him* rather than the robbery: she didn't want him to close up and withhold information out of fear that he might be under personal scrutiny. So as Ben pointed out the dig's unusual pits, the atypically large, octagonal tents, almost yurtlike in design, and the state-of-the-art gear, she nodded with enthusiasm. She admired the trenches, each one so precisely delineated it looked like it had been cut from the earth with scissors. She praised the speed with which he'd managed to build the substantial site. The compliments were no hardship for Mara: the bustling site thrilled and impressed her.

Mara thought she saw Ben blush at her mild praise. Though given the sandy film covering his skin, she wouldn't swear to it. As they continued the tour, Ben became like a proud new father, thrilled with this confirmation of the beauty of his offspring. Or maybe he was just relieved to be talking about something other than the theft.

Abruptly, he turned around and yelled out something to the small crowd following them. Though she couldn't understand the dialect Ben used, Mara assumed he'd bellowed out an order, as the pack dispersed.

"Sorry about the staring. We don't get many foreign visitors out here, and we have very few female workers. I hate to speak harshly to them, but I don't want you to feel uncomfortable."

Mara smiled at Ben's clumsy show of gallantry. For some reason, his attempt struck her as sweetly protective rather than patronizing. As she turned to thank him, it struck her that he was attractive beneath his unkempt exterior. She assured him. "Please don't apologize."

As they left the central excavation, she asked some gentle questions about the robbery. He told her the basics: the time of the robbery; the location of the theft; any damage done as a result; the site's security measures; who knew about the map. From his description, it seemed to Mara the usual bit of local-mafia-sponsored thievery, with which she hoped Paul's contact could help. If so, she felt confident about her chances of tracking down the map.

They approached the area containing numerous tents and drew near the largest, the only one with guards posted by its entrance. Ben held back the flap. As she entered, he said, "The map was stolen from here."

Mara walked into darkness. As her eyes adjusted, she observed the makings of a meticulously organized, ultramodern laboratory. "I haven't seen a lab like this outside of a university."

Though the light was dim, Mara was now certain

Ben blushed. "I know. We're really lucky to have such generous funding," he said, in his only reference so far to Richard Tobias. Then his face turned somber. "But our work demands it."

"I'd guess you'd need specialized equipment for an excavation dealing with first-millennium artifacts."

"You're right. Sometimes our most critical findings are scraps of fabric or manuscript fragments written on palm leaves. We need to be able to study and preserve fragile materials."

"Hence all the equipment."

"Yes. And the darkness."

Mara wandered around the room, studying the apparatus. "I bet the equipment you have is far superior to anything nearby. Even though Shaanxi Province is becoming quite the hot spot for archaeologists these days."

He nodded. "That's why Richard thought we should have all this. We couldn't trust the local labs, and we couldn't risk what shipping might do to sensitive findings."

"You must have felt pretty comfortable unrolling the map scroll here," Mara said offhandedly, as she continued to meander around the lab. She wanted to make their first real discussion about the map as comfortable as possible.

"Totally."

"Can you tell me about the map?" she asked, still keeping her focus on the room rather than Ben.

He hesitated for an almost imperceptible beat. "Would you like to see a picture?"

"I'd love to," she answered with a wide smile.

He pulled a crowded key ring from his pocket and walked toward a steel cabinet. "I have only one view, and it isn't the best quality. We were slated to take more pictures the day after it was stolen."

Mara counted back from the date of the robbery to the date of discovery—the number of days in which word about the finding could have leaked out from a variety of sources. "You must've waited several days to acclimate the map so you could unroll it and photograph it safely."

"I actually waited two weeks. I wanted to take every precaution," he said.

Ben pulled a drop-spine box from a drawer and brought it over to an examination table. Mara followed him and drew close as he reached for a light. A click sounded and an intense light shone down on an overexposed photograph.

The light revealed a map unlike any other she had ever seen. Even though the picture was too bright and showed only the lower left corner of the map, Mara knew at once that the map was a masterpiece. The right half of the photo depicted a brilliant blue, wavelike pattern that she believed must symbolize the ocean. The left portion of the picture was yellow, shot through with crimson, jade, azure, and amethyst emblems that Mara thought must depict land. A graceful script adorned the border.

The map resembled neither the fifteenth-century blackand-white calligraphed Chinese navigational charts Catherine had attached to her dossier nor the traditional European *mappa mundi*. It had a style entirely its own. She had expected a map perhaps formal and grandiose but primarily functional—not this master-work of colors and symbols and forms.

"It's—it's—beautiful," Mara said.

"Yes, I suppose it is. Even more so in person," he responded in a flat voice. "Up close, the land and seascapes contain tiny pictures of cities, rivers, forests, ships, even sea monsters. The illustrations were so detailed they reminded me of seventeenth-century miniature enamel portraits."

Ben handed her a magnifying glass and pointed to a specific stretch of ocean. From the crest of a sapphire wave, a dragonlike creature reared its head, so painstakingly rendered that its spine gleamed like pearls. "It's magnificent."

"Yes," he said quietly. "And it's the first fairly accurate Chinese map of the world they knew, from the early 1400s." Again, his response seemed curiously diffident. Perhaps the map's loss had diminished his enthusiasm.

"Do you have a spare copy of the photo?"

He pulled a sheet from the box. "This one is for you."

She circled the photograph, examining it from other angles. "How did a fifteenth-century map end up in a first-millennium archaeological site, anyway?"

"This dig's very close to the Silk Road, which starts nearby, in Xi'an. The Silk Road was heavily traveled for so many millennia that we often find artifacts from other centuries in the top layers." He paused. "But we're not expert in anything other than Tocharianism. We had the body to help us date the map and give it context."

"The body?" Mara hadn't heard anything about a body.

"Yeah, we found the map in a surprisingly well-preserved teak box on top of the skeletal remains, along with another scroll. Do you want to see it?"

Mara didn't know what light it would shed on the stolen map, but she nodded. "Did you find the body in a grave?"

"No, in a hastily dug hole. It looks as though he was murdered."

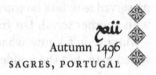

Autumn 1496

SAGRES, PORTUGAL

"Wake up, you lousy piece of dung. What did you do, bathe in ale?"

Antonio feels a rough shake of his shoulder. Without opening his eyes, he grabs the offending hand and shoves it away. "Get the hell away from me, Estêvão," he says as he rolls over, back into the haze of sleep.

"Christ knows I would like nothing more. But the Great Commander ordered me in here to wake you up. He wants you to meet him in the observatory the moment you are able." Estêvão pauses, and Antonio can envision him smirking. "Even though I informed him of your incapacity."

Antonio does not move. He can comprehend the import of the command, but sleep and pain and exhaustion from the long journey reclaim him.

"You leave me no recourse."

A bucket of icy seawater drenches Antonio, jolting him fully awake. He leaps from his bed, ready to pummel Estêvão. But Estêvão is prepared. A guard stands nearby.

"The observatory," Estêvão reminds him with a self-satisfied grin as he exits.

Antonio peels off his saturated clothes and unwinds the blood-soaked dressing from his wound. Only copious quantities of ale had dulled the pain from the injury enough for him to survive the days on horseback from Lisbon to Sagres. He knows he was lucky to escape with the single gash, but the alcohol is wearing off, and the pain sears.

He rebandages the still-oozing cut, puts on a doublet and cloak he had left behind in a wardrobe, and combs his dark, unruly hair with an ivory comb. Holding up a hand mirror, he looks at his dark eyes and his nose, a bit off-kilter from a recent brawl. He has no time to shave, but he deems his appearance respectable, though a bit simple compared to that of his beribboned colleagues. If only he felt the part. He wishes for a swig of ale to blunt the sting of his head and ribs and to take the edge off his nerves.

Antonio hurries down the long corridors from the residences to the study halls and observatory. Though geographers, cartographers, astronomers, captains, scholars, and shipbuilders have been studying and teaching at the School of Navigation since the time of Prince Henry, only in recent times have the halls been abuzz again. After long neglect, King Manuel has reinvigorated plans to find the sea route for the spice trade to India— by rounding the coast of Africa. And competition for involvement has been building.

With as much bravado as he can muster given his condition, he tells the page standing outside the observatory to announce him to the Great Commander, the head of the school. The page informs him of the long wait before his summoning, a delay of which Estêvão must have been aware. As Antonio lingers, fellow cartographers walk by, casting curious glances his way. He knows what they are thinking, with their fancy clothes and schooling: what could the Great Commander possibly want with him, the illegitimate son of a fisherman whose learning took place on the back of an undecked boat with one clumsy sail?

Antonio tells himself that he doesn't care, that his skills far exceed those of these poseurs who have barely seen the open water. But his rage grows. He is about to lash out at Pero, one of Estêvão's cohorts and the most priggish of the group, when the page calls for him.

He hustles into the observatory, the vast open space in which he typically spends hours nearly every day. Antonio has only a moment to scan the Great Commander and his guests before kneeling as custom demands. In that brief moment, he sees an unusually long beard and a floppy hat. The features could only belong to the appointed leader of the king's expedition: Captain-Major Vasco da Gama.

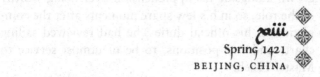

Drums thunder in the dark distance, and Zhi's heart pounds with them. He waits at the back of a long line of eunuchs and civil officials. They have been summoned to an audience with the emperor himself to commemorate the end of the Forbidden City festivities, and to bless the departing expedition.

Zhi tries to quell his nerves at entering the Forbidden City for the first time by reflecting on the past few months. Admiral Zheng had wanted his officers to begin working together without delay, so Director Tang had excused Zhi from the service of Master Shen. Zhi initially felt bittersweet pangs of guilt at the parting with his master, who had been so good to him, but Master Shen eased Zhi's remorse by telling him that he'd always known that a tiger lurked beneath Zhi's respectful catlike demeanor, and he had no wish to cage the wild beast.

Zhi had spent the next few months shuttling between the Imperial City and the port of Tanggu, on the coast of the Yellow Sea, where the fleet had been docked. He had begun his work as assistant to the *Ch'ing Ho*'s formidable chief mapmaker, Master Hsieh Chen, a legendary cartographer who had helped map Admiral Zheng's five previous expeditions. Zhi's excitement over participating in the celebrated sixth voyage had grown alongside his apprehension over being worthy of the role, so in his few spare moments after the completion of his official duties, he had reviewed sailing charts and star positions, to be of utmost service to Master Hsieh.

The keeper to a side entrance to the Forbidden City signals their permission to enter. The drums grow louder as the group walks to the next entrance. Zhi passes under the Gate of Luminous Virtue to the square in which the Hall of Supreme Harmony—the emperor's throne room—rests.

Zhi stares at the marble courtyard, so vast it defies his imagination. He hesitates for so long that he needs to be pushed along by the senior crew member behind him. His eyes are drawn across the immense square to the three marble terraces framing the staircases and ramps that lead to the hall. The tiers are already filled with tens of thousands of noblemen and senior officials, each flying flags designating their grades.

The guard instructs Zhi and his group to assemble at the base of the terraces. Snowflakes drift down onto Zhi's shoulder as they wait for the arrival of the emperor. A censor walks in and out of the carefully assembled audience, ensuring that not a single cuff is out of place. Such an offense would warrant the bamboo rod, or worse. Zhi starts an involuntary—and impermissible— shiver, before the sun finally appears on the horizon to warm him just enough to stop his trembling.

The snow begins to accumulate on the building rooftops. It dulls the bright imperial-yellow tiles and covers the dragons, phoenixes, and horses that prowl on the roofs' seams and edges. The shoulders and hats of the assembly turn white, until servants appear from the shadowy recesses to dust away the snow.

The red-robed master of ceremonies cracks the whip at noon, calling them to attention. In unison, the thousands shout, "Ten thousand blessings to His Majesty" and drop to their knees in the mandated kowtow. They prostrate themselves three times, knocking their foreheads on the flagstone nine times in honor of the emperor, hard enough to bruise.

An otherworldly song emerges from the Hall of Supreme Harmony. The scent of sandalwood and pine begins to fill the air from the eighteen incense burners in front of the hall, each representing a different province. Peacocks strut across the hall's marble platform.

The ceremonial official signals for the ambassadors to enter. The colorfully dressed officials disappear as they enter the haze of incense. Through the eunuch grapevine, Zhi has heard that the emperor will be bestowing farewell gifts of porcelain, jade, and silk upon the envoys, who have been enjoying the imperial celebrations of the Forbidden City's unveiling for several months. Each fleet of Admiral Zheng's armada is tasked with returning these ambassadors to their home countries as the first stop on their mission.

Returning to the hall's platform, the ceremonial official watches as the ambassadors file out. To Zhi's surprise, he cries, "The crew of Admiral Zheng is to approach the Hall of Supreme Harmony!" Guards appear and herd his group, along with several others from higher tiers, toward the hall.

Zhi shivers—no longer from the cold but from fear of being in the presence of the Son of Heaven, of being unworthy to appear in his presence. The assemblage walks down the long carpet covering the icy marble walkway and climbs the stairs to the hall.

As they enter, the voyage's officers throw themselves into postures of prostration before His Imperial Majesty, who alone is permitted to face south. In the fleeting moment before he flings himself to the floor, Zhi catches a glimpse of the famed Dragon Throne. A gold dragon coils around the throne's arms and legs in such a way that Zhi cannot see where the reptilian limb begins or ends. From his position on the floor, he strains to see more and is rewarded with a glimpse of the hem of the Emperor's silk robe; it is imperial yellow, a color he alone may wear. An embroidered dragon stares out at Zhi with ruby eyes, a spine of pearls, and five claws of emeralds.

The ceremonial master speaks for the emperor: "His Imperial Majesty gives Admiral Zheng He leave to rise and approach him for a blessing."

Though Zhi cannot see Zheng stand and move toward the emperor, Zhi knows he does so with lowered eyes. No one, not even Zheng, one of the emperor's closest confidants, dares look directly at the Son of Heaven. Zhi hears Zheng drop back down to the floor in a kowtow and utter compliments to the emperor.

On the emperor's behalf, the ceremonial master announces, "His Imperial Majesty wishes to bless Admiral Zheng He's voyage. May Zheng safely return the envoys to their honored homelands. May the emperor's civilizing goodness accompany you on the rest of your journey, allowing you to enlighten and collect tribute from the barbarians beyond the seas. May you bring His Imperial Majesty's sacred radiance to shine on All Under Heaven."

* * *

The senior crew members hurry out of the Forbidden City after their audience with the emperor, dispersing into the recesses of the Imperial City. Each rushes to his former quarters to pack his few remaining belongings.

As quickly as protocol permits, Zhi darts through the Xuanwu Gate, past the vast Coal Hill. He arrives at his sleeping quarters. It is the busiest part of the workday, and his fellow eunuchs are toiling in the agency building. Except Liang, who waits to say farewell.

Liang bows. "I have prayed to Allah that you have a safe journey and return." He hands Zhi a small, round bronze mirror with an eight-spoked Taoist wheel on the other side. The talisman is meant to ward off the evil spirits of the barbarians he will encounter. Though the friends are Muslim, the religious diversity and tolerance practiced in the Imperial City has softened them: in this way, the seemingly incongruous gift is not inconsistent with their Hui faith.

Zhi bows in thanks.

They pause, uncertain of what to say next. Zhi knows that he will not have a trusted friend like this in the long years to come, if ever. Someone he has known since his boyhood days, who suffered through the pain of losing his manhood with him, as well as the humiliation of their early eunuch training. Someone who understands his longing for Shu. Zhi also knows that, in a different way, Liang will be just as isolated upon his departure. And they both realize that Zhi might not return. Of the tens of thousands who will leave with him on the voyage, more than half will not come back.

Without words, the friends exchange a brief, awkward

embrace. After so long without any human touch, the gesture feels uncomfortable to both of them. Liang exits the building before any other emotions can surface.

Zhi watches his friend pass through the archway and out of his sight. He does not have time to indulge his feelings, so he hastens to his bed to gather his possessions. After placing the few items in his sack, he runs his hand along the wooden frame of his bed and dislodges his lotus blossom painting. He could not afford to have it on his person until now. Craning his neck to make sure no one has entered the building, he stores the illicit item in the teak box holding his *pao*.

Ben held the flap open so Mara could enter the tent. She walked into a surprising hub of activity. Two men in white lab coats, gloves, and surgical masks knelt in the pit, next to the body, she presumed. More men wearing similar gear worked in the back of the tent with a daunting array of scientific equipment. Mara was impressed that Ben had constructed all this in the few short weeks since the body's discovery.

Ben explained that his team had erected the tent around the pit where he had found the body. This way, they could examine it in situ and protect it from the elements. Though, he admitted, they had removed the teak box, since it sat on the body's chest cavity and blocked further study. That was how they had discovered the map.

He invited her to take a closer look. Mara approached the railing around the pit and peered over it. The fully dressed, intact skeleton was in a fetal position, with the exception of one hand, which rested on its brow as if warding off a blow. Even though the body was nearly six hundred years old, its pose and attire made it appear lifelike to Mara. She could nearly envision the poor man in his final hour.

"Do you think he's the mapmaker?" she asked quietly.

Despite the passage of time, it felt disrespectful to speak of the deceased in his presence.

Ben had no such hesitation. "Huang and I have been discussing that possibility. But I doubt it. His clothes are very modest, the kind of robes worn by someone poor. And the maker of the map would have been well educated and of a relatively high status."

"Could he have been a courier of some sort? He was on the Silk Road, after all."

"Maybe. But he isn't wearing a uniform or carrying any paraphernalia of a messenger. It's very curious."

She continued to stare at the body. "Regardless, it's a tragedy."

Mara was glad that it took them over an hour to reach the makeshift restaurant on the fringes of town. She had temporarily lost her appetite after viewing the body, and she needed the time to restore it, particularly since Ben had insisted that they dine in an establishment that did its best to match Xi'an's reputation for making the finest dumplings.

"Tell me about these Tocharians you study," Mara asked Ben. She was glad her desire for food had returned, since the *jiaozi* weren't just any dumplings. The restaurant, really just a lean-to adorned only with plastic chairs and tables, served savory dumplings shaped like swans and roosters, and sweet dumplings shaped like almonds and butterflies, among other confections.

Ben shoved in a steaming dumpling with his chopsticks before answering. He struck her as someone who became so engrossed in his work that he forgot to eat, only to find himself ravenous at day's end. As he chewed, he asked, "Have you ever heard of the Tarim mummies?"

The name sounded familiar, but she couldn't place it. She shook her head.

"In the 1980s, Chinese archaeologists exploring the southern rim of the Tarim Basin, a harsh desert on the outer edges of the Silk Road, uncovered a grave site with several thirty-five-hundred-year-old bodies. They were far better preserved than anything ever recovered in Egypt. The bodies were dressed in brightly colored garments—often in a twill or tartan weave like that found in Scottish kilts. The scientists shipped the bodies to a museum at Urumchi, where they sat until 1994, when some magazines published cover stories on them, complete with glossy photos. What everyone noticed immediately was that these bodies were clearly Caucasoid, not Chinese or Mongoloid, and that they were well over six feet tall."

"Who were they?" she asked.

"One possibility was that they were Tocharians. They were a people that originated in Celtic Europe but migrated east, to the Tarim Basin and very likely beyond."

"Prehistoric Celtic Europeans trekked east all the way to Asia?" Mara was skeptical.

He seemed not to notice. "It's one possibility. Because of my studies on the Tocharian peoples, I was asked to join an expedition in the 1990s studying the Tarim Basin mummies. The site leaders wanted to see if the mummies were indeed Tocharians."

"Were they?"

"I'd argue yes, as would others in my field. And if

we're right, the Tarim Basin mummies could change our perception of history."

"What do you mean?"

"If the Tocharians traveled from Europe to China, then China didn't develop its civilization in isolation from the West, but was influenced by prehistoric Europeans. If so, it might have been Europeans who introduced both the wheel and bronze metallurgy—two of the primary technologies of civilization—to the Chinese."

Ben continued, sharing the details about the site outside of Xi'an to which he'd been dispatched by Tobias's not-for-profit the very moment two Tarim Basin–like mummies had been found. Though not as perfectly preserved as the Tarim Basin dig because the climate was not as arid, the site held promise. His face was illuminated by the thought of his discoveries and their impact on history, by the very notion that history might have to be rewritten based on his findings.

As he spoke, Mara was moved by his excitement and his principled desire to contribute to the greater good. She sensed herself tapping back into her own childhood desire to uncover some long-hidden artifact critical to unlocking the past. So long in the company of opportunists, she felt a softening toward him and his ethics, and his enthusiasm for knowledge for its own sake, not for the sums it could garner.

Mara's back stiffened when she realized it. For the past three years, she'd worked hard at building a wall against such vulnerability. She had laid the bricks so close together that she thought not a crack of light could filter through. Yet somehow, while she was sitting in a ramshackle restaurant on the dusty outskirts of a remote Chinese village, a tiny ray had managed to penetrate.

Ben's expression changed as he continued: "On that first Tarim Basin dig, I experienced my first theft. When we arrived, we discovered that grave robbers had systematically ransacked scores of tombs spread over several acres of the site. The robbers had strewn about body parts and other artifacts, and destroyed the graves themselves. They rendered the entire section of the site incapable of evaluation." He stopped chewing and shook his head in disgust and anger. "It was devastating."

"I understand." She was sympathetic, but she had seen far too many thefts to be particularly moved by the Tarim Basin plunder.

"No, you don't. Mara, after that experience in the Tarim Basin, I swore I wouldn't allow another theft on one of my digs. I failed."

"Ben, you can't blame yourself. Grave robbery is a respectable profession in certain parts of China; I can't tell you how many thefts of this sort I've seen."

He raised an eyebrow. "How have you seen numerous archaeological lootings?"

"I recover stolen art for a living. Didn't Richard tell you that?"

"No. He just mentioned that his representative would be visiting my site, to find out about the robbery. I assumed you worked for one of his organizations."

"I work for myself. Richard hired me to find the map."

Ben sized her up, as if seeing her for the first time. He then signaled for the bill, and Mara gathered up her belongings. She'd reached out her hand to shake it in farewell when he asked, "Can I walk you to the police station? It isn't easy to find."

"No thanks." She was confused by his question. "Ben,

I'm not going to the police station. I won't be going to the authorities."

"Why not?"

"Look, you have your area of expertise and I have mine. Please believe that the only way I'll find this map is by going *not* to the authorities but to the criminals."

Mara spent the two precious hours before her meeting with Li Wen dealing with Ben. He could not understand why she refused to speak with the police about the theft, and claimed that he had held off contacting them himself only because Richard had asked him to wait until after talking with her. No amount of rational justification, cajoling, or pleading could bring Ben around to Mara's sensible—to her way of thinking—position that she needed to pursue the map in her own way. He could not conceive of, let alone condone, working with the very gang members who might have stolen the map, even if it was the only way of getting it back. And he did not believe that Richard really meant for her to keep the authorities in the dark permanently. The principles she had fleetingly admired during dinner now constituted an unyielding impediment to her plans.

Ben left her with no choice but to dial Richard. She felt like a child tattling on a sibling to a parent.

After working her way through a web of assistants, she got him on the line. "Richard, Mara Coyne here. I'm so sorry to disturb you, but I have a situation. Your archaeologist, Ben Coleman, is insisting that I contact the police."

"I thought I made my position on that abundantly clear."

"And I have shared your position with Mr. Coleman.

Regardless of your wishes, he says he will go to the police if I do not."

"Put him on the line."

Mara handed the phone to Ben, who rose from the restaurant table. He went off to a dark corner and started pacing. She strained to hear their conversation, but Ben spoke in hushed tones.

Ben returned to the table and gave her the phone. "Richard wants to speak with you."

"I'm sorry, Richard, about involving you—"

"Enough," he cut her off. "I've explained to Mr. Coleman my stance on governmental involvement, and he has come around. I do fund the dig on which he found the map."

"Good. Then I will proceed."

"Yes. Mr. Coleman has indicated that he would like to join you in your investigation."

"You mean at my meetings here in China?"

"Yes. And beyond."

Mara thought she must have misunderstood. "Surely he doesn't want to come along for my entire investigation?"

"That is what he said. He reminded me that, in fact, he is one of the only people who has actually seen the map. He may well prove critical in identifying it. Do you think you might be able to oblige him?" Richard's query seemed less of a question and more of a command.

Mara's initial reaction was to say no, to explain that Ben's presence would hinder her work. But then Richard was the client, and he was probably right about Ben's usefulness. "Of course, Richard. I think I can accommodate Ben's request."

A thickset man conducted Mara, Ben, Huang, and Paul Wong's man Lam to a private room at the back of a primitive restaurant. Two hulking guards stood in front of the doorway. They parted only when the man nodded.

Mara entered the room first, with Lam at her side, as she had arranged with Ben beforehand. Paul had informed his "important businessman" friend Li Wen about Mara and Lam. But not about Ben and Huang, whom Ben had suggested bringing along to help with local dialect translation.

A group of middle-aged men sat around a circular table, some in modern dress and some white-bearded and wearing skullcaps. The room was thick with the smoke and scent of unfiltered cigarettes. A light fixture lit by bare bulbs hung above them. A plate of cut oranges sat in the middle of the table, and each man had a toothpick between his teeth. This was a long way from Spring Moon at the Peninsula, Mara thought. And an even longer way from Severin, Oliver & Means.

The men stared at her, unblinking. Their eyes were black as obsidian and just as hard. For the first time since she'd entered the restaurant, the bold show she'd put on for Ben abandoned her, and she felt afraid.

Mara bowed low to the table in general, since she

had no idea which man was Li Wen. "My apologies for interrupting your meal," she said through Huang. She had only a rudimentary knowledge of Mandarin, enough to get by for traveling purposes. Huang would be useful to ensure that she grasped Li Wen's every nuance and, in turn, that he understood her. "Paul Wong said I should visit you."

Guttural grumblings came from the man in the maroon nylon jacket. She stayed in her stooped position, waiting for the exchange between Huang and the man she assumed to be Li Wen to finish. Her fear intensified as she watched Huang's demeanor transform from deferential to terrified. "He says he welcomes you and Lam as friends of Paul Wong. He asks who are these other people." Huang's voice was unsteady.

Mara stood up and faced Li Wen, whose eyes remained harsh and impenetrable. She was scared, but knew she needed to appear fearless or lose all footing. "They are also friends of Paul Wong."

After a seeming eternity in which Li scrutinized each of them in turn, Li spoke again. "He invites you to sit with him," Huang said.

Mara started toward one of the empty chairs at the circular table, but Huang quickly stopped her. "Over there." He motioned to one of the scattered side tables. Mara suddenly appreciated that these men would avoid sitting with a Western woman, particularly if they were Muslim. She sat at the designated table, keeping her head bowed as a sign of deference. Ben, Huang, and Lam stood behind her, and she was glad of their presence in that setting.

Li Wen hoisted himself out of his seat at the circular table and took a chair at the side table, the one farthest from her. He coughed and spat on the floor. Mara pretended it wasn't the sign of disrespect he intended.

Mara began. She pointed to Ben and said, "This man here works on an archaeological dig outside of town. He found an old scroll."

Mara waited for Huang to translate her comment and Li's response. "He says this is an ancient region. There are many old scrolls here."

"This is true," Mara said. "This old scroll, however, is missing. This man here may have mislaid it."

Through Huang, Li said, "When a site yields many goods, misplacing one is possible."

"Yes, that is true. It is also possible that this old scroll was stolen."

Huang's eyes pleaded with Mara not to make him translate her statement. She met his gaze, and Huang turned back toward Li. The men conversed for a while, but Mara's Mandarin could not keep up with their rapid delivery or local dialect.

"He says that progress has made the Chinese people greedy. Especially the younger people," Huang said with some relief.

"Please tell him this is a problem in all countries. Not just China."

Through Huang, Mara and Li conversed about the growing temptations faced by the very young. Several minutes into this chat, Ben started to shift behind her. She understood that all this small talk might seem pointless to the uninitiated, but it was building to the question at hand. Rushing to the point shut the door to information.

Mara said, "Please tell Li Wen that we do not care

how the old scroll left the archaeological site. We only come to ask his advice about its whereabouts."

It was Li's turn to talk, but he had grown silent. She watched as he smoked his cigarette down to the nub, until his fingers touched the burning embers. But he did not flinch. As she waited for him to speak, she grew more anxious, and not just about the chances of getting a name out of Li.

He let out a noise like a growl. "He says maybe he can confer with his colleagues to see if any wayward young people had a hand in this missing map," Huang translated.

"I would very much appreciate such a consultation."

Li Wen stood up and motioned for them to leave the room. They proceeded past the guards and waited in the adjoining public restaurant area.

The room was empty save for one family. Mara watched as the little group of father, mother, and adolescent son dug their chopsticks into steaming bowls of rice. Their faces were ruddy from labor and the rising heat of the meal after the chill of the brisk night. Their worn clothes and eagerness over the food showed their meager means. Mara realized that under such circumstances, grave robbery would be tempting. Even understandable.

One of the guards signaled for their reentry. They filed into the room and stood against the wall. Mara waited for the verdict: would Li share the name of the thief? He undoubtedly knew it, since no crime could be committed in this region without his permission.

Li signaled for Mara to take her seat. He began barking at Huang. From the furrow of Li's brow and the tone of his undecipherable voice, Mara knew he would never divulge the information she sought. When Li's torrent ceased, Huang turned to her and confirmed it.

Though she held her head high, as if such failure was anticipated, the humiliation bore down on Mara's shoulders as Ben, Huang, and Lam escorted her to the hotel. She had experienced disappointment like the one with Li Wen only a handful of times, and never with a client as a witness. Ben's presence compounded her embarrassment, especially after she had been so insistent about using her own methods.

Walking through the unpaved streets of the small outpost, the group did not speak. They passed an open-air market that offered livestock, bins of spices and herbs, handwoven carpets, and opulent fabrics side by side. Going by the slightly ajar door of a mosque, they glimpsed men at prayer on one side and veiled women on the other. Intoxicated by the rhythmic chanting of their prayers, Mara closed her eyes and imagined for a moment that she walked on the Silk Road of history, rather than the disappointing Silk Road of Communist China.

Huang held the door open for her as they entered the hotel lobby. Only a few mass-produced decorations and the starkest fluorescent lighting alleviated the bleakness of the Communist-issue concrete-block walls. Mara wasn't sure that the establishment even deserved to be called a hotel.

Huang walked over to reception—really just a wood-veneer student's desk dressed up with a vase of plastic flowers. With the recalcitrant Lam nearby, Mara and Ben stood alone. She tried to form the right phrase, yet words escaped her. Ben broke the silence first.

"That meeting didn't go so well, did it?" He said it without a note of sarcasm or a hint of gloating in his voice. Admirably kind, she thought.

"No. But I do have other leads," Mara quickly offered.

"Of course," he answered, just as quickly.

"I just need to make a few phone calls tonight to New York to firm them up." Her dossier did indeed contain a flow chart of the map-theft underworld and the paths by which the map might have left China, all of which were typical avenues of investigation. Mara had hoped that Li Wen might prove a time-saving shortcut through the usual drudgery.

"Should we just meet here in the lobby tomorrow morning, then? I'll bring my bags and passport."

"Sure. Do you have any personal arrangements to make? I don't know how long we'll be gone."

"No," he answered, with just a hint of wistfulness in his voice. "There's no one to notify; it's only me. And Huang can run the dig while I'm gone. We've been working together for years."

Huang returned and handed Mara her key. He told her where her room was and advised her not to open her hotel door for anyone. The hotel had a reputation for cleanliness and good security, but in the Wild West of newly open China, precautions were advisable. She reminded him that Lam would be on guard until she left the next day.

Mara and Lam trudged up the one flight of stairs and down the dimly lit hall to her room. Lam signaled that he would be waiting outside. The door creaked as she pushed it open and locked it behind her. She threw herself and her bags down on the bed.

The mental flagellation began. What had she done wrong with Li Wen? In a ritual that had become almost routine over the past couple of years, she solicited the right name from the right channel, and then money and information changed hands once she met the contact. Her reputation helped assuage any anxiety her contacts might have about the involvement of the authorities. On occasion, a physical threat loomed, as it had that evening, but it passed without incident. Was Ben the problem? His work would keep his team at the dig for the foreseeable future, and perhaps Li and his men wanted a second go at the site.

Mara had picked up her cell phone to commiserate with Joe when a knock sounded at the door. She froze.

The knock sounded again. Where was Lam? She assumed if Ben or Huang stood outside, they would identify themselves. Especially after Huang had warned her not to unlock the door for anybody.

The door shuddered from an even stronger pounding. Though she wanted to look through the peephole, Mara feared this would confirm her presence in the room. She looked for possible exits but observed only two tiny windows, neither large enough for her to squeeze through. She remained motionless while she weighed other options. What the hell had happened to Lam?

A heavily accented voice called out: "Miss Coyne, it is Li Wen."

The daylight has faded, and the study halls have long since emptied. The students and scholars have retired, rendering the night silent but for the crash of the waves on the cliffs below. The candlelight flickers in the evening air and provides scant illumination in the navigators' chambers. Yet Antonio continues to scrutinize the charts of Diogo Cão and Bartolomeu Dias, their practical portolan maps with detailed depictions of the shores.

Da Gama's predecessors, Dias and Cão had traversed West Africa by hugging the shore. Antonio is determined to glean every nuance of their coastline voyages by memorizing their day-by-day pilotage manuals. He does this not only because the Great Commander so charged him as pilot and mapmaker for the *São Rafael*, one of the four ships on da Gama's expedition, but mostly because he knows that this opportunity—rife with prospects of gold, jewels, and spices—will come once in his lifetime.

He must make himself indispensable to da Gama, and his innate sense of direction will take him only so far. Antonio knows that it was this strange, unerring voice inside his head that landed him at the School of Navigation after he guided the Great Commander's second-in-charge to safety on his uncle's boat during an unexpected squall. At the school, he has learned to make the charts and maps speak to him in their strange, fitful language, though if any of his arrogant fellow cartographers were to ask, he'd insist that at sea, as with women, he would rather go by hunch and experience than obey the books.

So Antonio works harder than ever before, committing the endless portolans to memory. He keeps his cravings for women and ale and dice in abeyance by imagining the indulgences he will be able to afford with pockets lined in gold from his travels. His riches might even provide him with the means to see Helena, who lives in his coastal home village near Sagres but might as well live in England for all his access to her.

Antonio pauses in his labors for a moment, thinking about the first time he saw Helena. He had been docking his uncle's fishing boat in the bay adjacent to the warehouses built by her father for his merchant ventures. As he unloaded the day's catch, he saw two women walking on the stone jetty her father had constructed. They carried parasols, and he could not see their faces at first. Yet some aspect of their carriage captivated him, and he waited.

After he'd busied himself with netting for a few moments, the younger woman lowered her parasol to speak to the older, and he was rewarded with a glance at her face. Her black hair gleamed in the sun, and her skin was pure white, so different from the tanned and weathered faces of the women he knew, even the young ones. It was his first glimpse of Helena.

He shakes his head to banish the taunting memories. He brings the candlelight closer to the rhumb lines on Dias's chart, but not near enough to singe the treasured document. He hears the march of footsteps but ignores them. In preparation for the expedition, the school over-flows at all hours with emissaries from King Manuel, visiting nautical scholars and shipbuilders, and military men.

The door swings open. A cadre of Order of Christ knights swoops into the room. Captain-Major Vasco da Gama, swathed in black, cuts through the knights' white mass like a storm cloud.

Antonio drops to his knees.

"Antonio Coelho," da Gama says and gives him leave to rise.

For a rare moment, Antonio stands eye to eye with his leader. He doesn't respect or fear many men, but Antonio has heard rumors that da Gama does not suffer fools, practices a rabid Christianity, and has a lightning-quick temper. He waits for da Gama to speak.

"I have come here to show you something."

Da Gama signals to one of the knights. Resplendent in a pristine tunic of white embroidered with a square red cross, the soldier carries a simple wooden box to the navigators' worktable. With a flick of his wrist, da Gama motions for the knights to leave them.

The knights depart, and the two seamen stand alone at the table. Da Gama lifts the lid off the long, narrow box and slides out a scroll. Laying it on the surface, he unrolls it by turning the two rods at either end.

The wavering candlelight reveals a strange map, re-sembling no chart Antonio has ever seen before. Yet he finds its strangeness beautiful. Other maps speak to him, but this one sings.

Mesmerized, Antonio forgets his station and asks, "What is this?"

Da Gama forgives the gaffe by deigning to answer. "It is Portugal's greatest burden and our utmost treasure, brought to us by Saint Vincent himself."

"I see," he says, though he does not.

"You will keep it secret, as have the knights of the Order of Christ, as have I, and have my predecessors."

"Certainly, Captain-Major." Since the days of Prince Henry, disclosing Portugal's maps has been punishable by death, so of course Antonio gives his accord. His assurance does not stop his mind from calculating the price this map would fetch from another kingdom.

"Antonio Coehlo, you will use this precious chart to find the sea route to India so that we may spread Christianity and fulfill Portugal's divine destiny."

Mara thought about opening the door and running, but then stopped herself. If Li Wen's intentions were nefarious, would he really announce himself to her? No, he'd send a thug in the dead of night. So she turned the knob and cracked the door, but left the chain intact.

There stood Li Wen, with the two enormous guards from the restaurant framing him like bookends. Lam stood beside them with a helpless expression on his face. So much for looking out for her best interests.

"Are you going to ask me in?" Li asked in English.

She must have looked at him with a comically incredulous expression, because he laughed. "I'm here for business only, Miss Coyne."

"You speak English?"

"One must speak the language of commerce if one wants to trade."

"If you are here to trade, you are welcome to come in."

Mara slid the chain off the hook, not that it provided any real protection anyway. Before he could enter the cramped room with his guards in tow, she said, "You can only come in by yourself. They must wait outside."

Li said, "If your man waits outside too."

Mara nodded her agreement and then stood aside to let Li in. They sat in the room's two uncomfortably small chairs. Without any pretense of small talk, he began.

"One of my colleagues did hear a rumor. I pass it on to you at great risk to myself, since he did not want me to share it with you. I do so only because you are a friend of Paul Wong."

Mara understood this meant that Paul now owed Li a favor. She also appreciated that she had to pay Li for his "great risk." She had brought a satchel full of yuan with her to the initial meeting for that very purpose, but had never had the opportunity to use it.

Nodding her assent to the unspoken terms, she reached to the bed and grabbed her bag off it. She laid it on the ground next to her chair.

Li started talking. "My colleague heard some gossip about this old scroll. It was indeed stolen from the archaeological site of the man who accompanied you today."

"Does your colleague know the name of the thief?"

He nodded. "As we suspected, one of our foolish young people took it. But the name of the thief is of no importance. This youth proceeded at the direction of another."

"Did your colleague tell you who instructed this young person to act?"

Li uttered a name. Through the haze of his accent, it sounded familiar. She thought her ears were playing tricks on her, so she asked him to repeat himself.

"The youth was employed by an Italian man."

"Can you repeat the name of this Italian?"

"He is called Ermanno Cavelli."

Hearing the name spoken again, Mara froze. She knew it well. During her work with Joe, she had dealt before with Ermanno Cavelli, a well-known agent for map thieves.

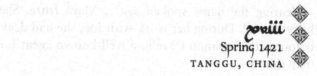
Zhi races to the carts waiting outside the east gates of the Imperial City to take the senior crew to the Grand Canal, outside the city. Once at the canal, he squeezes into a center seat in one of the already packed barges about to set out for Tanggu. The crew needs to reach the fleet in advance of the soon-departing ambassadors to ensure that the ships will be ready for them.

For more than a day, the barges make their way through the thirty-six locks to the Yellow Sea. Zhi hears his fellow officers exchange details about the audience with the emperor, the first for nearly all of them. While he shares their exhilaration, he spends the short trip mentally preparing for the first leg of their journey: across the Yellow Sea and Indian Ocean to the coast of Africa, a route traveled by Admiral Zheng's ships before.

As the barges pass through the final lock into the harbor, many of the crew rise from their seats to watch the entrance into the sea. Hearing gasps of wonder, Zhi, too, rises from his cramped seat and struggles to see. Even though Zhi has witnessed the assembly of the armada over the preceding months, he is unprepared for the sight of the ships decked out in their full regalia, sails unfurled.

Near to a hundred nine-masted treasure ships, enormous at five hundred feet in length and two hundred feet across, command the center. Vast red sails soar on the treasure boats, while menacing dragons' eyes stare out from the sides at any that dare look their way. Bronze cannons stand guard on the decks, but the sailors need not use any military might. The terrifying appearance of the treasure ships in the harbors will bend the barbarians' will without force.

Supply, horse, and merchant ships, smaller but still massive, encircle the treasure boats. Squadrons of sleek warships and troop transports guard them, though they are used more for intimidation than for military maneuvers. The armada, over seven hundred vessels in total, will sail in this configuration—treasure ships always in the heavily guarded core—until it reaches Malaysia. There, the armada will split into five fleets of over one hundred ships, each with their own, still undisclosed mission. Zhi is certain that the display will amaze even the most jaded of ambassadors.

In the days that follow, the crew waits for the arrival of the foreign envoys from the Forbidden City. In a little mountainside temple overlooking the sea, the officers take turns praying for a north wind. Without the northeast monsoon, the armada cannot gather enough speed to make the first leg of the journey. While most crew members burn incense and offer prayers to the Taoist goddess of the sea, Ma Tsu, Zhi breathes in the smell of the sea air, peers out at the harbor from their vantage point, and silently implores Allah. Though his years in the Imperial City have taught him that his Muslim faith need not be exclusive—or judgmental—of other religious beliefs, he still puts his trust in Allah.

He thinks he hears a gentle rustle in the leaves of the trees outside the temple. Yet no one stirs, so he continues with his private prayers. The rustling grows louder, and he swears he hears tree branches snapping with its mounting force. The Taoist chants persist.

Then a cry sounds out. The north wind has appeared, as Zhi had suspected. The crew hurries down the hillside and boards small rowboats to take their places on the ships. On board the *Ch'ing Ho,* Zhi dashes past Admiral Zhou's sea cabin and the staterooms for the ambassadors and their staff. He scurries past the concubines' rooms, located conveniently near the ambassadors' quarters. He hears a giggle and then his name: "Assistant Mapmaker Ma, please come here."

Taking a few steps back, he peers around the corner and into the concubines' luxurious chambers. They are hard at work painting their faces and donning elaborate gowns for the benefit of the arriving envoys. They would not dare invite a real man, other than an ambassador, into their rooms and a crewman could be killed for even daring to approach their rooms. But Zhi is not a real man.

A slender young woman wearing a silk robe the color of pink peonies steps forward from the group. Zhi is struck by her gown's color; it is the same hue as that worn by Shu on their last meeting. The woman's embroidered shoe peeks out from her hem, and he notices that her foot, unlike those of most women he has known, is large and unbound.

She bows, and her hair swings. "We are sorry to disturb you, Assistant Mapmaker Ma, but we were hoping you might tell us when we will depart from Tanggu."

"At dawn's first light," he says, and then bows in a hasty farewell. There is much to do before departure.

"Many thanks. I am Ke. I hope we will meet again."

Zhi turns back in surprise at the solicitous remark: it is an unusually friendly gesture, for as a eunuch he can do nothing to further a concubine's ultimate goal of securing the affections of an envoy who might free her. Her statement unsettles and confuses him, and he stammers, "I must go."

He rushes to the enclosed small bridge and adjoining cabins for the navigational crew. This is where Zhi will work, sleep, and dine for the years of the voyage, along with the chief navigator, Master Hong, and the chief mapmaker, Master Hsieh. Under the instruction of Master Hsieh, Zhi readies the private navigational bridge and cabins. Through the porthole, he sees other, final preparations under way. The supply ships collect stores of water and rice, the treasure ships amass stocks of dried fish, and the warships receive a last supply of gunpowder. As soon as the ambassadors board, the fleet will set sail.

In the dark hours before dawn, the envoys and their staff sleep in their silken staterooms with the ivory limbs of the concubines wrapped around them, Ke among them, he imagines. Admiral Zhou assembles the officers on the main deck.

Zhi stands by Master Hsieh and the navigators. They all lower their heads as the admiral offers a last prayer to the sea goddess, Ma Tsu. As Zhi returns to the navigational bridge to assist Master Hsieh, he watches the red sails of the armada's treasure ships billow with the monsoon winds. He says a silent farewell to China.

Present Day

ASOLO, ITALY

Mara floored the little rented Fiat down the open highway. Ben had wanted to drive, but Mara had insisted. She loved getting behind the wheel, especially when she had so few opportunities to do so in New York. And, as she'd explained, she already knew the way to Asolo. She had visited Ermanno Cavelli there on more than one occasion.

Over the roar of the engine, Ben asked, "Tell me more about this Ermanno Cavelli we're going to see." The mad dash to the Xi'an airport and the subsequent series of exhausting flights to Venice had left them with little privacy to discuss the developments. Plus, Mara thought it safer for Ben if she shared as little as possible with him.

"He's a fairly major player in the map and rare-print underworld. He acts as a middleman between collectors who desire certain pieces and those who will 'procure' them. So he probably arranged for your stolen map to go directly to the collector who'd commissioned the theft."

"Without even seeing the piece himself?" Ben asked.

"Possibly," Mara answered with a shrug, though she wondered why Ben would care whether Ermanno saw the map or not.

"How convenient that you know this Ermanno

Cavelli already." Ben's tone conveyed his skepticism at the coincidence—and his continued disdain over her pursuing the matter privately.

"The world in which I operate is very small. One with few players."

As they approached the medieval hill town of Asolo, not far outside of Venice, Mara reminded herself that, in effect, Ben was her client and deserved to feel comfortable with their agenda. She took a deep breath and tried to allay his concerns and confusion, hoping that knowledge might ratchet down his high-mindedness as well.

Mara explained a bit about the obscure world of stolen maps. The thefts ranged from amateurish, X-acto knife slicings of maps from atlases under librarians' noses to carefully planned, commissioned robberies from guarded collectors' homes or museums. More and more thefts fell into the latter category as rare-book libraries stepped up their security in the wake of high-profile plunder and as the market for antique maps continued to narrow. She finished her brief tutorial with instructions—couched as carefully phrased suggestions—on how best to behave in the presence of a map thief.

They quieted as they spied Asolo in the distance. Its medieval walls and castle clung to the steep foothills of a nearby mountain range. The town's red-tiled roofs nestled in and around the ancient ramparts and crumbling fifteenth-century fortifications. During earlier visits with Ermanno Cavelli, Mara had learned that Asolo became a royal court of sorts in the fifteenth century when Venice's leader sent the exiled queen Caterina Cornaro to the town to keep her from interfering with

Venetian politics. In the centuries since, aristocrats continued to live in the town, as did poets, musicians, and painters.

Mara pushed the Fiat to climb the long hill into the old town. She saw Ben cringe as she squeezed the little car around the impossibly narrow roads and into a tight space near the central piazza. As they strolled across the square, Mara watched as local townspeople and a smattering of tourists slowly sipped coffees and proseccos at outdoor café tables. Their languorous enjoyment of the drinks and the slight chill in the fall air almost made her wish she were visiting Asolo as a sightseer herself. But work prevailed, as always.

Ben and Mara meandered through the winding town streets, as if they were just like the visitors sauntering nearby. They passed under archways laden with vines that, Mara recalled, drooped with fragrant blossoms in the summertime. With ancient frescoes still visible on the buildings, the medieval atmosphere pervaded.

"It's so charming," Ben said, almost as though he was disappointed.

Mara laughed. "Not what you'd expect for the lair of a notorious map thief, right?"

They continued down the streets until they reached a dead end. Ben turned around, thinking they had taken a wrong turn, but Mara made a quick left up an even narrower road, more of an alleyway. She stopped to gaze at the street's sole store window, so dusty Ben complained that he could hardly see inside. Mara laughed to herself; she found his grumblings ironic, given that he looked as though the dirt from the dig still clung to his rumpled khaki pants, olive T-shirt, and backpack.

A small brass plaque bore the store name in a simple

script: *Asolo Arte di Cavelli*. Mara reached for the doorknob.

"This is it?" Ben asked, his voice brimming with disbelief.

"This is it," Mara said with a smile, turning the knob.

A gentle bell rang as Mara carefully closed the shop door behind them. She and Ben started wandering around the crowded little store. Books were piled on the tables and competed for space on the shelves. A few softly colored maps of Venice and the Veneto region hung on the walls amid the more recently rendered town views of Asolo.

Ben picked up a particularly large atlas and, while paging through it, inadvertently dropped it with a loud thud. A stocky, older gentleman wearing a patched brown cardigan materialized from the back room. He reached for a white cloth draped over his shoulder and wiped his hands on it, as if he were just finishing an afternoon meal.

He smiled and asked, in excellent English, "Can I help you, sir? Are you and the lady looking for something special?"

Mara answered, "We are indeed looking for something special. We are looking for a map thief."

Ben's eyes widened.

The man started to chuckle. "Some would say you need not look too far."

Mara laughed at his little joke. Ermanno had always been one of her favorites in the unseemly world of art thieves. He had a certain old-world charm and dignity she often found lacking in the younger set. "Ermanno Cavelli, so good to see you."

"Mara Coyne, always a pleasure."

The two walked toward each other, embraced, and kissed each other on both cheeks. After they exchanged pleasantries and Ermanno made inquiries about Joe, he locked the front door of the shop and invited them to the back room. There, they entered a space entirely different from the filmy, antique world of the shop: a well-lit and scrupulously clean room with a state-of-the-art computer system. They sat down at a table in the corner.

"Mara, what brings you all the way from the busy streets of New York City to my quiet little shop?"

"We really are looking for a map thief. One who has had recent dealings with a Chinese businessman by the name of Li Wen."

"Ah, I see." Ermanno gave a wry smile, then shot a look in Ben's direction. Mara understood from this glance that Ermanno would not be comfortable speaking directly about the robbery; oblique exchanges would have to suffice.

"We'd be grateful for any information you might have."

He rubbed his brow, as if considering her supplication. "What if this map thief who recently dealt with Li Wen had arranged for the theft at another's request?"

"I had suspected as much."

"Would you be satisfied with information about the man who commissioned the theft?"

"Of course. If I had such information, I would never need to mention the name of his intermediary to anyone."

Thus appeased, Ermanno said, "I have heard rumors that a well-known map thief ordered this theft."

"Can you tell me the name of this map thief?"

"Well, that is the tricky part."

"How is that tricky?"

"I have never heard his name mentioned. His real name, anyway."

Out of the corner of her eye, Mara saw Ben shake his head. Though she suspected that Ben might not swallow Ermanno's claimed ignorance, aliases and nicknames were standard practice in the art-theft underworld.

"He must be called something. By what name is he known?"

Ermanno hesitated, then said, "I know him only as Dias. I understand that he is called that after Bartolomeu Dias, the first explorer to round the Cape of Good Hope."

"Can you tell me what you know about this Dias?" Mara understood that Ermanno was conflicted. On one hand, he wanted to help her; in the past, she and Joe had done him some favors that had kept him from the authorities by negotiating for the private return of several museum-quality engravings. On the other, he did not want to reveal too much and risk losing future work as an intermediary by developing a reputation for exposing his clients.

Ermanno shrugged. "I do not know what help it will be, but I can share the gossip I have heard."

"I'd very much appreciate that, Ermanno."

"Ah well, Dias. I have heard that he is very interested in world maps and pays well and on time."

Mara prompted him to go on. "Do you know where this Dias is?"

"He is rumored to be in many places. Though I have heard he is in Portugal these days. In Lisbon."

"Do you know anything more about him?"

"No."

A silence heavy with unspoken requests descended upon the table. Mara let it hang between her and Ermanno, knowing that he needed to make the next proposal. And he did.

"Mara, I might be able to help if you told me precisely what you were looking for." Ah, Mara thought, this could be Ermanno's way around the quandary; he can help with information about the map rather than the man. She saw Ben roll his eyes in disbelief, but it was possible that Ermanno might have made the arrangements for the "acquisition" without being told any details about the object. Again, more protective measures.

Mara cleared her throat, about to describe the map, then noticed Ben's surprised look. Still, she had to reveal some facts to get more information in exchange.

"About two weeks ago, Ben dug up a map on an archaeological dig in Shaanxi Province in China."

"What kind of map?"

"A fairly accurate map of the world known at that time. Made by the Chinese in the early 1400s."

Ermanno paused, then reiterated the information very slowly: "A map of the world created by the Chinese in the early 1400s?"

"Yes."

The dealer grew quiet, and his brow furrowed.

"Is something wrong?" Mara asked.

"It is strange, that is all."

"What's strange?" She expected to hear Paul Wong's litany of impossibilities as to such a map's existence—chiefly, that early-fifteenth-century emperors had made the mapping of the world outside of China punishable by death.

"This map you speak of. It has long been rumored to exist. But not in China. Here, in Europe."

She shook her head. "I think you're confusing two different maps, Ermanno."

"No. It sounds like the map of legend. In my little world, we have heard that one of the earliest world maps came from China. But I have never met anyone who has seen it. And the rumors are very old."

"Ermanno, Ben found the map we're looking for in China nearly three weeks ago. It couldn't possibly be the same map."

"Maybe you're right, Mara." He paused before continuing. "It is too bad, though. If your map exists, it would explain many of the mysteries of the early European world maps."

"What mysteries?" Ben asked.

"Well, beginning in 1457, countries and seas not yet discovered by the Europeans started to appear on European world maps. For example, the tip of Africa was not discovered and rounded until the real Bartolomeu Dias did so in 1488. Yet thirty years earlier, in 1457, the Genoese World Map shows the coast of Africa as navigable and connecting to the Indian Ocean and the East. The Genoese World Map also shows a body of water to the west of Africa connecting to Asia—some forty years before Columbus's voyage when the prevailing map of the time, which was Ptolemy's, showed an impassable Africa joining some great southern continent. But this is not all."

"What else?" Ben interjected again.

"In the late 1450s, the Portuguese commissioned a map to commemorate their discoveries. The king hired Fra Mauro, a monk in the Camaldolese monastery of

San Michele in Murano, Venice, and supplied him with all the Portuguese maps and cartographical materials. In 1459, Fra Mauro created a beautiful map that—like the Genoese World Map—depicted Africa as a separate continent surrounded by water with a possible route to the East Indies around its southern tip. This was forty years before Vasco da Gama's voyage of 1497 that proved it.

"And then there is Martin Waldseemüller's 1507 *mappa mundi* that shows America as an island with an ocean beyond it, stretching to Asia. I could go on and on." He shrugged again. "How were the Europeans able to make these maps?"

Mara's head was spinning. Ben and Richard had described the map as representing "the world as it was then known"—not the world in its entirety. Yet that was precisely what Ermanno suggested this Chinese world map of legend—the map for which she might be searching—depicted.

"What are you implying, Ermanno? That this Chinese map is rumored to portray the whole world correctly—including America—some seventy-odd years before it was discovered by the Europeans?"

The furrow between Ermanno's brows deepened. "Now I am confused, Mara. I thought you said you were looking for a stolen world map, one from China in the early 1400s. I am describing to you the only such map I have heard of and, yes, the map is reputed to show the entire world. Does yours not?"

Mara knew she needed to backpedal. "My apologies, Ermanno. You understand that I could not share such information with you outright. I hope I can be forgiven for my little game."

His face softened, showing his relief that Mara had

tried deceiving him rather than having been the victim of deception herself. "Of course, my dear. We all have to play cat and mouse in this business."

"Thanks for understanding, Ermanno. I have just one last question. If Ben found this legendary map on the Chinese Silk Road three weeks ago, how do you make sense of the rumor that this map was in Europe for decades, if not centuries?"

"Perhaps the rumor was wrong. Perhaps this Chinese world map did not reach Europe. Maybe it stayed behind on the Silk Road, but the information on it traveled to Europe in advance of the Age of Discovery." He shrugged, as if indifferent. "Who knows? I have every faith that you will find out."

Ermanno escorted Mara and Ben to the shop door. They traded farewells, and he asked Mara to give Joe his best. Before unlocking the door, Ermanno hugged Mara. He whispered, "Make sure to tell me what you learn. It could change everything."

Mara stepped out into the dusky pink of evening. Twisting back for a final wave, she saw Ermanno watching her and Ben from his cozily lit shop window. She made a show of patting Ben on the arm and chatting collegially with him. Yet once they were out of Ermanno's sight and earshot, she veered down a rough, narrow lane, infuriated. Her instinct told her that Ermanno's description of the map was accurate. Ben hadn't told Mara everything.

She could hear Ben's footsteps hurrying to keep up with her. And his voice calling out to her.

"Mara, please wait. Talk to me."

She spun around, placed her hands on her hips, and

said, "You want to talk? Okay, let's talk. Why did you lie to me about this map?"

"I didn't lie exactly."

"Oh, I see. You want to play more games with me. Let me rephrase. Why did you fail to tell me that this is the first map *in history* to accurately show the entire world?!"

Ben didn't answer immediately. She turned around and started back down the path.

"Mara, I wanted to tell you, but I couldn't," he yelled to her.

"What do you mean you couldn't?" she shouted back, continuing her march down the uneven lane.

"Richard asked me not to tell you."

Through the light streaming through the stained glass
windows of the Chapel of Santa Maria de Belém,
Antonio sees the expedition's four ships anchored in
the Tagus River. He watches as sailors finish loading
the vessels—the flagship *São Gabriel,* a four-masted
carrack nearly ninety feet in length; the slightly smaller,
lateen-rigged caravel *Berrio;* the storeship; and his
own *São Rafael,* of like size to the *São Gabriel.* He
wonders which chest holds da Gama's map. The salty
scent of the sea taunts him, and he itches to get on
board, to lead the boats toward their discoveries.

But Antonio must withstand the service and vigil first.
He hears the trumpets heralding the arrival of King
Manuel and looks toward the front of the little chapel
built by Prince Henry on the banks of the Tagus River.
The king finishes his procession down the nave and settles into his gilded throne, glorious against a vermilion
banner emblazoned with his coat of arms of castles and
sapphire shields. It looms on the altar larger than the
bishop's chair.

The priest blesses the congregation. The king's
companion-in-arms summons Captain-Major Vasco da
Gama to King Manuel's throne, and commands his officers to join him. Antonio, as the most junior, takes a

place at the back of the line. They approach the throne, and da Gama kneels at its base.

The king's voice booms: "Do you swear as the principal motive of this enterprise to serve God our Lord? To exalt the holy faith of Christianity and convert the Moors and other natives?"

"I do," da Gama answers.

"Do you vow to utilize this expedition to the advantage of our kingdom of Portugal?"

"I do."

"Do you pledge fealty to your Dom Manuel, by the grace of God king of Portugal and of the Algarves on this side and beyond the sea, and in Africa?"

"I do."

King Manuel stands. A knight of the Order of Christ walks toward the king, head bowed, and furnishes him with a skein of fabric. The king unfurls the heavy white cloth and holds it high: it is a banner bearing the square red-and-white cross of the Order of Christ.

He drapes it over da Gama. "May it please God in His infinite mercy to speed you on your voyage."

The bishop echoes King Manuel's consecration with a lengthy prayer. The king departs and, with him, his entourage, save for the knights. Vasco da Gama and his mariners are left with the bishop and priests and the Order of Christ to sweat through the evening vigil, which will last until morning.

Dawn breaks. Newborn sun filters through the image of Saint Vincent etched in precious glass. To the God he claims to disavow, Antonio says a silent prayer of thanks that the tedious, incessant chanting of the night watch is over.

Da Gama and his officers file down the nave behind the knights and the bishop's men. Each takes a lit candle from a priest. The bishop motions for his liege to open the chapel's bronze doors. Waiting their turn behind the knights and religious men, the seamen step from the darkness of the church interior and into the burgeoning day.

Antonio squints as his eyes adjust to the light. He is unprepared for the sight that lies in store. Hundreds, nay thousands of Lisboans await them, among them elderly men stooped over canes and babies strapped to their mothers' backs. From the disheveled state of their clothes and their bleary faces, Antonio knows the crowd had stood vigil through the night along with them.

He is unexpectedly moved. The masses follow them as they progress to the place of embarkment. The bishop begins a litany, and the people chant the responses along with the priests, the knights, and da Gama's men. Antonio is swept up in their fervor, feeling for the first time that he is part of some larger plan than filling his own coffers.

The procession reaches the riverbank. Da Gama and his men begin boarding the small rowboats provided to take them to the anchored ships. As he waits, Antonio fills with pride looking at the four ships and thinking that nearly one hundred and fifty men will man them. Antonio secures the last seat in the final boat to push off from the shore.

The Latin chanting grows louder as they cut into the chop of the Tagus River, heading toward the *São Gabriel*, *Berrio*, *São Rafael*, and the storeship. He turns back to the gritty coastline and watches Lisbon recede.

Present Day
ASOLO, ITALY

Mara halted. In her line of business she had learned to expect falsehoods and omissions from all sources, but not usually from the client. Clients understood that if she didn't know the truth about what she was looking for, she couldn't very well find it.

"Did he tell you why?" she asked without facing him.

"Only that he thought it best to keep the full nature of the map limited to as few people as possible."

"I see." She saw something else too. "That's why you wanted to come with me, isn't it?"

"Yes."

"And that's why Richard insisted?"

"Yes."

Ben appeared at her side. "Please, Mara. I'll tell you everything I know."

Mara had trouble believing him. "Why would you defy Richard now?"

"Because I want to find it and figure out why Richard wants to keep the facts secret even from you. And because you won't tell Richard what I'm going to tell you."

Mara deliberated, weighing her hunger for the whole story against her unwillingness to trust Ben. His omission could be explained by his reliance on Richard's excavation financing. Still, she wondered why he'd put his site funding in jeopardy by imparting the truth to her. Particularly since he seemed so judgmental of her unorthodox methods.

"Why would you risk the bankroll for your dig?"

"Mara, remember what I told you about why I'm drawn to my work; I want history to be rewritten based on *my* discoveries. I found this map. If it really shows the entire world, then the Chinese must have circumnavigated the globe before the Europeans. This discovery would have a much greater impact on history than would proving that the Tocharians introduced the keystones of civilization to the Chinese. If you're going to be recovering this map, *I* want to be there."

This seemed genuine. Especially since it revealed a self-serving side to the moralistic Ben. What other choice did she have? She nodded her assent to the arrangement.

They continued in silence down the lane until it joined with a wider street, one dotted with quaint cafés and restaurants coming to life as the sun set. Ben motioned for them to enter the first bistro they encountered. They sat down at a table for two in the darkest, quietest corner. Mara ordered a prosecco, a rarity for her these days, and Ben asked for a Peroni.

His posture relaxed, as if he were relieved to drop the duplicity. He reached into his bag and pulled out an envelope. Spreading its contents on the table, he invited Mara to examine the photographs of the entire map.

Mara studied the overexposed pictures but couldn't make sense of them. "Can you tell me what I'm looking at?"

Ben pointed to lands and waters that history declared undiscovered until long after the map's creation: a navigable Africa, the borders of Antarctica, the form of Australia, the outlines of the Americas, and an ocean connecting America to Asia. The scale was off and the coastlines were askew, but it captured the world in its entirety. All in the same rapturous detail she'd seen in the first photographs.

Mara shook her head in awe. "Could the Chinese really have undertaken a journey this big? They would have had to send out a massive fleet in the early 1400s, before Emperor Yongle's successors shut China off from the rest of the world. And they must have had scientific and nautical skills well beyond the Europeans'."

"The Chinese definitely had the capability to make the voyage. We know they had gargantuan ships, much larger than anything the Europeans produced during this time; the vessels had highly efficient sails and gigantic rudders, and were specially designed to survive the fiercest storms on the open ocean. The Chinese possessed advanced navigational techniques: a sophisticated sense of astronomy, an understanding of latitude, the ability to use the compass, insight into the currents and wind systems, an excellent grasp of cartography, and six centuries of maritime experience."

"But why did they want to try?"

"They had a desire for discovery—before Emperor Hongxi took the throne, anyway. His predecessor, Emperor Yongle, was determined that after years of foreign Mongol rule, the Chinese should believe in themselves and their glorious past. He resolved to unite the entire world—All Under Heaven—and bring it into his tribute system. Heaven being Yongle, of course."

"How do you know all this? I thought your expertise was Tocharianism."

He hesitated. "We found the map two months

ago—not three weeks ago. Once we unrolled it, I realized the importance of the artifact. I delayed telling Richard until I had a real handle on the history."

A begrudging smile appeared on Mara's face. She wanted to get mad at him for the deception—and the hypocrisy of taking the high road when he was guilty of lies himself—but she couldn't. She would have done the same thing. "And here I thought you were ethical to the core."

Ben looked away.

An unexpected white botanical motif, outside the border of the map, in the scroll's right corner, caught her eye. "What's that?"

"I'm fairly certain it's a lotus flower. Huang tells me that the inscription underneath says that the map is dedicated to a young woman named Shu."

"What else can you tell me about the map? Any details on the mapmaker, the patron, its intended use, or any symbolism contained in the paintings?" These elements were the ones Mara relied on to detect who really owned the map and who'd stolen it.

"I wish I could tell you more, Mara. Aside from the dedication to Shu and a tribute to the late emperor Yongle in the top left corner, I can't tell you much else. I can interpret some of the map symbols, and the lotus, of course."

"What's its meaning?"

"Well, the lotus is a type of water lily. It grows from the mud to blossom; this makes it a symbol of purity within the material world. It's also a female symbol and means binding or connecting in marriage. Taken together and in context with the accompanying inscription, the lotus likely represents a pure, young woman—"

Mara interrupted him. "Shu is the mapmaker's love."

"Something like that."

The thought of Shu struck Mara as incredibly sad. If indeed the body Ben found was that of the mapmaker, then he'd never reached his lotus.

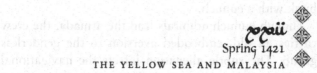
The *Ch'ing Ho*'s crimson sails fill with the north wind. The gusts ferry them away from Tanggu, into the Yellow Sea. As the sun crests over the horizon, Zhi's work begins.

He starts in the airless compass room, taking readings with the iron fish to ensure that the *Ch'ing Ho* holds its course. He moves to the private navigational bridge, making observations on the color, speed, currents, depths, and scent of the water. As night falls, he brings out the jade disk to survey the constellations, constantly measuring the location of the polestar to calculate latitude. At day's end, he retires to the study, where he records all the details of their route in a sailing chart, folding in the information culled by the junior navigational crew on the other ships and shuttled over on small boats. This mapmaking task is one that he enjoys performing above all others.

Zhi performs the same cycle day after day, week after week. The routine stops only when the incense stick marking the hours of his watch burns down and others relieve him. Exhausted, he stumbles to his tiny cabin for a rest before his next shift. He need not worry about disturbing any fellow cabin mates; he is the only member of the eight-man navigational and cartographical crew to have his own compartment. No one wants to bunk with a eunuch.

Though eunuch admirals lead the armada, the crew carries an old, embedded aversion to the genderless group. The subtle alienation infects the navigational crew's shared evening meal. There, the other officers banter comfortably with one another but address Zhi with a formal politeness, and only when necessary. Except for Master Hsieh—though always the superior, he treats Zhi with respect.

Zhi leaves the evening meal as quickly as decorum permits. From time to time, when his schedule permits he takes solitary strolls on the main bridge, enjoying the play of the moon on the waves. After meeting him by chance during one of his nighttime walks, Ke occasionally joins him in his promenade, when her duties allow. Her desire to accompany him surprises him at first, but he comes to believe that she welcomes their meetings as a safe respite from her obligations to the envoys and the petty jealousies of the other concubines. He is a haven for her.

Ke tells him of her people, the Tanka, who had emigrated from China's landlocked center to the coast to work as pearl fishermen. She shares with him her belief in Buddhism, and even chants her favorite mantra for him. She recites lines from the plays the concubines perform for the envoys, and sings parts of songs. She never mentions the Cantonese floating brothels from which she was hired, or the prohibition against her ever going ashore, but he has heard of these things. Though he welcomes her companionship, the swing of her hair and the pink of her gowns remind him of Shu on some evenings, and pain him.

When he's not slated for night watch, after his walks, he retires to his compartment, where he offers the small rosebush permitted in his chamber a part of his water ration. In these moments when he's not crowding his mind with maps and sailing charts, thoughts of home creep into his consciousness. He imagines his parents and brothers in an elegant wooden house sharing a meal of roast mutton with scallions, all provided by the taels of his eunuch salary. He reminds himself that the rise in the Ma family position is the reason he entered imperial service and that the quiet repugnance of his fellow officers does not matter. The thought comforts him—as long as he does not allow himself to think of Shu, a difficulty if Ke has walked along with him.

Near the end of the sixth week, his charting tells him that they should be reaching Malacca, Malaysia, a trading port and forward base established by Zheng on a previous voyage. Zhi does not need navigational calculations to tell him they are nearing land. The change in the smell and character of the air—from brisk and clean to heavy and salty—reveals this to him as well.

Zhi consults with Master Hsieh on the best route to the shore, as Malacca lies through the treacherous Lung Ya Strait. They review the sailing charts and decide upon the safest passage for the season and weather— avoiding Niu Shih Rock, the stony islets, and the shallow, sandy shoals that line the passage—and inform the admiral's deputy. Several anxious hours later, Zhi hears drums in the distance welcoming the fleet to Malacca.

Master Hsieh is pleased with Zhi's assistance on the passage through the hazardous strait and gives him rare leave to go ashore. Zhi boards a rowboat with other crew members from the *Ch'ing Ho*. As they approach the city wall, he spies a row of spikes, like the back of a dragon, following them in the water. He leans down for a closer look.

"Stop!" the sailor next to him yells, pulling him back with such force that the boat rocks. The others on board stare at Zhi with reproach.

"What have I done?" Zhi asks, confused by the reaction over his small movement.

"Don't you know? That creature is an iguana-dragon. He will eat a man at first sight."

After Zhi offers his gratitude and apologies for putting them at risk, the familiar-looking sailor explains that he is a helmsman on the *Ch'ing Ho* named Yuan. Zhi introduces himself and his role in turn.

Bells ring out in greeting as they near the city wall. As they disembark, Yuan brags that he knows Malacca from an earlier voyage with Admiral Zheng. "Come, let me show you through the port town," he invites Zhi.

Unused to friendly gestures except from Ke, Zhi does not answer. He wonders whether Yuan does not know that he is a eunuch.

"Is an assistant navigator and mapmaker too proud to let a helmsman guide him for once?" Yuan teases.

"No, of course not!" Zhi insists, horrified that such a thought would cross Yuan's mind. Even in jest.

"Then let me guide you through Malacca."

Thus encouraged, Zhi agrees.

Yuan leads Zhi to the wooden bridge over the Malacca River. He weaves Zhi in and out of the more than twenty merchant booths where all the trading takes place. Each stall contains a different ware unknown to Zhi; Yuan

identifies the blocks of tin, the ebony, and the golden am-
ber *ta-ma-erh* incense. The two men fall into comfortable roles: Yuan as the lighthearted storyteller, and Zhi
as the eager but quiet observer and listener. Zhi gazes
around in wonder; even the influx of envoys from tribute lands to the Imperial and Forbidden Cities has not
prepared him for the immense range of complexions,
dress, and language they encounter.

As Zhi inhales the aroma of unknown spices, he hears
the familiar cry of the muezzin. All around him, in the
middle of the marketplace, merchants face Mecca, drop
to their knees, and pray. Never before has Zhi been in a
place where the practice of his faith is so prevalent. Or
accepted. Moved, he kneels, joins the white-turbaned
merchants in prayer, and entreats Allah for forgiveness.
He has neglected his religious duties while on board the
Ch'ing Ho, forgoing them for the creed of cartography.
Yuan stands close by, waiting for his new friend.

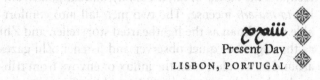
Mara stared out of the window as the plane circled over Lisbon. Somehow the view before landing made her think of Hong Kong. Perhaps the precipitous terrain that cascaded into the ocean reminded her of Hong Kong's dramatic setting. Or maybe it was the way both cities had bravely built themselves into inhospitable hillsides. Regardless, she hoped that Lisbon offered more answers and less deception than Hong Kong. Or Italy, for that matter.

As Mara and Ben rode to their hotel, she stared at the Portuguese capital through the taxi window. The antiquated grandeur of its buildings, dotted with Moorish blue-and-white tiles and arched doorways, struck her as both regal and exotic. Even though closer examination revealed a few patches worn from history and economic strife, Lisbon dazzled from afar.

They entered the lobby of the Ritz Four Seasons. The marble foyer was beautifully appointed, but they did not linger. They rode up in the elevator to their respective rooms and made plans to meet in the lobby bar in three hours. A chime sounded. The doors to her floor opened, and she stepped off.

Mara sank down into her hotel room's plush club chair and called Joe. She let him ask her a dozen questions about the way she had handled Ermanno; she knew he wanted to be sure she'd preserved him as a future contact and ally. Then she revealed Richard's critical omission about the map. Mara had formed some theories about why Richard had held back the full truth—the most benign of which was Ben's suggestion that Richard wanted to limit the dissemination of such shattering news—but she knew Joe would be able to decipher the dishonesty better than anyone. He hopped off the phone to do some research, warning her to stay alert.

Tired, overwhelmed, and inwardly still furious with Richard, she decided to head to the bar early for an afternoon coffee and a sugary sweet. As she walked into the red velvet and book-lined lobby bar, looking for a host to seat her, she sensed the eyes in the room upon her. She felt as though she had intruded on the inner sanctum of local businessmen, their private place to have a drink and discuss deals, politics, maybe their latest mistresses.

She asked the host if she could sit on the patio she'd spotted in the background to escape the uncomfortable stares. Though the fall day had a chilly bite, Mara guessed that the shining sun warmed the outdoor space, since the patio bustled. The host led her to a corner table for two.

Mara ordered coffee and a chocolate cake. The simple label did not do justice to the decadent four-layer tartuffo, resplendent with berries and sauce, that arrived. She dove into it, only to have a bloodred drop of the raspberry syrup land on her lap.

As she tried discreetly to dab away the stain, she gazed across the Ritz patio. Six tables over, behind a bobbing sea of dining businessmen, Mara spotted a familiar face.

The man was Asian, not unusual in cosmopolitan Lisbon, but she knew she had seen him somewhere before. She looked away, trying to place him, when it came to her. As she and Ben had rushed out of the Cathay Pacific business-class lounge to board their flight from Hong Kong to Venice, she had slammed into a man standing outside the lounge entrance. She had spilled hot coffee on his suit and, after apologizing profusely and momentarily leaving him in Ben's care, had run into the lounge to get some napkins. In the seconds it had taken her to grab some toweling and dash back into the terminal, the man had left. Ben had been unable to detain him.

It was the same man. Mara turned back in his direction. But the man was gone.

While she scanned the patio, trying to locate him, Ben bounded over to the table. She thought about sharing the sighting with him, then thought better of it. Perhaps she had been mistaken. After all, she had only seen the man in the Hong Kong airport for a moment.

"I found someone we need to meet with," Ben announced.

Mara doubted that anyone Ben might suggest could further their search, but she wanted to play nice. "Who's that?" she asked.

"Professor Luis Silva, from the University of Lisbon. He's reputed to be an expert on cartography during the Age of Discovery. A friend from Harvard worked with him and recommended him."

"A friend recommended him?" A red flag went up.

In an instant, he identified and allayed her concerns. "Don't worry. I haven't told anyone but you and Huang about the map."

"And Richard," she reminded him.

"Yes, Richard," he said, with a downcast look. She really did find it hard to stay mad; the dishonesty had not sat well with him.

To reassure him, she asked, "Do you think this professor knows anything about the Portuguese map-theft underworld?"

"He might be able to give us some direction."

"Okay. Let's meet with him after I've talked to my contacts here."

The waiter arrived to take Ben's order. Mara was just about to recommend the chocolate cake when her cell phone rang. She reached into her bag to grab it. Seeing her father's name on the screen, she ignored it. The phone rang and rang until Ben asked, "You're not going to get that?"

"No. It's my father."

"Why wouldn't you pick up his call?"

"It's complicated."

"Whose relationships with their parents aren't?"

"It's a little more complicated than the average parent-child relationship."

"At least your dad calls you. I was raised by two Princeton professors—a geneticist and a linguistics expert—who believed and spoke only in the language of science. So normal parental phone calls are kind of out of the question."

"I wouldn't characterize my father's calls as 'normal.' He usually phones to learn my whereabouts. Once he figures that I'm safe, he chastises me for wounding him and my mom by throwing away a white-shoe partnership for 'other people's problems,' as he likes to call my work."

"I'd take a chastising phone call any day. It's better than no contact at all."

Ben's remark made Mara think twice. When the phone rang again, she flipped it open, assuming it was her father again.

"Mara, it's Sam. We need to talk."

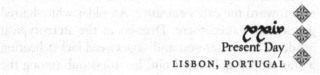

A day passed, and the knot in Mara's stomach that had formed with Sam's call became more and more entangled. He'd told Mara that the Chinese government had overheard rumblings about the discovery of a momentous map that had been taken from the country. Undoubtedly, they had sent the man she'd spotted on the Ritz balcony.

The knot was worsened by Mara's futile dealings with her Portuguese contacts, particularly given the onerous precautions Mara now needed to take to protect the privacy of their meetings from her Chinese friend. Like Ermanno, her associates had heard of Dias. They were familiar with his thirst for museum-quality early world maps and his willingness to go to great, expensive lengths to procure them. But they had no insights as to his true identity.

Mara agreed to Ben's suggestion that they meet with Professor Silva. She figured they had nothing but precious time to lose before they left Portugal to meet with some of her other European contacts.

Professor Silva suggested they meet at the Antiga Confeitaria de Belém rather than his offices at the university. As Mara and Ben approached the celebrated nineteenth-century café, she saw tourists lined up outside and bristled a bit. They were not here as sightseers.

Ben noticed Mara's hesitation and guided her by the arm toward the café's entrance. An older white-haired gentleman waited there. Dressed in the stereotypical academic's sweater vest and sage tweed jacket bearing a star-shaped gold lapel pin, he stood out among the T-shirt-clad visitors. As they approached, he waved and smiled at them, his eyes crinkling at the corners; he was indeed Professor Silva.

After they made their introductions, he led them to a reserved table in a room that seemed to be designated for locals. "My apologies for the tourists," he said, his English perfect but heavy with the lush Portuguese accent.

"No worries," Ben replied.

"The café is famous for good reason. May I order you some coffee and *pastel de nata*?"

"Please, Professor Silva," Ben answered. Mara bit her tongue; they didn't have hours to squander on pleasantries and pastries. From experience, she knew that as time elapsed, the chance of recovery diminished. Yet the professor seemed so kind and gentlemanly, she felt rude rushing him. And he quickly made clear that he had not chosen their meeting place on the basis of its pastries. He'd selected the café for its proximity to the Museu de Marinha. The Maritime Museum was an ideal setting, he explained, to discuss mapmaking in the Age of Discovery.

After they finished their deservedly renowned pastries, they walked the few blocks to the Mosteiro dos Jerónimos, the monastery in which the museum was located. Sun illuminated the ornate, almost lacelike stone façade of the sixteenth-century church and monastery. The rays accentuated unusual architectural elements on the complex's face, such as ropes and nautical motifs. Even Mara, her mind distracted, found its artistic elegance hard to ignore.

Ben asked about the curious design. The professor straightened his posture and launched into a mini-lecture about Manueline architecture. He explained that King Manuel I had commissioned the design in the early 1500s as a tribute to Portugal's maritime domination. As they walked to the museum, Ben and the professor talked about the style—rich in royal, Christian, foliate, and maritime imagery, she heard one of them say. The conversation was interesting, but Mara tuned them out. She needed to concentrate on their next steps, once the meeting with the professor ended.

Professor Silva exchanged nods with the security guards, and they walked into the museum. The professor paused in front of a life-size bronze statue of a man wearing a wide-brimmed hat, grinned with pride, and pronounced, "It all began with Prince Henry the Navigator.

"Henry, the son of King John I and the English noblewoman Philippa of Lancaster, was born in 1394. As a young military officer, he led a successful expedition against the Muslim stronghold of Ceuta, in Morocco. This experience seemed to have sparked a dual obsession within Henry: the desire to spread Christianity throughout Africa, the Holy Land, and Asia, and the thirst to discover trade routes to African gold and Asian spices. He believed that, as the most southwestern country in Europe and with God's special blessings, Portugal was uniquely situated to lead the exploration efforts necessary to accomplish these goals."

The professor ushered them into the Discoveries

Hall. They stopped at glass cases holding replicas of ships, navigational instruments, and artifacts from various fifteenth-century voyages. "In 1419, Prince Henry arrived in the Algarve region in southern Portugal to serve as governor. He decided the time was right to act. Henry founded the School of Navigation in Sagres, the most southwesterly point in continental Europe. He gathered together the most advanced maritime and nautical learning available in Europe, attracting the best seamen, shipbuilders, cartographers, astronomers, and makers of navigational instruments. They taught currents, wind systems, and navigational methods and invented tools like the compass. Even Christopher Columbus studied at the Sagres school in its later years."

The professor walked over to a glass case showing the development of seafaring vessels. "At the Sagres school, they created a new type of sailboat, the caravel. This ship utilized the Arabic lateen sail, which made the ships much more maneuverable and capable of traveling longer distances." He pointed out the ship models of the four vessels from Vasco da Gama's famed first expedition to India, as well as the portable altar and statue of the archangel Rafael that da Gama had kept in his private quarters during certain voyages.

Mara liked the enthusiastic professor and found the history lesson intriguing, especially when she compared the Portuguese accomplishments to the presumed achievements of the fifteenth-century Chinese fleet. But she didn't want the professor's little talk to drift too far, so she said, "As Ben may have mentioned, we're very intrigued by the role cartographers played."

The professor practically skipped over to a wall on

which several maps hung. "I'm so glad you said so. Cartography is where history gets really interesting. Existing maps had an impact on the direction taken by the Portuguese in the Age of Discovery. In turn, the Portuguese discoveries of the African coastline, the Cape of Good Hope, and the sea route to India and Asia greatly shaped the history of mapmaking."

His eyes glimmered; he was fully in his element. "At Sagres, Prince Henry assembled a team of spies whose job was to travel throughout Europe collecting all the available maps and charts and amassing narratives from travelers. Henry hoped that this information would provide his mariners with the best routes to Africa and Asia. Despite all this subterfuge, the dominant map used by Henry's men in the early years of exploration was the world map of Ptolemy."

"It's interesting that the Portuguese used a second-century world map," Mara said. She had seen the name and a picture of the Ptolemy map in Catherine's dossier, and she had heard the name mentioned by Ermanno. But she wanted to get the professor's take on it.

"Yes," he answered with a grin, pleased with her knowledge. "At the time of Prince Henry, Europe was just emerging from the Middle Ages, a period when science was eschewed and religious fervor embraced. The Middle Ages maps were spiritual in nature, not geographic; these ecclesiastical maps showed the earth as a record of divinely planned events.

"Then, in the fifteenth century, there was an abrupt change. Maps emerged with a new concept of orderly geographical space, containing coordinates of latitude and longitude. Now, this could be attributed to the rediscovery of Ptolemy's map by a monk in Constantinople in the late 1300s. Ptolemy's world map depicted eight thousand places and three continents, Europe, Asia, and Africa; showed longitude and latitude; and presented a star catalog. The map had flaws, of course, but it became the authority for the discoverers. And their inspiration.

"Using Ptolemy's map as a rough guide, Prince Henry pushed his sailors to round Cape Bojador—the bulge on the West African coast—starting in the 1420s. That way, the Portuguese ships could bypass the Muslim states of North Africa and trade directly with West Africa by sea, and then, presumably, sail to the East. As they sailed south, they discovered and colonized the Madeira Islands in 1420 and the Azores in 1427. But as for rounding Cape Bojador itself, fourteen expeditions failed between the years 1421 and 1433, causing Henry to grow increasingly angry and impatient. When he dispatched Gil Eanes in 1434, on the fifteenth attempt, Henry made him promises of great riches if he succeeded. And Eanes did. In the late 1430s and 1440s, Henry's men continued their southern progress down Africa's western coast, uncovering Cape Blanco and Cape Verde."

"But they didn't round Africa's tip until 1488, right?" Mara asked.

"That's true. Unfortunately, the discoveries stalled a bit after Henry died, in 1460. It wasn't until King John II succeeded to the throne in 1481 and King Manuel I in 1495 that the Portuguese interest in exploration rekindled. Under their auspices, Diogo Cão reached the mouth of the Congo in 1482; Bartolomeu Dias rounded the Cape of Good Hope in 1488; Vasco da

Gama arrived in India in 1498; and Pedro Álvares Cabral reached Brazil in 1500. By this point, Portugal had become the world's leading nation in trade." He finished his history lesson with a little flourish, then directed them to a wall covered with reproductions of maps.

As they walked, Mara processed something the professor had said. She asked, "You mentioned that the Portuguese mariners used Ptolemy's map as their guide to sail south?"

"Yes," he answered without turning around.

"With the ultimate goal of reaching the East?"

"Yes." The professor continued his progress.

"But Ptolemy's map showed Africa as impassable, as joining a southern continent. The Portuguese wouldn't have had any reason to think that they could reach the East by going south if they were using Ptolemy as their guide."

Professor Silva turned and met Mara's gaze. "That's true, Miss Coyne. How very perceptive of you to have pieced together one of history's little mysteries. We'll never know why Prince Henry was motivated to push his sailors south." He smiled. "But I'm certainly pleased that he did. Aren't you?"

"Of course," she agreed, nodding.

"Shall we talk about the way in which the Portuguese discoveries influenced mapmaking?"

Mara and Ben said yes, and the professor was off and running, extolling the role Portugal had played in the history of cartography. As he talked—pointing to the various map reproductions on the museum walls—Mara wondered how indeed the Portuguese had known about the true configuration of the African continent.

Was there some truth to Ermanno's speculations that the Europeans had caught wind of the discoveries shown on the Chinese map? She looked over at Ben, but he seemed engrossed in the professor's speech. She could not believe that the import of her exchange with the professor escaped him.

Professor Silva paused and made a sweeping gesture across the room. "And of course, they had the funds for the Sagres navigational school and all these voyages from the Order of Christ." He pointed to the red crosses that appeared on model ships, maps, and even carved stone markers. "The Order of Christ cross became the flag under which all these expeditions sailed."

Mara asked, "What's the Order of Christ?"

The professor puffed up and said, "The Order of Christ was a religious military order formed by King Diniz of Portugal in the early 1300s. Some say the Order of Christ succeeded the Templars when they were dissolved in 1312, because Pope John XXII passed a papal bull in 1323 granting the Templars' property and assets to the order. Others would argue that the order was an entirely new creation. Either way, it is certain that—starting with Prince Henry, who became grand master—the Order of Christ's resources and manpower were utilized for expanding Christianity in Africa and the East and for discovering trade routes. We know that this trend continued after Henry's death because, thereafter, all grand masterships were held by someone from the royal family, someone whose goals were aligned with Henry's."

Here she stood with a cartographical expert in the place where a legendary map thief was thought to reside. She found it hard to believe that Professor Silva hadn't heard some gossip about the infamous Dias figure. Yet she couldn't ask directly.

Instead, she said, "What if I were interested in buying a world map from this Age of Discovery time period?"

The professor chuckled at Mara's seeming naïveté. "Miss Coyne. There is no such world map to purchase. There are only a handful of these charts in existence, and I can assure you they are all accounted for. They hang on the walls of museums and rich private collectors' homes, or they're in church and state vaults."

"What if one of these 'accounted for' world maps was stolen? How would I go about buying it?"

The professor's brow knitted in confusion. "Miss Coyne, I am an academic. I can only tell you the history of maps from the Age of Discovery. Not how to buy a stolen one."

Before any offense or discomfort could register, Mara smiled. "Sorry, my imagination got the better of me. I'm just curious as to how these maps change hands, if they ever do."

Professor Silva's grandfatherly smile returned. "I understand, Miss Coyne. We'd all like to own a part of history. I really have very limited experience with the 'trade' side of the cartographical world. The only thing I've ever done is authenticate two minor maps from the early 1500s for a local collector before he made a purchase."

They began walking toward the exit. Ben and Mara expressed their gratitude, and the professor shook their hands in turn.

Before the professor pushed open the glass doors to the museum's courtyard, Ben hurried after him. To Mara's surprise, he asked one last question, one she should have asked herself. "Professor Silva, who is this local collector for whom you authenticated those maps?"

"Gabriel da Costa, the Viscount of Tomar." Mara knew the name. She remembered it from Catherine's dossier.

The first months at sea pass as if in a good dream. The armada leaves the Tagus River and arrives at the Cape Verde Islands off North Africa within a month. From there, the vessels swing far west, out into the sea rather than clinging to the coast of the dark continent, as had their predecessors Dias and Cão, and reach a bay near the tip of Africa by November. This unprecedented route is of Antonio's design, and allows the ships to avoid the southeast trade winds and currents of the coastline and capitalize on the favorable ocean airstreams.

As the boats near the broad bay, the first sighting of land in three months, Antonio receives word in the pilot's bay to don his gala clothes. He leaves the chart he is preparing of their journey and locks da Gama's map away in a hidden compartment. He rushes to the officers' accommodations in the room below that of *São Rafael*'s captain—Paulo da Gama, the captain-major's brother—on the quarterdeck. The officers bump into one another as they change in the cramped quarters, apologizing to each other but not to Antonio. The disdain of his origins he had experienced at the Sagres school trails him here, though it angers him less as he has not the time to dwell on such small slights.

Nearly fifty men, the officers, sailors, soldiers, and a

priest—all but the convicts—scramble up the ladders to join the captain on the deck of the *São Rafael*. The four ships of the armada align, all dressed with flags and standards, though none as pervasive as the Order of Christ banners. The *São Rafael* salutes the captain-major on board the *São Gabriel* by firing its bombards.

The men break into cheers, and a soldier passes out ale and cider. They divide according to station and then further, according to friendship. As usual, Antonio stands alone. He fits with neither high rank nor low: the officers revile his easy way with the sailors and his ability to calm them during the long, three-month stretch of open water, and the sailors despise his title because he's a peasant and they believe he should remain one. He tells himself he would spit on their company if they offered it.

The ship's priest, João Figuerado, a former prior of the Lisbon monastery, approaches. With his like background of humble parentage and lofty education, he has become an improbable friend to the impious Antonio. They discuss safe topics: the propitious voyage and the sheltering properties of the bay.

A clerk draws close to the men and bows to Antonio. "Pilot Coehlo, Captain-Major commands you to the *São Gabriel*."

He hastens to the rowboat, which is already manned and ready for lowering. It splashes when it hits, and the men on deck rush to the rails to see the source of the noise. Antonio knows this singling out by the captain-major will only fuel their contempt, though he is as ignorant as they are about the reason for his summoning.

The ship's master greets him on board the *São Gabriel*. He leads Antonio through the celebrating men to the captain-major's cabin. He announces him to da Gama, who is kneeling at his personal altar with his back to Antonio.

"Our map, is it safe?" da Gama asks, though he keeps his face toward his red-and-black wooden altar, which gleams with gilt flowers and a painting of the Crucifixion. Antonio can discern only his dark cloak and hat.

"Yes, Captain-Major."

"Is it still a secret between us?"

"Yes, Captain-Major." Da Gama had entrusted him with the safekeeping of the strange map on board the *São Rafael*. The captain-major wants the map to remain secure if harm befalls him and the *São Gabriel*, and he doubts the motives of his own navigator, long a pilot of Bartolomeu Dias's who da Gama thinks cannot keep secrets.

"I am well pleased with your piloting, Antonio Coehlo."

"Thank you, Captain-Major," Antonio answers with a smile to da Gama's back. He had formulated the unique route using the secret map's wind and current markings and the portolans' coastline rendering and warnings. He wants none of Dias and Cão's cowardly creeping along the shores.

"I will bestow a private honor upon you in recognition of your efforts."

"Thank you, Captain-Major." Antonio wonders whether he will be granted a share of their spice haul or gold bullion, and his mind whirs.

"You may name the bay."

"The bay?"

"Yes. This bay will need a Christian name."

Antonio thinks little of the "honor" da Gama confers

upon him. But he knows he must appear grateful, and
he has achieved his goal of recognition in any event. He
hopes it will serve him well when da Gama doles out
remuneration at the voyage's end.

He muses too long on his eventual hoard, for da
Gama prompts, "The Christian name?"

Antonio refocuses and answers without hesitation:
"Helena. I would like to christen the bay after Saint Helena, Captain-Major."

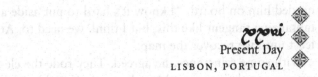

They wedged themselves into cordovan chairs at a corner table in the lobby bar. She hadn't broached her speculations, but Mara had thought of nothing else on the cab ride back to the Ritz Four Seasons. She wondered whether the same was true of Ben.

After they ordered drinks, she couldn't wait any longer to bring it up. "The European mapmakers had too much information too early. They had to have gotten the knowledge from somewhere."

"I've been thinking the same thing."

"But it doesn't make sense that the European explorers learned of the discoveries from a Chinese map that lay buried in the Silk Road for over five hundred years."

"Unless travelers to Asia heard rumors of the Chinese voyages and brought those tales back to the Europeans. Ermanno made that suggestion, and the professor told us that the Portuguese rulers had spies trolling for just such information."

"True."

They grew silent. Each downed their drink, thinking through the ramifications of their theory. "It's intriguing to hypothesize, but I don't think it's going to help us find Dias," Mara said.

Ben didn't say a word. Mara sensed that the academic sleuth in Ben—the one clamoring to change history with his findings—wanted to pursue this path. But she needed him on board. "I know it's hard to put aside a tantalizing tangent like this, but I think we need to. At least until we recover the map."

With some reluctance, he agreed. They rode the elevator up to their rooms. Mara hopped off and hustled into her room just as her cell phone rang, with Joe on the line. She hoped that Joe had some intelligence on Dias or Richard that would guide her next step.

She picked up.

"Ever hear of the Committee for National Policy?" he asked.

"No. It sounds like some kind of university think tank," she answered quietly as she strode across her room. She pulled back the curtains for a glimpse at the sun setting over the spectacular vista of the Marquês de Pombal monument, the Tagus River, and Saint George's Castle. She opened the terrace door and stepped out.

"You're supposed to think it's a bunch of smart professor types holed up in some room spouting grand theories over cups of crappy coffee."

She cut him off before he could launch into one of his usual tirades about the uselessness of academia. "Something in your tone makes me think that's not what the committee does."

"What gave it away?"

Mara laughed. "So what does this committee really do?"

"They hop on their private jets and meet from time to time to fix little things like presidential elections. Just this past week they all flew out to Amelia Island, Florida, where they probably axed a few senators over martinis." His voice grew serious. "It's a secretive club of extreme Christian conservatives and their political allies."

Republicans, presidential elections, a stodgy resort: it bore all the hallmarks of her client. "Let me guess who attended the committee's meeting. Richard Tobias."

"You got it."

"It sounds right up his alley. Except that I hadn't thought of him as a supporter of the far right. I had him pegged as more of a moderate Republican, like my father." Though, she thought to herself, her father might just righten up his politics if he were asked to join an elite power cabal like the Committee for National Policy.

"In the years since he and your father worked their magic in Boston, he's marched to the right." Joe launched into a litany of rigid Republican candidates Richard had allegedly championed.

Mara interrupted him. "So how do Richard's politics bear on his reasons for not telling me the true nature of the map?"

"Why don't you tell me?"

Mara smiled into the phone. Joe wasn't afraid to take her down a few notches when she got impatient. "Let's see. If Ben's right about what's on the map, then it just might prove that the Chinese discovered much of the world—including America—before the Europeans. The Chinese would try to use the map as part of some publicity campaign showing off their early world dominance. They might try to tie together their historical openness with the 'New China.' And if Richard's really that conservative, his political agenda wouldn't have any room for the idea of the Chinese reaching America before the Europeans." She chuckled. "Imagine Richard's face if New England was redubbed New China."

"Bingo."

Mara spun out the webs of her theory. "Richard would want to recover the map. And then destroy it." She paused. "I take that back. He'd hide it. Something that valuable might come in handy one day."

"You got it."

"How do I figure in all this?"

"I'd say you're in charge of the recovery part."

"What about the hiding part? If he knows my views at all, he knows I'd be in favor of sticking to the law and returning the map to the Chinese. Or brokering some deal whereby he'd garner discovery credit but it'd remain in Chinese control. I'd never agree to keep it hidden."

"That part I'm still trying to piece together. While I do, be wary of Tobias. Keep your communications with him very simple."

"Will do."

"Back to the Chinese: have you spotted your friend?"

"I haven't seen him lately, though I've been taking all those precautions you taught me."

"He's out there, Mara. He's just getting more careful since you nailed him on the Ritz patio."

The sun finished its descent, casting a glow on the terrace. The temperature dropped. Mara walked back into her messy room, closing the door tightly behind her.

As she tidied up, she updated Joe on their meeting with the professor. He feigned yawns as she shared the history lesson about the Age of Discovery, the Order of Christ, and all the oddities involving early world maps. Until she mentioned the viscount of Tomar. "I know that name from somewhere," he said.

"He's a fairly prominent Portuguese map collector,

among other things. I've been trying to get an appointment with him. Pull out the dossier Catherine prepared."

Half-listening as Joe recapped the biography, Mara bent down to pick up one of her shoes. That's when she saw it. The invisible tape she'd run along the desk drawers—one of Joe's little tricks—looked split. She ran her finger across the seam. The drawers had indeed been opened. She supposed the cleaning staff could be responsible, even though she had hung the Do Not Disturb sign on her door that morning.

Gingerly, she slid open the drawer. Earlier that day, she had arranged a number of inconsequential items in a particular order, keeping all documents of any importance on her person. It served as a test to see if anyone had rummaged through her belongings.

The objects were nearly in the same place. Nearly. One pen lay in the wrong groove, and a pamphlet was askew. Someone had searched her room.

The armada divides into five fleets as they leave Malaysia. Admiral Zhou's flotilla traverses the famed ports in the Indian Ocean and Arabian Sea to return ambassadors to their homelands. Then, using the tail end of the northeast monsoon for speed, it heads to the eastern coast of Africa.

Many of Admiral Zhou's sailors have traveled the route before. For them, the trip is routine, particularly since the fleet is blessed with fair weather and favorable winds. For Zhi, the excursion is anything but usual. He is overwhelmed with compass readings, constellation and latitude calculations, and relentless charting.

Master Hsieh cannot spare Zhi long enough for him to go ashore, so his only relief comes from Yuan, who, as a helmsman, has less work to do in the ports and thus has liberties to visit land. During Zhi's periodic evening strolls on the main bridge, Yuan shares stories about the barbarian towns, acting out the scenes he has witnessed. Zhi learns how the crewmen trade their personal stores of porcelains, silks, and lacquerware for ivory, spices, and precious stones. He hears tales of curious creatures: the giraffe, the black-and-white-striped *fu-lu*, and the ostrich. He revels in Yuan's description of the rubies, sapphires, and diamonds the king of Calicut presented to Admiral Zhou in tribute to Emperor Yongle.

Yuan takes special care to describe the religious practices of the port towns, as many of the peoples are Muslim. He tells Zhi how, on days of worship, trading in the market is stopped before midday. Instead of working, the people fast; bathe themselves in rose water, incense, and oil; and go to temple to worship. Zhi marvels at these customs; while practice of his faith is tolerated in his home country, certainly no labor is stopped on its behalf.

Zhi feels pangs of guilt when he learns that Admiral Zhou's fleet will not be stopping at Mecca. When he was a boy in Kunyang, the haji returning from their long pilgrimages shared stories of the holy city. They had told of the Great Mosque with its Heavenly Hall, aglitter with layers of colored stone and shelves of gold. They had shared stories about the mosque's wonderful fragrance, emanating from its walls made of clay mixed with rose water. They had recounted their circuits around the Kaaba and, when begged, showed the small pieces of black hemp-silk they'd cut from the Kaaba's cover. Listening to their tales, Zhi had dreamed about hearing the call to prayer from the four towers of the Great Mosque. To be so close and not make the pilgrimage—when others spent years undertaking the journey by land—seems sacrilegious. Especially when having another haji in the family would bring further glory to the Ma name.

Zhi stores up Yuan's tales to share with Ke, as Yuan could never regale Ke with them in person. Zhi and Ke both stay on board in the ports—though for very different reasons—and he enjoys giving her a view into the exotic life ashore. She claps with delight when he describes the strange animals Yuan has touched at the market and widens her eyes in disbelief at the details of the egg-size jewels given to Admiral Zhou by the Calicut king. Yet as she revels in the world beyond the treasure fleet, Zhi sees the young girl hidden behind the heavy makeup, the elaborate hair, and the silken gowns. And he grows sad at the sacrifices they have both made for this voyage.

Late one evening, Zhi is familiarizing himself with the sailing charts for the route down the eastern African coast to Kenya, and from there to Mozambique. Master Hsieh interrupts him, ordering him to report to the navigational bridge. Zhi hurries to the deck to find Admiral Zhou and his deputies waiting with the rest of the navigational crew. The visit is extraordinary; protocol demands that they report to the admiral in his chambers. Zhi drops to his knees in deference, remaining there until one of the admiral's deputies gives him leave to rise.

The admiral holds a scroll in his hand. Zhi recognizes the emperor's seal from his days in the Imperial Ceremonial Directorate. The admiral announces, "His Imperial Majesty, Emperor Yongle, has entrusted a special mission to us, his worthless servants. Our fleet will finish transporting ambassadors to the eastern coast of Africa. Then, in accordance with the emperor's desire that Admiral Zheng's armada visit all lands under Heaven and bring all into his tribute, we will travel south down to the end of the coast of Africa. From there, we will continue westward to find the land of Fusang and bring it into His Imperial Majesty's domain."

As Zhi listens, he sees the typically composed Master Hsieh shudder. All Chinese seamen have heard the legend of the land of Fusang. A thousand years earlier, a

Buddhist monk called Hoei-Shin returned from a twenty-thousand-*li* journey to convert others in which he claimed to have discovered a civilized country rich in copper but without iron. The priest named the place after its trees, which bore an unusual purplish-red fruit and provided the people with bark to construct paper, cloth, and homes.

Zhi understands why Master Hsieh trembles. To voyage beyond Mozambique means sailing without charts or maps. It means traveling on rumors and the word of mouth of Arabian sailors. It means journeying on nothing but the thousand-year-old declarations of a Buddhist monk.

The admiral continues: "You will tell no one of this mission. I repeat this: no other crew member is to be informed that we are seeking Fusang." His deputies in tow, the admiral leaves the bridge.

No member of the navigational crew needs to be told the reason for this prohibition. They appreciate the hysteria that the other sailors will experience if they learn the precarious, unfixed nature of their route. It is best to leave the news until they can no longer keep it quiet.

The small crew retires to their dining room to plan. Zhi is unnerved to see the experienced seamen so shaken by the prospect of guiding the fleet into uncharted waters. They cull their collective knowledge about the writings of Hoei-Shin and the world beyond the African coast, but the dearth of information demonstrates that they can do little. So Master Hsieh stops their nervous chatter. He decides they should focus on maintaining their route, but not think beyond that for the time being.

* * *

They sail to the East African coast and return the remaining ambassadors. Though they cross the Indian Ocean with relative ease, the journey beyond looms before Zhi. Before all of the navigational crew.

The night they leave Mozambique, the sky is pitch-black but clear. As if it is an ordinary evening, Zhi is on watch, alone. Yet he knows that the rest of the navigational crewmen are below in their cabins, waiting, watching, and praying. He mounts the bridge and, as is his routine, brings out the jade disk to locate the polestar. He scans the horizon but cannot locate the guiding star. This does not faze him, for the star has eluded him many times before. So he tries to find it again. And again. And again. The polestar has vanished.

Zhi runs to waken Master Hsieh. The disheveled master races to the bridge with him. With an expert hand, the master holds the jade disk up against the horizon. They both hope that Zhi's relative inexperience is to blame, but they are wrong. The polestar is gone.

Without the polestar, they have no way to determine latitude. They can still use the Southern Cross for direction, as well as the compass, but otherwise they will be without a guide.

Master Hsieh and Zhi have no choice but to inform Admiral Zhou. The master composes himself and returns to his cabin to don his uniform. With Zhi a few respectful steps behind, the two approach the admiral's stateroom.

The guard demands the reason for the interruption of the admiral's rest. After he is told of the polestar's disappearance, he rushes to waken their leader. Master Hsieh and Zhi are given leave to enter.

The two men kowtow to the admiral, who sits in a

horseshoe-shaped receiving chair in the back of the room, some distance from the men. Though the admiral is fresh from bed, he is dressed in his full uniform of a long red robe and a tall black hat. A vice admiral stands in front of him and asks for a report. In hushed tones, Master Hsieh informs the vice admiral of the development. The admiral bellows his response from his chair: "The priest must conduct a prayer service for Ma Tsu. The sea goddess will guide us."

Master Hsieh and Zhi wait outside the closed door to the prayer cabin. When the priest emerges, he scuttles off to the admiral's stateroom to give him Ma Tsu's answer. The two men follow. After a seeming eternity, the vice admiral opens the door. "Master Hsieh, Admiral Zhou orders you to continue pursuing a southerly course."

The master dares to question him: "Using only the compass and the Southern Cross for direction?"

"Was the admiral's command not clear? Do you think you know more than Ma Tsu herself?" the vice admiral scolds.

Master Hsieh bows low. "Of course not, Vice Admiral. Please forgive your humble servant. We will sail as the admiral directs."

Within a few days of southerly travel, the ships pick up speed as a current grips them and pulls them. After another consultation and prayer service, the admiral concludes that Ma Tsu guides them and commands the fleet to hold its course.

The next night, as he scans for the Southern Cross, Zhi spies Yuan approaching the private deck. Though he has not been told of the plan to find Fusang, as a helmsman Yuan knows that they are in uncharted waters.

Zhi walks toward him, away from the prying eyes of any sailor. Yuan steps forward and says, "My friend Zhi, I am certain you understand that we have become restless. We have passed Mozambique, and yet we sail on. Surely you know where we are going?" Yuan's eyes do not bear their usual gleam.

Zhi cannot lie to Yuan; he and Ke are the only friends he has made on the long months of the voyage, and Yuan is the only man who has not made him feel like an anathema. He wants to tell him the truth but knows he may not. "I cannot say."

"Do you know?"

"Yes."

"Have you been ordered to keep silent?"

"Yes."

Yuan knows better than to ask Zhi to break his vow. "Is there any reassurance you can give us?"

"Only that we are in the hands of Ma Tsu herself."

Yuan nods in understanding and withdraws. Zhi is left alone with the strange night sky.

For days the ships ride the current. Waves taller than the treasure ships crash near them. The ships fall into troughs deeper than themselves. Fear takes hold of the crew, and the admiral orders constant prayer services to appease Ma Tsu.

One morning on dawn watch, Zhi notices that the waves are settling. He smells a now-familiar, humid scent in the far distance: the first sign that the fleet is approaching land. He signals the rest of the crew, and the lookout sounds the cry.

Soaring yet oddly flat mountains loom on the horizon. From the ship's distant vantage point, they seem to form a round tip surrounded by a ring of crashing white waves. Zhi guesses that they have arrived at a cape, perhaps the very tip of Africa.

The crew rejoices at the sight of land. Though the familiar seabirds circling and cawing should appease him, Zhi feels ill at ease. As if the fleet has arrived at the end of the world.

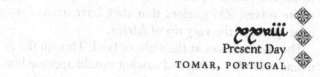
Mara lost an entire day trying to arrange a meeting with the viscount of Tomar. Out of desperation, she mentioned it to Richard, who spoke to a Portuguese political contact who knew Gabriel da Costa from their work finagling Portugal a place in the European Union. This colleague of Richard's, Paulo Montiero, secured them an invitation to a benefit hosted by the viscount of Tomar.

Mara and Ben sat in a limousine climbing the steep, winding road to the Castle of Tomar and the adjoining Convent of Christ. The Tomar complex, a former holding of the viscount of Tomar's ancestors outside of Lisbon, was the location of the gala. The normally reclusive viscount had agreed to host the event only because it would raise much-needed money for the restoration of the complex, now a UNESCO site. In exchange for her engraved invitation, Mara's firm had made a five-figure donation to the Tomar Fund.

As the car rounded a hairpin turn, Mara caught a glimpse of the castle's towers and mammoth stone fortifications rising from the mountainside. The complex dominated the right bank of the river Nabão. With each squeal of the tires and accompanying new vista, she spotted ramparts, turrets, watchtowers, and parapets looming over the hillside like ancient sentinels. It seemed picture-perfect, straight off a movie set.

"I didn't expect it to be so impressive," she said.

"The Tomar complex was the Portuguese Templar headquarters until the pope disbanded the order in the fourteenth century. Then it became the seat of the Order of Christ," Ben said in an offhand way, looking out the window.

"Really?"

"Yeah." He turned toward her with a smirk on his face. "I spent the day researching. What did you do today? Shop for your dress?"

Mara was thankful that nightfall concealed the blush creeping across her face. She had indeed squandered several hours finding a dress for the event and unconsciously tugged at the fruit of her efforts: a black strapless Ana Salazar gown. "Very funny," she said, in a tone of mock anger.

"It looks nice on you," Ben said, only making Mara blush deeper. She ignored the compliment. Ben's tone was light. An obligatory partnership and shared revelations had caused a comfortable relationship of sorts to develop between them. So much so that Mara needed to watch herself.

"Do you remember that Professor Silva mentioned that the pope transferred the Templar assets to the Order of Christ in 1323?"

Mara nodded.

"The Tomar complex is one of those Templar assets. Once the Portuguese royals took charge of the Order of Christ, beginning with Prince Henry, they began making changes to Tomar."

"Like what?"

"Prince Henry constructed cloisters to serve the Tomar monks and friars as well as the knights of the Order of

Christ. After Henry died, the building spree died off until Kings Manuel I and John III got involved in the late 1490s and early 1500s. With the help of architects Diogo de Arruda and João de Castilho, those kings made extensive additions and renovations; they altered the Charola into a more crosslike shape and added more cloisters. All to commemorate the Portuguese nautical discoveries made under the Order of Christ flag."

"What's the Charola?"

"The Templars built an octagonal church at Tomar in the late 1100s and called it the Charola. Legend has it that the Temple of the Rock in Jerusalem, where the Templars had their mother church, inspired it. The Templars, and the Order of Christ knights after them, prayed in the Charola before they took off on their missions." He laughed. "Some rumors even say that the Templars found the Holy Grail and hid it in the Charola."

The limousine stopped; the driver explained that cars could go no closer to the complex. Mara and Ben slid out into the night lit by the moon and the glitter of other guests' evening gowns and jewels. Mara smoothed out her dress, which had crumpled a bit after the long car ride, and Ben pulled at his bow tie.

"Does this look all right?" he asked, turning toward her.

Mara laughed out loud at the now-vertical tie. "It looks terrible. Let me fix it." She reached up to adjust it, really looking at him for the first time that evening. With the last vestiges of the dig scrubbed away, his curly hair tamed, and his thick glasses replaced with contacts, he was handsome.

Mara and Ben gazed at each other for a split second, before she broke away. She muttered something about finding the entrance to the party and wandered ahead. He quickly caught up to her.

They were not sure where to go, so they followed the seemingly better-informed couples toward a narrow arched entryway cut into a rough-hewn castle wall. As they neared it, Mara made out a sign announcing the entrance as the Sun Gate, one of only two passages into Tomar. They waited their turn and then squeezed through the gate onto the wide pebble walkway that led from it. Though Mara could not understand their Portuguese, she could read the female guests' faces; they were not pleased to be subjecting their Yves Saint Laurent and Chanel gowns to Tomar's rough conditions.

Once through the gate, Mara and Ben were rewarded with a floodlit view of the manicured hedges and topiary trees leading to the complex's entrance. The sound of the lady revelers' stilettos crunching on the stones accompanied Mara and Ben as they approached a set of steep stairs ascending to the base of an oddly shaped building topped by a bell tower.

"The Charola," Ben whispered. Mara was surprised; she had expected the famed structure to be grand, not squat.

Mara and Ben followed the crowd to the staircase. She watched as the ladies teetered on the uneven, almost wavy steps and clutched onto their escorts' arms. She laughed at the drama, sure that she didn't need anyone's arm to help her with the stairs. She started up alone, only to catch her heel on a centuries-old groove, and she tumbled forward, landing hard on her palms. When Ben stooped down to help her up, she waited for a mocking gibe, but he said nothing as she took his offered arm for support. For someone who'd been raised by cold scientists, Ben was unfailingly empathetic and kind.

Inside, pages collected their invitations. For Mara and Ben's benefit, they explained in broken English that the party was in progress in all the complex's public rooms, except the Charola and church. Those spaces were open for viewing, but not revelry.

Mara and Ben wandered into a vaulted gallery tiled in blue-and-white enamel that ran around four sides of a courtyard where a string quartet played. The cool night air did not deter the bare-shouldered revelers from swishing the voluminous skirts of their ball gowns round the lemon trees and lavender in the simple courtyard's center.

As Mara took a glass from a waiter's tray, she learned that they were in the Washing Cloister, one of Prince Henry's additions to Tomar. Drinks in hand, Mara and Ben passed into an adjoining area called the Cemetery Cloister, which Ben recognized as another work by Henry. It served as the burial place for the convent's religious men and knights of the Order of Christ.

She watched in disbelief as a tuxedoed man put out a cigarette on an elaborate stone tomb built into one of the otherwise plain gallery walls. Mara walked over to scold him, but seeing the fiery look in her eye, he scooted off before she could reach him. She bent down to brush off the ashes with a tissue from her purse. There, amid the Latin lettering, she saw the name da Gama. She looked up at Ben, who clarified that the burial monument was for Diogo da Gama, one of the brothers of the explorer Vasco.

The bejeweled guests gravitated into the adjoining New Sacristy, and Mara and Ben trailed after them.

Mara felt as though she'd stepped into a knight's treasure chest. The barrel-vaulted ceiling reached high, and its wooden panels were decorated with an intricate, shimmering design of gold motifs, shields with coats of arms, square red crosses, and unusual-looking globes.

Mara craned her neck for a better look. Ben followed her quizzical expression. "Wondering what those are?" he asked.

"Yeah. Some of the symbols look familiar," she said.

"You've seen them all before. At the Maritime Museum." He reminded her that the distinctive red cross was the emblem of the Order of Christ and flew on all the sails of the Portuguese Age of Discovery ships; it was the chief symbol of the discoveries. The odd globe was an armillary sphere, a navigational instrument that had served as the personal badge of King Manuel I. The shield had smaller shields in a cross shape at its center and a border of castles, representing the vast conquests of the Portuguese. "Together, these symbols proclaimed the sovereignty of Portugal. In the Manueline period, anyway."

Just as Mara had begun to wonder whether they'd ever locate the viscount of Tomar, they turned the corner and bumped right into his receiving line. Taking their place at the back of the queue, Mara watched the elderly gentleman greet his guests. By his side stood an older woman wearing a regal violet gown and splendid ruby tiara and earrings; Mara assumed this must be the viscountess of Tomar. Over his tuxedo, their host wore a red sash with a gilt cross pinned on his right shoulder and a gold star with many asymmetrical arms on his left chest. Mara recalled that the cross represented the Order of Christ.

The receiving line moved slowly. Mara entertained herself by surreptitiously looking at the other guests in the queue. The dazzling array of gems and couture ball gowns drew her initial attention. Only after she'd scanned the female guests did she notice that many of their male escorts also wore versions of the viscount's gold star, though in different places on their tuxedo jackets.

Mara was about to ask Ben about the star's particular meaning when she saw him: the Chinese man from the Ritz patio. At the back of the line.

She spun forward, praying that he hadn't seen her spot him. Stepping into the crowd, she tried to blend in with the other guests. Yet as they neared the front, a page inquired as to their names and places of origin and announced them.

Mara winced at the loud proclamation. Then she realized that if the Chinese government's spy was in attendance at the gala, she and Ben were the reason. There was no reason to hide.

The viscount of Tomar extended his hand in welcome. "A pleasure to have guests all the way from America." He nodded, shook Ben and Mara's hands, and turned to greet the next guest.

Mara did not release his hand. "We're friends of Paulo Montiero and Richard Tobias. They send their regards."

He turned back toward her with a smile. "You know Paulo Montiero? I haven't seen him since we worked on the Portuguese European Union directive together."

Mara had only limited knowledge about Montiero at her disposal, so she nodded and said, "He sends his best. In fact, there's a small matter he asked us to discuss with you." She gestured to the long line. "When you have a minute, of course."

He paused, scanning the queue. "The receiving line will finish in half an hour. You can find me in the Charola thereafter."

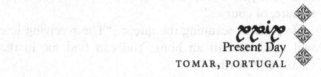
Mara and Ben left the receiving line and wandered down a long, dark hallway. Though part of her wanted to hear the page announce her follower, she thought it best to leave the area before they came face-to-face. The ruse was easier to maintain if she could pretend he didn't exist.

The hallway emptied into the Charola and the main body of the church. The famed building was surprisingly devoid of partygoers. Perhaps the prohibition on drinking in the sacred space kept them away. Whatever the reason, Mara was thankful for the emptiness and the guards that flanked every doorway. She would be able to comfortably observe anyone entering or exiting.

She and Ben stopped in the nave of the church. He asked, "Should we walk through the Charola while we wait for the viscount to finish?"

They went under an arch etched with faded paintings of saints and crosses and entered the Charola. The octagonal structure was broken by a series of arches, supported by wide buttresses, and topped by a cupola.

They walked around the gallery at the Charola's perimeter. These peripheral walls were covered with trompe l'oeil architectural features, faded sixteenth-century tempera artwork of saints, scenes from the life of Christ, and the ubiquitous Order of Christ cross and shield. Side altars dotted the walls: some contained paintings or statues, and some were conspicuously empty.

She passed under the open arch into the eight-sided center of the Charola. Her eyes immediately rose to the magnificent, highly arched ceiling, adorned with a powerful gold pattern of fleurs-de-lis, armillary spheres, and more crosses. In the ceiling's center, the motifs converged on a multirayed star, similar to the pin on the viscount's jacket, emblazoned with the letters XPS, a designation for Christ. The opulence continued on the lower walls in a dazzling array of gilt woodwork and polychromatic statues of angels and saints, as well as frescoes. For a brief moment, Mara allowed herself to be seduced by its exquisite excess and forget about the map.

Leaving the Charola, Mara joined Ben in the nave of the church. She pulled her wrap tight around her shoulders; the chill in the night air had turned frigid in the vast stone space. He asked, "Do you mind if we take a quick stroll into the main body of the church? Through the choir and sacristy?"

Mara nodded. As they walked up the stairs to the even emptier choir, they chatted quietly about the beauty of the Charola, with its pervasive Manueline emblems, nearly as prominent as those of Christ. Ben observed that the original Charola must have been simpler; the ornate decoration was a sixteenth-century overlay, an attempt by the Portuguese monarchy to provide ideological support for their Age of Discovery dominance.

Stepping into the choir, Mara felt as though she'd

entered a tranquil painting: a lofty vaulted ceiling, soaring windows, and natural sandstone, all streaming with touchable light. A rose window presided over all of it. None of the patterned gilt, trompe l'oeil, or deep somber colors they had seen in the Charola. "It's so simple and serene in here," Mara said.

"Look closer," he said.

Braided ropes overlaid the ceiling's sail-like vaulting; maritime rigging rimmed the windows; winged figures supported Manueline insignias of armillary spheres and badges at the bases of columns. Ben commented, "I'm sure you won't be surprised to hear that King Manuel I commissioned this two-level addition to the Charola. He wanted Tomar to symbolize and honor the maritime adventures that gave Portugal its wealth and supremacy."

They walked down a flight of stairs back into the nave and then down another set of steps to the floor below the choir to the sacristy. The room had the same plain look as the choir. On first glance. A nearer inspection revealed that cables, nautical knots, coral, and sea flowers climbed every masonry border. "My God, Manuel was really determined to make Tomar look like a product of the sea," she said.

"The renovated Tomar *was* a product of the sea; the Age of Discovery voyages provided the funds for it. Wait until you see the famous Manueline window." Ben pointed to the large west-facing window crisscrossed with iron grillwork. "This must be the inside of it." He took her hand. "Come on. Let's go outside and take a look at it."

The outside air seemed warmer than the frigid church interior. They walked around terraces and parapets to find the perfect spot on one of the exterior terraces for viewing the floodlit Manueline window. Patterned coral, seaweed, and algae crusted the borders; spiraled cords and ropes wrapped around the finials; nautical knots tied every corner; and fishing floats and buoys dangled off edges as if they bobbed in a rolling sea. At the base, a bearded, ancient figure supported a gigantic tree root. Mara felt as though it had arisen from the sea like some long-wrecked treasure ship.

She broke the silence. "It deserves to be one of Portugal's masterpieces."

Ben didn't answer her. He started walking around the terrace, looking at the two levels of the church from different angles.

"Ben, what are you doing? We really need to stay near the Charola, so we can get a minute with the viscount." She needed to keep them focused on their goal.

"Do you see how the Manueline window sits in a perfect line under the rose window? Which in turn sits under the Order of Christ cross and Manueline shield on the church roof?"

Mara stepped back and looked. "Yes."

"Do you see how the rose window appears to be on the third floor, where the choir is, and the Manueline window seems to be on the second floor, where the sacristy is?"

"Yes."

"Well, where is the first floor?"

She peered around. "I don't know. I can't see the first floor because it's under the terrace we're standing on."

"Precisely."

Mara was confused. "I don't understand."

"The first floor should contain something magnificent,

or at least momentous—on which the other treasures rest. Just like the Manueline window rests on the shoulders of the bearded figure. The first floor shouldn't be buried in the dark under some terrace," Ben said.

He walked off to the right of the Manueline window, mumbling to himself. Mara ran after him. Together, they found a set of stairs to the lower level that emptied out into two cloisters: Saint Barbara's and the Hostelry. The "first floor" of the church appeared to consist of a stone wall with no windows, decoration, or doorway of any kind.

Ben stated the obvious: "There isn't an entrance to the first floor down here."

"So I see," Mara said, irritated. They needed to watch for the viscount in the interior of the Charola, not run around the exterior.

"Maybe we have to access the first floor from the inside of the church." He raced back into the church with Mara in tow. After a fruitless search of the interior, they ended up back on the same terrace where they'd begun—looking at the Manueline window.

"This makes no sense. There *must* be a first floor," Ben said.

Mara spotted a large group of partygoers walking onto the terrace. "Let's go back into the Charola, Ben. It looks like the receiving line has broken up; maybe the viscount is inside."

"Just one more walk around, then we'll go in. I promise." This time, he headed to the left of the window. There, cut into an enormous column, they discovered a dark staircase leading down. No light illuminated the stairway, and they could not see its bottom in the blackness.

Ben started down, and Mara followed him. His hand darted out from the darkness to restrain her progress. "Mara, just stay there. Your heels weren't meant for these stairs."

Mara watched as Ben descended slowly into the pitch black. The chatter of the revelers passed, and Mara was left in silence. Then she heard the steady, rhythmic thud of approaching footsteps. She feared that it might be the Chinese man following her. Rather than turn around to see whether it was an innocent partygoer or her Chinese friend, she headed down the stairs.

She placed one hand on the wall to steady herself. Her fingers recoiled involuntarily; a slimy moss covered the stones. She forced them back down on the slippery surface and inched her spindly shoes forward.

Mara listened for the dreaded footsteps, and heard them pace back and forth. She longed to race down the stairs, but she couldn't speed up without falling. Finally, they faded off into the distance.

At the base of the bottom stair, she edged her foot forward, and encountered only flat, stone flooring. She had reached the landing at the staircase's bottom, and when she took another step she ran right into Ben.

"Mara," he whispered. "I told you to stay put."

"I heard footsteps. I thought I'd be safer down here."

"In the pitch black?"

"Let's not stand around and talk. Where's the exit?"

"There isn't one."

In disbelief, Mara ran her hands along the four walls bordering the landing, feeling for a doorway. Ben was right. The stairs came to a dead end.

"I guess we'll have to go back up. Come on, Ben." She grabbed his arm.

"This staircase should lead somewhere," Ben muttered.

"Ben, let's go. These steps don't go anywhere."

He paused. "Not now. But Mara, these stairs used to lead to the first floor. There must be something hidden down here."

After the fleet rounds the tip of Africa, the wind and current sweep it northward, up the continent's western coast. The terror that had gripped the sailors diminishes. Though the seamen understand that the fleet sails into unexplored waters, they are reassured by the fact that the shoreline appears from time to time and that the admiral anchors the fleet and sends advance parties to land. Even Zhi's unease lessens and his excitement builds as he immerses himself in the monumental task of charting the new coast of Africa.

The sailors seem to surrender to their work, into a pattern of peacefully accepting the unknown. In truth, they all wait for the lookout's call of land, Zhi along with them. He strains to hear the sailor's cry amid the waves lapping against the outer walls of the *Ch'ing Ho*.

When, from time to time, the shout sounds, Zhi releases the breath he's been holding since they last left the African coast. He longs to rush to the deck, but he knows that as an officer he must maintain protocol and await the end of his shift. Admiral Zhou orders the high-ranking crew to behave as if sighting any uncharted land is as ordinary as hearing the welcoming drums of Malacca. It is an effort to maintain the sailors' confidence in the admiral's command.

Yet none of the fleet's seamen, from the most senior

officers to the lowest galleymen, can mask their anticipation at hearing the scouts' reports on this western
African coast. After one visit, the men return with tales
of small, tawny-colored inhabitants who dress in skins
and shells and gather honey from the bases of bushes.
After another, they divulge details of tall, nearly black-
hued natives of amazing strength. None of the popula-
tions they encounter have fine cloth, valued minerals, or
legendary animals like the giraffe that Admiral Zheng
had presented to Emperor Yongle after an earlier expedition. Their societies do not seem as sophisticated as
those the fleet had met on the eastern coast of Africa.
Admiral Zhou deems none of the peoples worthy of
bringing into the emperor's tribute system, though he
orders the men to treat the natives and their strange
ways with respect. Perhaps the dark heart of the continent bears priceless fruit, but not the accessible shore.
So they leave the coastal communities of West Africa
alone and sail on.

Overnight, the wind shifts, blowing the ships westward.
The lookouts no longer see land. After a full cycle of the
moon with only whitecaps and the sea for company, the
admiral cannot deny the conclusion Master Hsieh and
Zhi have reached. The fleet has entered the boundless
waters of a new ocean: the Atlantic.

A tiny part of Zhi is thrilled. To have charted a new
coast of Africa, to have outlined a continent near in full,
is a pleasure. But to discover and map an ocean is an
unprecedented privilege. Even Admiral Zheng might
take special notice.

He understands that the rest of the fleet does not share
his private delight. The seamen fixate on the frigid

temperature of the ocean deep. They worry about when their supply of fresh water will run out. They worry that they might never return home. Even Yuan and Ke begin to believe that the myth of the end of the world is true.

Master Hsieh and Zhi are in the study, at work on a sailing chart of this new ocean, when a deafening boom sounds on deck. They have become accustomed to storms and oceanic squalls, so they continue with their challenging latitude calculations. Then they hear another boom, and the cry of their names by one of the sailors on duty.

They rise and race to the study door, but they cannot force it open. The door frame has warped from the impact. The *Ch'ing Ho* begins to pitch in violent, heaving rolls that treasure boats are designed to never suffer. Zhi tries to calm himself by thinking about the ship's myriad protective features: the reinforced bows, the water-resistant sectioning, and the stabilizing anchors. Surely the boats will level soon.

Yet lamps, writing brushes, and instruments begin to fly around the small room. The men rush to secure the irreplaceable tools in bolted-down chests but are thrown to the floor from a powerful lurch. They struggle to stand but cannot.

They crawl beneath the study desk, which is fastened to the floor, for protection. Zhi clings to one of the desk's legs as the ship reels back and forth as if it were in the jaws of an iguana-dragon. He beseeches Allah to protect them, and he hears Master Hsieh pray to his gods as he grips another leg of the desk.

A terrible roar sounds. The ship tilts until it is nearly vertical—poised to dive to the ocean depths. They slide

toward the wall. Master Hsieh screams, "We have angered the gods with this pursuit of Fusang! Heaven
protect and forgive us!"

Defying the ship's protections, water rushes into the
study. It climbs and climbs until Zhi and Master Hsieh
must inch out from beneath the desk and cling instead
to its surface. Zhi begins to think of the study as his
burial chamber.

Then, as suddenly as it had begun, the rolling sub-
sides. Zhi hears the voices of sailors and pounding on
the study door. He is loath to release his grip on the
desk, but he forces himself. He wades through the hip-
high water to the door and yells out that he and Master Hsieh are alive within.

He hears the sound of an ax on the door, and an
opening begins to appear. The sailors reach their hands
through the hole to pull Zhi and Master Hsieh through.
They stagger above board.

The deck is covered with bodies. Behemoth surges,
dwarfing those at Africa's tip, had engulfed the treasure
ships and overwhelmed the vessels' designs. The waves
had flooded the watertight compartments in the hulls,
sending hundreds of drowned sailors to the decks. Many
smaller grain ships and warships did not survive the
deluge; some simply did not resurface after a swell. Zhi
is appeased only by the knowledge that Yuan's and Ke's
bodies are not among those of the unfortunate sailors
on deck; they've survived.

By nightfall, the waves calm. The winds soften. But
the sailors do not relax along with the elements. The
loss has been too great and too immediate for them to
loosen their defenses.

Not withstanding his entreaties to his gods and his

cries about the quest for Fusang, Master Hsieh returns to his behavior before the storm. He orders Zhi to continue with his routine tasks, despite the loss of hundreds of men and ten ships. As he walks the navigational bridge, Zhi considers that his efforts may be futile, that his elation over charting the fleet's discoveries may be pointless. For they may never escape from this new ocean and return to China.

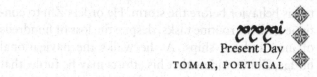

Mara brushed a smear of moss from Ben's tuxedo sleeve as they reentered the Charola. She didn't want to draw any unnecessary attention to themselves, though she needn't have worried. Guests from the receiving line buzzed around the sacrosanct structure, against which their entrance was insignificant.

The vaulted space seemed less vast now that it teemed with visitors. Mara and Ben weaved in and out of the partygoers as they searched for the viscount of Tomar. She spotted him near the archway to the Charola. He was holding court to a phalanx of glittering guests.

Mara drew near, eager for their host's rendition of Tomar's past after hearing the history-book version from Ben and Professor Silva. Yet his tales, told in English and Portuguese for his multinational audience, seemed torn right from the pages of a classroom text. The only insights he offered related to his family's project to transform the southwest cloister of the convent into a neoclassical palace in the 1800s, after his ancestors became stewards of the complex upon the extinction of the Order of Christ.

When he was asked about the interior decoration of the palace, the viscount's face lit up. He launched into a keen description of the hand-painted silk wallpaper in the ballroom. Mara's eyes glazed over at the loving minutiae. She'd begun to wonder whether they'd ever get him alone when one of his security detail approached. The viscount held up his hand as he listened to his guard, then excused himself from the circle gathered around him.

The guests waited politely for a few minutes, but when the conversation with the guard dragged on, they dispersed throughout the church. Mara and Ben studied an archway painting of a saint so they could stay close to him.

The viscount finished with his guard. For a rare instant, he was alone. Mara seized her opportunity.

"Viscount, I don't know if you recall us from the receiving line?"

He smiled graciously, but his eyes betrayed his boredom at chatting with yet another guest. "Ah yes, our American friends."

"Yes. You suggested that we speak to you about a private matter when you arrived in the Charola."

"Of course, of course. I haven't much time to spare, though. As you can see, this is a very busy night for me."

"Our apologies. We wouldn't dare interrupt such a meaningful occasion unless the matter was of some urgency. We need to speak with you about a stolen map."

He looked startled. And, simultaneously, inexplicably furious. He signaled Mara and Ben to follow him down one of the Charola's empty galleries.

"Has one of my maps been taken?" he asked, regaining his composure and showing concern.

"No, no." Mara reassured him that this matter had nothing to do with his renowned art collection.

"Then what could this urgent matter have to do with me?"

"You have the reputation for being the most important map collector in Portugal, and we were hoping that you might be able to talk to us about the Portuguese map community. We've heard rumors that the stolen map we seek may be here."

He paused, scanning them up and down. "Who are you people?"

"As I mentioned in the receiving line, we're colleagues of Richard Tobias and Paulo Montiero."

"You're working with Richard Tobias and Paulo Montiero on this map business?"

"Yes, we are."

The viscount's rigid stance relaxed a bit. He hesitated for a moment and then reached into his pocket. "Come to my home tomorrow evening at eight." He handed Mara a calling card. "Here is the information you'll need to reach me."

"Thank you, Viscount. Again, our apologies."

He bestowed a curt nod of dismissal upon them and tore away. Before he'd reached the crowd, however, he pivoted back. His already dark eyes blackened with reproach. "But I do not want to hear one word of this map business mentioned again at this affair. I don't want the evening spoiled. Do you understand me?"

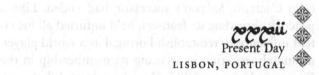
Present Day
LISBON, PORTUGAL

Mara and Ben's cab whizzed through the Lisbon streets. Through the window, Mara saw signs for the Vasco da Gama Bridge, the longest in Europe. It struck her that the Age of Discovery lived on in modern-day Lisbon: in the monuments, in the street names, in the names given to restaurants and stores, even in the people. Current Portuguese national pride harkened back to the long-past time of world supremacy.

The taxi sped through the ancient roadways and lurched to a stop on the Rua das Janelas Verdes. Mara and Ben stumbled out of the cab and headed up the stairs leading to a palatial yellow-and-white building: the National Museum of Ancient Art. The museum had the largest collection of paintings in Portugal, but Mara and Ben had not come to see its excellent assemblage of early religious works. They had come to the museum for a special exhibit.

Mara and Ben meandered down the long hallways to the designated gallery. As they did, she thought about her conversation with Joe. In advance of their appointment with the viscount, Joe had called in some favors to flesh out their limited profile on Gabriel da Costa. It seemed that the dictator Antonio de Oliveira Salazar had ousted his family's claims to rule, but the now-reclusive viscount had been a political force in Portugal

and Europe ever since 1974, when the regime of Mar-
cello Caetano, Salazar's successor, had ended. Like a
peacock spreading its feathers, he'd unfurled all his la-
tent influence to reestablish Portugal as a world player,
ultimately assisting in securing its membership in the
European Union in 1986. Once he achieved that goal,
he faded back into the rich tapestry of Lisboan life,
serving as a quiet but potent reminder of the power of
monarchy and historical ties. He surfaced only when
his sway was needed for a worthy cause, like the 1998
Expo in Lisbon or the Tomar benefit.

An ardent collector of antique maps and medieval
Portuguese art, the viscount had loaned a few pieces
to a temporary cartographical exhibit at the Museum
of Ancient Art. Mara thought that a stroll through
Views of Lisbon: A Walk Through Time might give them
some insight into the viscount as a collector, rather than
a politician. So she'd suggested a visit to the museum to
Ben.

They reached the entry to the exhibit. Handing their
tickets to the guard, Mara realized with delight that they
would have the gallery all to themselves. She lost herself
in the pictorial history of Lisbon. The exhibit featured
cityscapes and town scenes rather than maps, ranging
from the fifteenth century to the eighteenth. She was
fascinated by how much had changed—the Jerónimos
Monastery once sat on the banks of the Tagus River,
rather than a distance away—yet how much remained.

Mara took in the entire exhibit, then circled back to
the engravings loaned by the viscount, hoping to get
a sense of the man who owned them. The views of
the Torre de Belém, the fortress built in the middle of the
Tagus River in the early 1500s, were magnificent. The

drawings showed the imposing tower rising from the crashing waves of the river, allowing Mara to conjure up the fear the Torre must have inspired in sailors visiting Lisbon for the first time. She jumped when Ben touched her shoulder.

"I'm going to the archives," he said.

"The archives? Why?"

He hesitated. "They have some of the original architectural plans of Diogo de Arruda and João de Castilho."

Now Mara understood why he'd been so willing to join her at the museum; he had planned on coming to see the archives all along. "The architects for the renovation of the Charola?"

He nodded.

"Think you're going to find the missing first floor?" she teased.

He blushed. "You never know."

"I thought we'd agreed to put aside that riddle for now."

"We did. But we're here. The plans are here. What would it hurt?"

Mara had to laugh; he was beginning to sound like her. "All right. I'll meet you there in an hour."

She finished her study of the viscount's engravings. Exiting the exhibition, Mara hunted around for a docent who might point her toward more literature on the show. As she wandered around, she kept seeing signs pointing the way to the *Adoration of Saint Vincent*, the museum's most famous piece. She decided to take a peek.

Grabbing a pamphlet as she entered the gallery, she read about the celebrated polyptych of the patron saint

of Lisbon by Nuno Gonçalves, an enigmatic figure who
was court painter to King Afonso V. Lost for centuries,
it was rediscovered in 1882 in the Monastery of Saint
Vincent. While working at the monastery, the painter
Columbano found the altarpiece hidden under some
wooden scaffolding in an abandoned chapel. He extri-
cated the painting and sheltered it in one of the corridors of the monastery, where it went unappreciated for
another decade.

Now considered the most important fifteenth-century
Portuguese painting, the *Adoration* had recently become
a symbol of national pride in the Age of Discovery. The
literature claimed that the controversy surrounding the
altarpiece and its meaning approached that of the *Mona
Lisa*. The *Adoration* presented a singular emblematic
depiction of the moment in time when the religious and
the worldly joined to further a common goal: the epic
objective propelling Portugal into the seas to spread
Christianity and assert its material dominance.

Mara looked up from the pamphlet. No amount of
hyperbole could have prepared her for its visual impact.
Exquisitely, realistically rendered portraits of Saint
Vincent, King Afonso V, King John II, Prince Henry
the Navigator, and even Gonçalves himself stood out
against a backdrop of figures, many of them ordinary
fishermen, monks, and soldiers. These mysterious figures were each individually portrayed. Gonçalves's
brushwork and treatment of light and color were masterful, yet given Mara's fascination with iconography,
the carefully placed encoded objects intrigued her most
of all, the Panel of the Infante in particular.

In the panel, Saint Vincent held open a Bible for the

benefit of King Afonso V, King John II, and Prince Henry the Navigator. Its open page read:

> *Hereafter I will not talk much with you; for the prince of this world cometh, and hath nothing in me. But that the world may know that I love the Father, and as the Father gave me commandment, even so I do.*   JOHN, CH. XIV, 30–31.

Mara thought that perhaps the quote, from Christ encouraging the apostles in their coming struggle with the devil, was meant to give the Portuguese courage as they braved new worlds full of "infidels."

The disruptive arrival of a tour group made her think to look at her watch. Over an hour had passed since Ben had left for the archives. Amazed by how time had slipped by, she was reminded that it was the art itself that drew her into this life and kept her there. The sleuthing was only a means to an end—solving the riddles of art and history.

She left the *Adoration* with reluctance, museum floor plan in hand, and found the archives. At first, she didn't see Ben anywhere. Then she noticed a small, glass-paneled room off to the side. There he sat, with a pretty librarian with dark hair and eyes hovering by his side. Though they seemed intent on a document and not each other, she felt a wave of jealousy.

Pushing open the glass door, she entered the room. They looked up simultaneously. She whispered, "What are those documents?"

Ben answered her: "These are Diogo de Arruda's original plans of the Charola renovation."

Mara drew proprietarily close to Ben. She watched as he turned the pages with a gloved hand. She thought she could make out the nave, the choir, and the sacristy.

Ben gazed up at the librarian. "Where is the plan for the first floor? The floor that lies underneath the sacristy?"

"I don't understand," she replied with a heavy accent.

He repeated his question, this time more slowly and emphatically.

"I understand your English. It is your question that I do not comprehend. You have before you the entire plan."

Ben nodded in seeming agreement, but Mara watched as he slowly turned through the architectural plans again. His attention was focused on the bottom right corners, where the page numbers were located. The numbers skipped. A page had been removed.

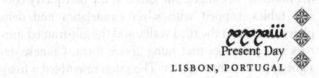
"You've made us late for this appointment," Mara whispered to Ben as they waited for the viscount of Tomar's door to open. Ben had disappeared for a few hours after they'd returned to the hotel to freshen up for their meeting, and despite his repeated apologies, she was still furious.

"I needed to meet with Professor Silva, Mara," he whispered back. "He is the only person I know who might be able to help track down the full architectural plans of the Charola addition."

"Ben, we're not here to go on some wild-goose chase to solve the puzzle of the Charola. We are here to find your stolen map."

"What if I told you that—" The door creaked open. Mara painted on a smile for the viscount, and she readied her apologies for their late arrival. But the dour, craggy face of a butler greeted them. The attendant took their coats and ushered them into the salon. He motioned for them to sit on delicate side chairs with backs shaped like violins that flanked an enormous rosewood cabinet.

Mara perched on the edge of one of the chairs, fearful of resting her full weight on its spindly legs. She noticed that Ben assumed the same uncomfortable position. As they waited in silence to be summoned, she tried to take

her mind off her anger. She gazed at the marquetry con-
sole tables, topped with silver candelabra and delft
plates, that lined the tiled walls, and the gilt-framed mir-
rors and paintings that hung above them. Chinese designs appeared throughout. The salon resembled a fussy
drawing room of the seventeenth or eighteenth century,
she guessed.

The loud tick of a porcelain clock kept them company.
While they waited. And waited.

After three-quarters of an hour, the butler reappeared. "The viscount and viscountess of Tomar," he
announced.

Mara and Ben jumped up, and suddenly she realized
she did not know the proper greeting. She wondered
whether a bow was expected or if a handshake would be
acceptable. She straightened her now-rumpled skirt
and waited for their cue.

The viscount of Tomar, with a gracious manner bearing no traces of the loftiness of his title, answered the
unspoken question for her. He approached Mara with
his hand outstretched in welcome, while the viscountess of Tomar did the same for Ben. Then they switched.

As they bantered about the sites of Lisbon and the
glorious weather, Mara took in the couple. Without his
tuxedo and her ball gown from the benefit, they resembled many of the older couples she'd seen in the finer
restaurants and shops around Lisbon. As the couples
aged, the men thinned and dressed more nattily, while
the women grew stouter and wore pricey but matronly
ensembles.

The viscount and viscountess were no exception. The
viscount wore a V-necked cashmere sweater, a handmade shirt complete with French cuffs, flannel slacks,

and loafers; the only concession to age came from the reading glasses dangling around his neck on a chain. The viscountess wore an A-line skirt, comfortable shoes—though they looked expensive—and a cardigan sweater that she constantly fussed over to keep her large bosom covered. Still, her legs remained shapely; Mara imagined they were as slender as they'd been on her wedding day, when she'd had a twenty-inch waist.

Pleasantries completed, the viscount and viscountess escorted Mara and Ben into their home. The viscount took the lead, explaining a bit about its history and bringing them into a vast space that served as a ballroom. Maps lined its walls. Hundreds of maps.

He walked them by the charts, pointing out certain pieces. His collection seemed to focus on a singular theme: the celebration of Portugal. He concentrated on a portolan chart painstakingly represented in color on parchment by Pedro Reinel. He highlighted maps from one of the six surviving atlases of Fernão Vaz Dourado, dating from the 1570s. Explaining that Dourado was not only a cartographer but an artist, he proudly indicated the maps' elaborate borders and decorative devices.

Ben stopped in front of the Dourados. "These are exquisite. Mara, I think Professor Silva mentioned Dourado the other day, didn't he?"

"Professor Silva?" the viscount asked.

Before Mara could rein Ben in, he spouted off: "Yes, Professor Luis Silva from the University of Lisbon; he's a noted cartographical expert. We spoke with him the other day about maps in the Age of Discovery. He mentioned that you two had met."

"Very briefly," the viscount answered, and then returned to the discussion of Dourado.

Watching the viscount, Mara was reminded of the portraits from Gonçalves's *Adoration of Saint Vincent*. He had the same long face, black eyes, and resolute jaw of many of the subjects in the background frieze.

As they reached the end of the tour, Mara stated the obvious: "Your collection is magnificent."

"Thank you. But this is not my entire collection."

"How could I forget that you have some beautiful engravings on loan to the National Museum of Ancient Art? I saw them today. They're lovely."

"I have many other pieces beyond that, but I rotate their display for preservation purposes."

"Is it hard to select the maps for display?"

The viscountess giggled. "We joke that it is like picking a favorite of your children."

They grew silent. Mara wanted to ask some pointed questions about Dias and the Portuguese map community, but she felt uncomfortable doing so in the presence of the viscountess. Not because the questions were so confidential, but because her gentility made the questions seem crass.

The viscountess seemed to sense Mara's dilemma. She excused herself, saying, "I will see that Maria is readying the coffee and pastries."

The threesome strolled into an adjoining study and settled into a small conversational area around a roaring fire. Strains of harpsichord music wafted through the air. Mara could almost imagine that musicians, rather than a stereo, were playing the Mozart piece in the next room.

Before she launched into her questions, Mara complimented the viscount on his political work, his success in securing Portugal a place in the European Union, among other endeavors.

"It was my pleasure to help put Portugal back on the map," he answered, chuckling at his own joke. His expression then turned serious and proud. He explained to Mara and Ben the degeneration of Portugal under the tyranny of Salazar, a name he spat out like a curse. After the dictatorship toppled, Portugal had needed to demonstrate its economic and cultural assets to the world and to regain some of the status it had once had: a prominence unchallenged during the Age of Discovery. Though the viscount doubted that Portugal would ever again achieve its fifteenth-century heights, he was thrilled to assist in inching the nation closer toward the goal of reestablishing its standing.

"I have spoken to my old friend Paulo Montiero," he interjected.

"Oh?" Mara held her breath. She was fearful that Paulo Montiero might have told the viscount he had never heard of Mara Coyne and Ben Coleman.

"Yes. And he thinks very highly of your colleague Richard Tobias."

Mara exhaled. "I'll be sure to share that with Richard."

"He also spoke admiringly of the work *you* have done lobbying for legislation to prevent the export of antiquities from their countries of origin. That is an effort I support wholeheartedly."

The compliment rendered Mara momentarily speechless. It was rare that her public work as a negotiator and lobbyist collided with her private investigative work. Mara recovered and thanked the viscount for his praise.

"So, how can I help you? A stolen map is an affront to the entire cartographical community."

"As I mentioned last night, we've received some information that the map is here in Portugal. I'm hoping you can describe the players here."

The viscount listed dealers, fellow collectors, auctioneers, and museum directors. As Mara took notes, she realized that many of the names were familiar. They appeared in Catherine's dossier, and she had already spoken to a fair number of them.

"I am not certain my descriptions have been of much assistance."

"Oh, they have," she lied.

"Perhaps if you could give me more details, I might be able to help further. Maybe a description of the map? I might be able to identify interested collectors and relevant dealers."

Mara hesitated. She glanced at Ben, who nodded slightly. "Have you ever heard of a man called Dias?"

The viscount started and then stopped. In that brief span, Mara wondered how to interpret his silence; had she offended him in some way by daring to mention a map thief in his presence?

The tension broke with the viscount's chortle. "Oh, the legendary Dias. Please do not tell me your information indicated that this Dias has your stolen map?"

Mara nodded.

"Let me guess. You were told that Dias might be here in Portugal?"

"Yes."

He let out a deep belly laugh. "I am sorry. I'm afraid you have been led down the proverbial garden path."

"In what way?"

"To start, I have heard about this infamous Dias since I was a small child and my father collected maps. So that would make this Dias quite old, well past the age of active thievery I would guess. Also, I have heard rumors that he is based in Lisbon, Madrid, Milan, Florence, Paris. I could go on and on. Most of us believe that Dias never really existed, that thefts attributed to him were commissioned by a host of criminals who took advantage of the legend to divert attention from themselves."

Mara averted her eyes from the viscount. She had stumbled into a novice's trap.

During dawn watch, somewhere behind the continuous lapping of the waves, Zhi thinks he hears a faraway caw. He stops his surveying and listens, harder than he has ever listened before. He hears the sound again. "I hear a bird," he whispers to himself. He says again, even louder, "I heard a bird!"

The battered, weary seamen working nearby cast a skeptical eye at him. Yet within hours, the first sight of verdant green islands greets the ship—the Caribbean— and the sailors signal the rest of the fleet with bells. As they wait for the armada to join them, Zhi breathes in the change in the air, watches brightly plumed seabirds circle around the boat, and relaxes into the moment.

As the ships draw close to the craggy coast of the first island they reach, Admiral Zhou assembles the crew on deck. He is generous with his liberties; he gives all sailors leave to go ashore when they are off duty. Even the concubines are permitted to touch land for the first time since leaving Tanggu, though they must travel in pairs and cannot associate with the men. Except for the eunuchs, of course.

Rowboats depart from the *Ch'ing Ho* and its remaining squadrons. They carry sailors eager to walk on firm soil. The men roam through uninhabited lands teeming with fruit, fish, and birds so tame they can be picked up by hand. Zhi is determined to enjoy the idyllic days, and he joins Yuan. They pass tranquil hours exploring the new island, each happy to exist in the moment.

Zhi tries to push from his mind thoughts of Fusang. Yet as he and Yuan hike over hilly inland terrain and swim in coastline waterfalls, while they watch from afar Ke and her fellow concubine Tschen retire to the shade of palm trees and the breeze of the beaches, he cannot help but look for the fabled trees described by the Buddhist monk Hoei-Shin. When he does not find them, he knows the serenity will not last. After the ships are re-stocked and the sailors are refreshed, the admiral will order a return to the ocean, to the likelihood of more squalls, to the unknown. For the island is not Fusang.

The fleet stops at many islands in the Caribbean chain, but not every one. The admiral singles out those isles with visible, plentiful waterfalls for easy restocking and shuns those with looming volcanoes. The tropical climate yields unexpected thunderstorms, though the islands afford the ships shelter. And not every island is as unpopulated as the first. Tribal people occupy a few of the islands, though the admiral regards them as too backward to bring into the imperial tribute system.

The ships set sail from an island with air so dense and humid it can nearly be seen wrapping around the branches of trees and the limbs of men. A strange illness takes hold of the boats as they leave, an illness as thick and torpid as the island air.

The sickness leaves no physical trace at first. It merely slows the pace of the men, such that even punishment cannot hasten them to their duties. Only then do the fevers come and the pustules form on their faces, hands, and feet. The doctors know of no treatment for the disease, though they try every herb and every remedy at their disposal. Still, the sailors die in droves.

The admiral orders a hasty departure from the island chain. For a time, the navigational crew seems to be spared. Zhi and his colleagues give thanks for their separate deck and living quarters. They cling together, shunning contact with others as much as possible. For the first time, they fold Zhi into the protective shield of their ranks—out of necessity rather than kindness. Zhi wonders how Yuan and Ke are faring.

A few moons pass. In the stultifying air of the compass room, the rocking of the boat lulls Zhi to sleep. He nods off for the first time during his many watches, then jerks himself back to alertness, blaming it on the stagnancy and the rhythmic sway of the ship. Then he falls back to sleep.

He awakens covered in a sweat. Not the pervasive perspiration to which he's become accustomed in the oppressive tropical climate, but a saturation. Sleep overcomes him again. He drifts in and out; for how long he does not know.

Pain sears him to consciousness. As it courses throughout his body, the stabbing sensation evokes the neverforgotten pain of his knifing day.

On that day, Zhi had journeyed to the capital with his father, Liang, and Liang's uncle. His father had held in his hand a copy of Admiral Zheng's decree, requesting that young men from Kunyang volunteer for the imperial eunuch service. The document detailed the taels the young men's families would receive and the honor such service would bestow upon their family name.

Zhi watched as his father glanced down at the scroll

and then stared off into the distance. He could almost
envision his father's thoughts: the fields he could purchase with the extra taels, the new home he could build,
the restoration of the Ma standing in Kunyang. While
Zhi had agreed to the sacrifice, he had also thought
how the decree made no mention of any personal
surrender—in his case, the love of a woman.

On the critical day, the four men entered the Imperial
City and made their way to the Hsi-hua Gate. Lost in
the maze of the Imperial City alleys, they caught the arm
of a worker rushing by and asked for the location of the
chang-tzu. The man's eyebrows arched in surprise at
the question, but he directed them to the shabby building of the *tao-tzu-chiang*, or knifers, who performed the
castrations.

Zhi's heart pounded as they pushed open the rough-
hewn wooden door. Showing the decree, they stated
their business and paid the six scarce taels for the operation. With reluctant tears, Zhi's father said his farewell
and handed Zhi over to the knifers. Liang's uncle did
the same.

Zhi and Liang were taken down a hallway. It seemed
very long to Zhi, who turned back to Liang just as he
was about to be ushered into a separate room. Liang
stared back at him with eyes filled with terror.

Two men entered Zhi's chamber and placed him on a
chair. One man bandaged his waist and thighs, while
the other applied hot pepper water to the entire region
three times, to numb the pain. They then held him down
firmly.

A third man came into the room: the *tao-tzu-chiang*.
He asked Zhi the ritual question: Do you willingly
agree to this operation? Zhi gave his assent. The knifer

approached him with a small, sickle-shaped blade. Zhi screamed.

Zhi turns away from the memory, toward his rose-bush, bare and wilted, with its petals brown and curled on the floor. He is confused; he last recalls seeing it in full bloom.

He falls back on his bed, exhausted from the effort. He looks around the room. Master Hong sits in a chair by the door. Zhi tries to sit up and assume a respectful posture, but he is too weak. The chief navigator rises and places a calming hand on his shoulder.

"Stay still. You have had the fever," Master Hong says.

Zhi tries to answer. He has many questions, but his voice, long unused, will not obey.

"Many of the fleet's sailors have died. Hundreds. More than during the storm."

Zhi nods in understanding.

"The sickness infected some of our own navigational crew. They did not fare as well as you."

Zhi's eyes widen. He had hoped he was alone in his illness.

"Including Master Hsieh."

"Master Hsieh?" Zhi croaks. Though he had seen Master Hsieh at his weakest, during the ravages of the tempest, it is still unimaginable to him that the master could succumb to any sickness.

"Yes, Master Hsieh. You are now the chief mapmaker of Admiral Zhou's fleet, Master Ma."

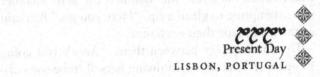

"The past two days have been an utter waste of our time." Mara threw her bag down on the banquette. They had gone directly to the hotel's lobby bar after their meeting with the viscount.

"Did you really think he'd know the identity of Dias?" Ben asked.

"No, but I didn't think I'd be humiliated by mentioning him." Mara shuddered at the memory of the viscount's laughter.

"At least he gave us some names," Ben offered.

"Sure. Names that I've already heard of and contacted." She paused. "I'm just surprised that Ermanno would give me such misleading information. Joe and I have a solid history with him."

While Mara reached into her bag and compared her notes with the dossier list, the waiter delivered the drinks they had ordered: a Sagres beer for him, and a Vilar da Galeira for her. As she e-mailed the upshot of their meeting to Joe, the concierge scuttled into the bar. "Mr. Coleman, I have an envelope for you."

"You can just put it down, please," Ben said, as he poured his beer into a glass.

"I was instructed to place it directly into your hands," the concierge answered.

Ben put down his glass and reached into his wallet as

Mara rolled her eyes. She assumed the staff member was attempting to glean a tip. "Here you go," Ben said as the men made their exchange.

The envelope lay between them. "Aren't you going to open it?" she asked, knowing herself to be too curious to ever allow an envelope to sit unopened.

"No. It's just the latest site plots from Huang."

"Any developments on the dig?"

"No. They've found some other later artifacts, but nothing else from the early 1400s or the Tocharian era. It's odd that Richard's scouts found that initial intact Tocharian mummy and fabric samples but we've been able to uncover nothing else. Normally, there'd be a host of related objects—it's supposed to be a burial site, after all."

They chatted for a while about the excavation, and Mara was relieved to converse about a subject other than the map—or Ben's Charola wild-goose chase. Inevitably, though, the topic returned to their next steps. As Mara conceded that they'd have to leave Lisbon to meet with other European contacts, Ben slid open the envelope.

He pulled out a sheet of paper and unfolded it. Mara asked him a question about their travel plans as he studied the page, but he didn't answer. "Ben, did you hear my question?"

Still he did not respond.

"Ben, what is it?"

He looked up. "Mara, it's a note from Professor Silva. He stopped by the hotel while we were out. He wants me to meet him in his office first thing in the morning. He says he can show me what I'm looking for."

* * *

Mara dressed with more care than usual the next morning. As she selected her favorite pair of boot-cut black trousers and a fitted merino wool sweater, she told herself she'd chosen her favorites because the day held so much uncertainty. She might be called upon to do any number of things. Underneath her little white lies, though, she knew another reason existed: Ben.

She met him in the lobby and immediately launched into a description of the security measures they'd have to take en route to the University of Lisbon. Except for her initial meetings with her art-theft contacts, she hadn't much cared if her Chinese friend followed her and Ben. But now she wanted to take precautions, and she couldn't keep the Chinese involvement from him any longer.

"What do you mean we're going to have to take the train, a cab, and then walk to get to the university?" he blurted out.

"Ben, some representative of the Chinese government has been following us for days. Maybe even longer, since I think I saw him in the Hong Kong airport. Remember that guy I spilled coffee on?"

"Yeah. What does he want?"

"I think the Chinese know that an important map has been found and stolen. And I think they want us to lead them to it."

"Why didn't you tell me?"

"I didn't want to worry you. And I didn't have to hide any of the actions that you and I have undertaken until now."

Ben shook his head in disappointment. "Mara, I thought this was a partnership, based on trust and a common goal. I've confided all my knowledge in you, and I expected the same from you." He started toward the door. "Let's go."

They took their train and cab and then walked in silence. He was right, and she was humbled. By circumstance, an alliance had formed between them, and he'd deserved to know the reality of their situation. Not some censored version she judged him capable of handling. "Ben, I'm really sorry."

He craned his neck so that he looked directly in her eyes. "Are you?"

"I am." Without thinking, she said what she felt: "I want us to have the partnership you described."

"You do?"

Keeping his gaze, she said, "I do."

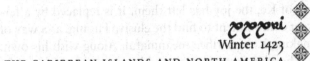

Zhi learns that he passed two cycles of the moon in the grip of the fever. Two moon cycles during which Admiral Zhou's fleet traveled northeast hundreds of *li* past new islands and coastlines. Two moon cycles during which the ships encountered peoples with customs and skin very different from any they had seen in the Indian Ocean or Africa. Two moon cycles during which Master Hsieh commissioned junior navigational crew members on the fleet's other ships to gather information on the newly discovered lands. Before the fever took Master Hsieh—and Ke along with him.

When he is strong enough, Zhi wants to say a proper farewell to Ke by performing a Muslim burial at sea. He waits until he has a mealtime shift and all other navigational crew members leave the private deck. Standing near the railing with his head pointing toward Mecca, he chants over and over, "Allah is great." In Ke's memory, he tosses a white cloth into the gentle roll of the waves—her body has long since been sent to the depths—and wishes her a safe journey to the afterlife. He waits until he can see the cloth no more. As he turns away, he sees Yuan watching from a nearby deck, saying his own farewells to Ke, the friend he was never permitted to have.

Zhi returns to his responsibilities—but with the passing of Ke, the joy has left them. It is replaced by a fervent commitment to find the elusive Fusang, as a way of making Ke's sacrifice meaningful. Along with his own.

The vice admiral assigns him an assistant from the pool of lower-ranking navigators on the other ships. His assistant is not trained in mapmaking, so Zhi undertakes all the cartographical work.

As the fleet continues northeast on the strength of the winds and current, Zhi charts the ships' progress during his fever, as well as their new discoveries. He plots islands, reefs, bays, waterways, and vast shorelines. A cohesive map of another new continent—one running parallel to part of West Africa—emerges. Zhi reaches a startling conclusion, one he is afraid to say aloud.

The current begins to pull the fleet farther northward. The ships anchor in a bay shaped liked a hook. In its protective arms, which shield the fleet from the blustery winds and the threat of snow, the admiral will plan the next stages of their route.

Before Admiral Zhou makes his final determination, Zhi decides that he must share his map—and his deduction—with the admiral. The vice admiral grants Zhi a brief audience with their commander. Zhi pays his respects to the vice admiral and requests leave to approach the admiral, who sits at a table. The vice admiral nods, and Zhi approaches the admiral. He spreads his map out before the admiral; the vice admiral hastens over to the table.

Hands shaking, Zhi explains, "Admiral Zhou, your humble servant Chief Mapmaker Ma believes that, for the past two moon cycles, the fleet has sailed the coast of a new continent."

The vice admiral answers for Admiral Zhou: "We are aware of that, Chief Mapmaker Ma Zhi."

Zhi continues in the face of the vice admiral's derision, directing his comments to the admiral himself. "I have consulted the crew's collective knowledge of the writings of the monk Hoei-Shin. And I have calculated the *li* we have traveled since leaving Tanggu."

"Yes?" the vice admiral says, again speaking for the admiral.

"Based on my calculations and a comparison of our discoveries with those of the monk Hoei-Shin, I believe this new continent is Fusang."

The vice admiral does not answer, but the admiral asks, "How can that be? We have found no Fusang trees on shore bearing fruit like a red pear."

"So I understand, Admiral. But all the other descriptions match, such as the details of the people and their homes and clothing. And, most important, the *li* distance reckoning from China to Fusang is identical. I have noted the similarities on the text columns of the map."

Admiral Zhou reaches for the map, pulling it closer to him and studying it. The vice admiral rushes to the admiral's side, as do their assistants. One assistant orders Zhi to wait outside while they consult the map and one another. Leaning against the deck railing, Zhi watches as the sun sits high in the skies and then makes its journey to the seas. He observes small rowboats being dispatched with communications for the other anchored treasure ships. He waits and prays that Admiral Zhou will agree with his conclusion.

The day is nearly over before Zhi is called back into the admiral's chambers. Admiral Zhou himself announces, "Chief Mapmaker Ma Zhi, I wish to inform you that I agree with your calculations. Thus, I have ordered the fleet to divide: one half will undertake further explorations to the north, while the other half—your half—will return home to China under the command of the admiral. You are commanded to report to Emperor Yongle that Admiral Zhou's fleet has found Fusang."

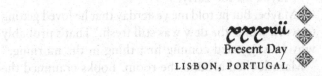

Once Mara was sure no one was following them, she and Ben walked onto the University of Lisbon grounds. The campus was barren first thing, making her surveillance task easier. They found the professor's building with relative ease. No guard stood on duty at the entryway, so they let themselves in and trudged up the three flights of stairs to his floor. They wound their way through the labyrinth of cubbyholes and offices until they reached the end of the hall.

Outside Professor Silva's office an engraved brass plaque was hung, more august than any other on the corridor. They had hoped to have his assistant announce their arrival so as to avoid interrupting him but, unable to locate a secretary—or anyone else, for that matter—Ben just knocked.

No one answered.

"Try again."

Another knock and another silence.

"Should we just go in?" Ben asked.

"I guess so."

He turned the knob, and the door pushed open a crack.

"Professor?" Ben said into the gap.

When no one responded, Ben opened the door wide and stepped into the office. Mara followed.

It was empty.

"Maybe it's too early?"

"Maybe. But he told me yesterday that he loved getting to work while 'the dew was still fresh.' That's probably why he suggested coming first thing in the morning."

Mara looked around the room. Books crammed the shelves lining the walls, and heaps of papers were piled up on the floor. It was the typical office of a busy academic.

"I wonder where he is."

"This is odd," Ben said. "Yesterday, his desk was cluttered with papers and books. We even joked how both of us are pack rats. Today, it's clean."

"Except for that book." Mara pointed to the one tome on the desk.

Ben picked it up and looked at the spine. *"Lives of the Saints."*

Mara noticed a tiny scrap of paper sticking out between two pages. "What's that?"

He opened the book. "It's a marker for the chapter on Saint Vincent."

She walked over to his side and looked at the page. The margin contained penciled notes in a language she could not discern. "Do you know what it says?"

"It's just a prayer to Saint Vincent. In Latin."

"Can you translate it for me?"

He opened the page wide and started reciting:

> *Oh, adored Saint Vincent,*
> *Forgive me.*
>
> *What secret you bade me keep*
> *Under dark cover and arms red and white*
> *Honor bade me illumine.*

Wash away my sins
So that I might join my brethren in Christ.

"Ben, the professor knew you read Latin?"

"Yes."

"He must have meant you to see that."

"I guess. But it doesn't mean anything to me. And he knew that I was looking for the Charola plans."

"Maybe he left them for you. Somewhere around this office."

They started to look around the room. A small cylindrical tube lying at the back of one of the shelves caught Mara's attention, and she wondered if it might contain the plans. She picked it up and handed it to Ben.

He took the lid off the top and slid out the rolled paper within. He spread it out on the clean desktop.

He stared up at her. "Mara, it's a copy of the missing pages from the Charola architectural plans."

Voices of a man and woman echoed down the long hallway leading to the professor's office. Mara and Ben froze until the conversation trailed off and the hall grew silent again. They opened the door a tiny crack and looked down the corridor. It was empty—for the moment. Mara motioned to Ben, and together they started running.

Antonio begins to believe that the rest of the voyage will pass as auspiciously as the first leg, with its successful rounding of the tip of Africa. Under his guidance, the ships start to career up the east coast of Africa. He sights the *padrãos*, stone pillars inscribed in Latin, Portuguese, and Arabic, left by Dias on his 1488 journey, and the fleet erects a few of its own, though these bear the markings of King Manuel and the Order of Christ.

He conveys his uncharacteristic optimism to da Gama in their increasingly regular meetings. His sanguinity infects the usually reserved and pious captain-major, who names a major river the Rio dos Bons Signaes, the river of good omens. Antonio permits himself to envision Helena's black hair and graceful movements, and the few secret afternoons they had spent together before her father discovered their relationship and forbade their meetings. The hope that he might call upon her again takes firm shape.

The omens turn. They are forced to break up the storeship. The *São Rafael* runs aground on a shoal a few days after the fleet leaves Mozambique. Arabic pilots are brought on board to assist the coastal sail since the portolan charts can no longer help, and they proclaim that Christians live alongside Moors in the nearby bustling port city of Mombasa. A kingly welcome lulls the armada to complacency in the Mombasa harbor. At midnight, two *almadia* boats full of men approach in silence. They cut cables, ensnarl the riggings, and try to board. Da Gama's sailors thwart the attempted treachery, and the captain-major himself stands by as boiling oil is dropped upon the Moors to make them confess any further treachery. Antonio watches the torture through sideways glances, but notes that da Gama's stare is unflinching.

Yet Antonio has no time to focus on the deceit or its impact on da Gama. He must keep constant counsel with the secret map. It alone advises Antonio in fixing the route for the *São Gabriel*, the *São Rafael*, and the *Berrio*, across the Indian Ocean—the first European ships ever to so cross. He does not permit himself to think about Helena.

Even with the map, the route challenges Antonio. He must guide the ships before the wind, and find the best course for the monthlong open-water sail. He rejoices at the reappearance of the North Star, an old astronomical friend lost in the sky for many months, yet it does not ease the way. Though land comes into view, heavy rains and thunderstorms prevent their anchor. When Antonio finally navigates the armada into Calicut—the shining spiced jewel of their journey—the seamen are so relieved that even his fellow officers yell out congratulations.

Da Gama sends two messengers to the king of Calicut, announcing their arrival. After receiving an invitation to visit with the king, da Gama and thirteen of his men, Antonio among them, set out in their best attire. A palanquin and armed men receive da Gama and his men on shore and take them to the palace. Excitement builds as men beating drums and blowing bagpipes join their progress, as do great lords.

At an hour before sunset, they pass through a gate into the shimmering palace. The king, dressed in fine linens, draped in rubies, and holding a great golden cup, receives them from his couch of green velvet under a gilded canopy. The king and da Gama exchange introductions while Antonio and the other men taste strange fruit resembling melons and figs. Their welcome is felicitous, and Antonio begins to imagine again that he will indeed return to Portugal with gold and spices lining his purse. Finally, he allows himself to envision Helena.

Well satisfied with their reception, in the days that follow, da Gama instructs the men to ready the gifts for the king: sugar, oil, honey, coral beads, and washbasins. One by one they present them to the king's representative in a solemn ceremony, with Antonio handing over the canisters of honey. To their surprise, the representative scorns the goods, telling da Gama that they are not things to offer a king, that even the poorest merchant would make a present of gold. Humiliated before his men, da Gama demands another audience with the king, another chance to make his offering.

They wait for days, days in which da Gama grows angrier at the injury to his pride and Antonio grows anxious about da Gama's mounting rage. When they are finally granted admittance, the king laughs at the gifts of sugar, oil, honey, coral, and washbasins, and ridicules da Gama. Da Gama sees this as a mockery of his God, and Portugal itself, and demands that they be returned to their ships. But the king demands gold in exchange. They have no gold, so they make their way back to the ships on their own.

Da Gama orders the fleet to set sail back to Portugal. He announces to the sailors that he has secured his prize—the sea route to India—but will not waste further time fostering relations with the heathen king. Yet Antonio knows that da Gama's bullishness is all show. Beneath the surface, fury simmers.

The open sea does not soothe da Gama. Antonio hears tales of da Gama pacing the deck of the *São Gabriel*, searching for a suitable object for his rage. The captain-major orders unjustified floggings and cuts the men's rations without warning. He commands the sailors and soldiers to attack the natives before they assess the population's intentions. Even the most stalwart of mariners start to fear da Gama.

Then the armada sights a ship. Da Gama commands the men to overtake it.

Antonio guides the ships through the dangerous shoals indicated on the map. The fleet nears the lateen-rigged vessel. They lie in wait.

Antonio makes some adjustments to his astrolabe and, through it, sees that the boat harbors pilgrims from Mecca and that many women and children are on deck. He disregards the time-consuming protocol demanding that he inform Captain Paulo da Gama first and sends for a clerk instead. He instructs him, "Get word to the captain-major that women and children are aboard. We should halt the mission."

Antonio watches as the clerk dispatches a rowboat to the *São Gabriel*. He remains fixed at the rail until he witnesses its return to the *São Rafael*. He rushes on deck to receive the word from da Gama.

The sailor is panting from his exertions. Antonio enjoins him, "Speak, man. Do we have the captain-major's orders to cease our progress?"

The sailor freezes.

Antonio shoves him. "Speak."

The trembling sailor shakes his head. "I am sorry, sir. The captain-major orders all three ships to proceed apace against the Muslim vessel."

Antonio staggers away from the sailor and the clerk, who stare as the usually brash pilot falters. He retires to the navigators' deck, determined to shield himself from the horrors about to unfold. Yet he cannot close his ears to the screams, and he cannot protect his skin from the searing heat. Da Gama commands the ship to be set aflame, burning alive the innocent women and children on board.

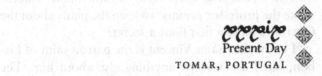

Present Day

TOMAR, PORTUGAL

Mara and Ben sped away from the university in a cab. She told the cabdriver to take them to the train station. She thought the train would be the safest way of traveling to Tomar. And they both agreed they had to go to Tomar.

They spread out the plans and the prayer between them. "You were right that a first floor existed, Ben."

"Yeah, but I'm so confused. Where is the professor, and why didn't he just give us this information himself?"

"He obviously wanted you to have it but couldn't give it to you directly for some reason."

"I hope he's all right."

"He very carefully arranged that office so that you'd find the prayer and the plans. So I'd say he's fine, wherever he is."

They studied the plans, but Ben grew frustrated because they did not show a means of access to the first floor. He turned his attention to the *Lives of the Saints*. "What's the meaning of this prayer?"

"I'd guess that the prayer links to the architectural plan," she said. "But how?"

"The 'secret' mentioned in the prayer must be the plans he left."

"I agree. But what's this reference to Saint Vincent? The prayer says the secret *you*—meaning Saint

Vincent—bade me keep. Why would Saint Vincent make the professor promise to keep the plans about the Charola's hidden first floor a secret?"

"I know that Saint Vincent is the patron saint of Lisbon, but I don't know anything else about him. The catechism wasn't part of my upbringing."

"He was a deacon of the church and martyred in the third or fourth century after being tortured on a gridiron."

"How do you know that?"

"I spent a long time studying the saints with a very Catholic grandmother."

"I still don't see what he has to do with the Charola plans. Saint Vincent doesn't have any overt association with the Tomar complex, and his history predates its construction."

"Maybe it's not supposed to relate to Tomar. Maybe the professor prayed to Saint Vincent. My grandmother always offered up her prayers to Saint Brigid because she was the patron saint of her homeland, Ireland."

Then an idea struck Mara. "Can I see the prayer again?"

Ben handed her the paper, and she studied it. "It says, 'Oh, *adored* Saint Vincent.' Did you tell him we'd been at the National Museum of Ancient Art?"

"Yes. We looked over the copies of the architectural plans I got from the museum."

"I bet he's referencing *The Adoration of Saint Vincent* by Nuno Gonçalves. It's the masterpiece of the museum."

As she rummaged through her bag for the museum pamphlet, she described the polyptych to Ben—its multiple panels; its unusual, individually rendered portraits of noblemen, religious, and commoners; and its references to biblical verses calling followers to stay faithful in the face of the infidels. She explained the controversy surrounding its meaning and the prevailing view on its symbolism: the painting represented the devotion of late-fifteenth-century Portuguese society to the ideal that they were sanctioned by God to go forth into the world, conquer, and disseminate their faith. And amass wealth along the way, of course.

"Given its iconography," she said, "I can see some connection between the painting and the renovations to the Charola in the architectural plans. Both are late-fifteenth-, early-sixteenth-century tributes to the Portuguese role in leading the Age of Discovery."

"But I still don't understand how the Saint Vincent of the *Adoration* commanded Professor Silva to keep secret the first floor to the Charola," Ben said.

"Or how breaking that vow—by giving the plans to you—would trouble the professor. Or require that he give you this information so surreptitiously."

Apologizing for the early hour, Mara called Joe to get his guidance. She then rang Catherine to ask her for more information about the painting. Catherine turned on her home computer and read aloud from her specialized database of art-history research, interpreting some of the other emblems from the painting. The object in Saint Vincent's left hand in the Panel of the Archbishop was a subject of scholarly debate; some claimed it was a staff representing military action, while others believed it was a martyr's palm. With his right hand, the saint allegedly pointed to the kneeling knight Infante Don Ferdinand, a grand master of the Order of Christ. Finally, Catherine asserted that the coiled cord under

Saint Vincent's feet was the whip commonly associated with him.

Mara took a close look at the whip. "Could that be a knotted rope, Catherine?"

"It could."

"If so, that would really tie this painting into the iconography of the Manueline era that we saw in the Charola renovations—indicating that the Portuguese achieved their goal by the sea." She paused. "The only problem is that my pamphlet says Gonçalves painted the *Adoration* in the 1470s, but the Manueline iconography of ropes and nautical emblems didn't develop until after 1495, with King Manuel I's reign."

"Actually, Mara," said Catherine, "there is some evidence that the *Adoration* was painted later, maybe by the school of Gonçalves rather than Nuno himself. Listen to this: 'a late-sixteenth-century codex called the *Retrato dos Reis q Estáem Lisboa* states that the figure of Saint Vincent has the features of the son of King John II, who died in 1491.' So maybe the *Adoration* was created in the late 1490s or early 1500s, making it fit within the time frame of the Manueline additions to the Charola."

Mara read the text of the professor's prayer to Catherine, hoping that she might be able to add further clarification. As Catherine asked for more time to research, Joe clicked onto Mara's other line. "Mara, I just sent you an e-mail. Hang up and take a look at it."

Mara picked up her BlackBerry and opened Joe's message. In the text, he described the Order of Christ, as it existed in the fifteenth and sixteenth centuries and as it continued in modern times. Then she opened the attachment. He had scanned in an official document of some sort. At the top, the document bore the heading "Order of Christ Members." On the list below, the names appeared—including Professor Luis Silva and the viscount of Tomar, Gabriel da Costa.

Their taxi pulled into the station.

On Admiral Zhou's order, the fleet splits into two
squadrons of over sixty ships each. While one half ventures north, seeking further uncharted lands, Zhi's half
leaves the shelter of the bay in search of an identifiable
route back to China. The fleet makes plans to reunite
in Tanggu, along with the rest of the armada. Without
a return sailing chart in hand, the reunion seems im-
plausible to Zhi.

Zhi needs to find a way to guide the ships back across
the Atlantic Ocean, back down the coast of West Africa,
and around the ominous cape. The squadron begins to
retrace its steps by heading east when the current takes
them—east and then south. After a few moon cycles
pass, Zhi begins to recognize landmarks: a rocky outcropping here, a coral reef there, and familiar island
chains. This allows Zhi to plot the flotilla's progress on
the maps he created on the outbound journey. He can
direct them home.

Armed with charts, Zhi finds the return trip manage-
able. Long stretches in the open sea no longer worry
Zhi. The view of the towering cape of Africa does not
fill him with dread, for he knows where next to point
the ships.

The sailors erupt in celebration as they reach well-
known ports in East Africa and the Indian Ocean. As

they draw closer and closer to China, even Zhi allows himself to imagine a triumphant welcome home. The armada has achieved more than Emperor Yongle had asked of it. Admiral Zhou's fleet has found Fusang and discovered lands of which His Imperial Majesty had never dreamed. Perhaps, Zhi thinks, when word of his role on the sixth voyage of Grand Eunuch Admiral Zheng reaches Kunyang, the Ma name will be restored to its former glory. Maybe even Shu will hear of his achievements and believe that his abandonment of her merits her forgiveness.

They reach Tanggu. The ships dock in the harbor already crowded with the other fleets and wait weeks for Admiral Zheng to arrive. They reunite not only with the other fleets but with the other half of their own fleet, which has sailed to icy lands far, far north. Zhi stands on the bridge and looks out over the twinkling lights of the port town, realizing that after all he has seen, Tanggu now appears small to him.

The crewmen spend their days mending and painting the battered ships so they will look good for Admiral Zheng; they spend their nights reveling on land. All except Zhi, who works hard finalizing the official maps of Admiral Zhou's voyage and hears about the sailors' merriment only from Yuan. He dreams of presenting the maps to Admiral Zheng himself.

A knock sounds on the study door. Zhi gives the visitor leave to enter, and a junior crew member announces the arrival of Admiral Zheng in Tanggu. The admiral has ordered the officers of the armada's treasure junks to meet with him on board the deck of his ship that evening.

At dusk, the sailors assemble on the vast bridge. The

cool night air rumbles with the excited voices of the sailors, until they see a swath of red on the bridge platform. In unison, they stop speaking and drop to their knees in deference to their leader.

Admiral Zheng's voice booms: "Rise." He waits for the men to reassemble. "I welcome home the officers of the Sixth Expedition of Admiral Zheng. You have honored your admiral and Emperor Yongle during your long voyages. You have traversed more than one hundred thousand *li* of immense waters and have beheld huge waves like mountains in the sky. You have set your eyes on barbarian regions far away, while your sails, unfurled like clouds day and night, traversed All Under Heaven. His Imperial Majesty Emperor Yongle ordered us to discover and chart the entire world, including the legendary Fusang, and to bring those lands into Confucian harmony with China, into tribute where worthy. Your fleets have accomplished Emperor Yongle's directive, bringing honor to you and your families."

Admiral Zheng pauses. When he resumes, his voice is quieter. "In less than one moon cycle's time, we will return to the Forbidden City. Before we depart, you must learn of the events that occurred during the years of your absence. Two moon cycles after our armada left China the heavens erupted in a furious rage. Lightning lit up the skies over the Forbidden City, and the heavens hurled a single, burning bolt onto it. The blaze destroyed three of Emperor Yongle's new palaces—and burned the imperial Dragon Throne itself. Many were killed in the terrible flames.

"The mandarins interpreted these awful events as a

sign that the gods had abandoned Emperor Yongle. They claimed that the fire's destruction of the most extravagant parts of the Forbidden City was a message that the gods were displeased with His Majesty's expensive projects: the creation of the Forbidden City, the reconstruction of the Grand Canal, the rebuilding of the Great Wall, and, especially, the construction of our great armada and its expeditions. The mandarins called for a new emperor. An emperor who would no longer spend the country's funds on foreign-focused endeavors, an emperor who would focus only on the areas in their control—finance and home affairs—and forsake the eunuch domain of the armed forces and foreign policy.

"Emperor Yongle tried to prove that the gods still favored him. When the Mongol leader Arughati rejected requests that he pay tribute, the emperor assembled an army to defeat Arughati and led it himself. But Emperor Yongle died a hero's death on the battlefield. And the emperor's son Zhu Gaozhi ascended the throne; he is now called Emperor Hongxi. His Imperial Majesty has since issued the following edict."

Admiral Zheng stops and extends his arm. A vice admiral places a scroll in his outstretched hand. He turns his attention to it, unrolls it, and reads aloud: "'All ships moored are ordered back to the capital, and all goods on the ships are to be turned over to the Department of Internal Affairs and stored. All overseas trade and travel is banned. All voyages of the treasure ships are to be stopped. All accounts of the expeditions of Grand Eunuch Admiral Zheng He are to be burned, and the voyages are never to be mentioned again. Violations of this edict are punishable by death.'

"In our new emperor, Hongxi, the mandarins received the emperor they requested. An emperor who will focus China inward and close the doors to the outside world."

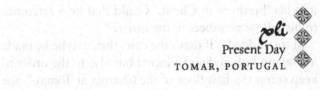

A group of English tourists crowded the station platform. From their conversations, Mara gleaned they were headed for Tomar as well. She and Ben boarded their car of the train and sat down among them. Though Mara hadn't spotted her Chinese friend anywhere, she wanted to make sure they had ample cover if he materialized, and the tour group would provide it.

Under the camouflage of the chattering throng, as they waited for the train to fill, Mara and Ben whispered about the puzzle that the professor had left them. They knew that Tomar had served as the Order of Christ's headquarters and understood that the order had served as the financial and manpower resource for the Portuguese nautical expansion into Africa and the East. Yet the links between the order, the professor's prayer, and the plans continued to evade them.

"I thought the Order of Christ was long defunct," Ben said.

"Joe mentioned in his e-mail that it still exists as an honor for outstanding service to the republic. It makes sense that the viscount is a member since his family homestead was the order's former headquarters. But maybe it continues on differently than the way it's represented to the public."

"Maybe that explains one of the lines of the prayer.

It asks Saint Vincent to forgive him his sins so he can join his 'brethren in Christ.' Could that be a reference to his fellow members in the order?"

Mara nodded. "If that's the case, then maybe he made a vow not only to Saint Vincent but also to the order to keep secret the first floor of the Charola at Tomar." She thought back to their tour of the Maritime Museum and the complex at Tomar. "Isn't one of the emblems of the Order of Christ a cross? Outlined in red with a white center?"

Ben was with her. He quoted from the professor's prayer: " 'Under dark cover and arms red and white . . . ' "

"Further support for the theory that he promised the Order of Christ to keep the architectural plans confidential."

"What's so important about this hidden floor?"

The English tourists overflowed into the aisles, and a man squeezed into the sole open seat facing them. Mara and Ben couldn't keep talking about the information that Catherine and Joe had provided. Each was left to their own thoughts as the train clicked down the tracks leading away from Lisbon, north to the countryside and Tomar. Mara stared out the window at the rolling hills, resplendent with autumn foliage. She imagined the tranquil landscape thundering with horses carrying members of the Order of Christ from Tomar to the coast—and onto caravels taking them to Africa.

As soon as the train pulled into the station, Mara walked up to the tour guide, frumpy in a shapeless rayon dress, boxy jacket, and orthopedic shoes. She asked her if they could join the group. After the guide pocketed a tidy sum, she welcomed Mara and Ben onto the bus with more animation than Mara had witnessed on the entire train ride. They settled into seats in the middle of the bus and watched the picturesque town of Tomar recede as the mammoth tour bus climbed the winding hill to the Templar Castle and Convent of Christ.

The Tomar complex took on a different cast in the bright glare of midday, with the tourist hordes in tow. Tips of bows and arrows no longer seemed to peer out from the parapets. The arched Sun Gate no longer intimidated. The castle walls and structure still impressed, but the light exposed the complex's crumbling, weathered walls and the dire need for the viscount's fund-raising gala.

The guide held her yellow flag aloft to gather her flock together after they filed through the Sun Gate. Then she started the long march across the gravel entryway and past the topiary gardens to the admissions desk adjacent to the Charola. Leading them into the Cemetery and Washing Cloisters first, she recited a rather tired narrative about Prince Henry the Navigator's renovations. As they moved into other rooms, Mara listened intently in case some helpful nugget about the Tomar complex history or the order emerged, but the stale lecture disappointed her.

Mara's BlackBerry buzzed with a new message. Catherine wrote:

Research indicates two new pieces of information. First, the alignment of the painting suggests that the two panels with Saint Vincent images—the Panel of the Infante and the Panel of the Archbishop—turned toward a center object.

*Tradition suggests that a niche containing a statue
would have sat in the center of the polyptych,
between the two Saint Vincent panels. Second,
X-radiographs of the painting demonstrate that
the staff in Saint Vincent's hand in the Panel of
the Archbishop was damaged during the
painting's creation. It was repaired and repainted
shortly thereafter, before its completion. The
object in Saint Vincent's hand was once thicker,
though still cylindrical in shape.*

Mara handed the BlackBerry to Ben as she pulled her
picture of the *Adoration* from her bag. "Could the Saint
Vincent in the Panel of the Archbishop have been holding the architectural plans of the Charola renovations?"

He nodded. "That works. If the professor learned
through the Order of Christ that *The Adoration of Saint
Vincent* once depicted the plans, and the order charged
the professor with keeping the plans secret, then all the
references in his letter fit together."

"We just need to find out what's on the first floor."

"Oh, that should be easy," Ben answered acerbically.
"We just need to access a floor in a world-famous
UNESCO building that may have been concealed for
centuries."

The guide interrupted them with an unexpectedly
perky announcement. "We are about to enter the
Charola."

Unlike the exterior of the Tomar complex, daylight
did not alter the gilded, ethereal interior of the Charola.
In fact, the thick swaths of sun heightened its beauty.
Mara blocked out the drone of the guide and allowed
herself to savor the Charola's decadent excess.

Their work began in earnest the moment they entered the vestry. Mara prowled around the room, mentally comparing every window, every column, every cornice, every nuance with the architectural drawings. She confirmed that no obvious entrance to a lower floor existed in the interior and tried to imagine creative means of access, other than drilling holes in the stones.

Mara moved back to the south wall. Recollecting some passage in the tourist literature stating that, until the 1930s, entry to the vestry was made by the south window facing the main cloister, she wanted to reconsider it.

Then she saw it. A small stone washbasin above a substantial ironwork grille jutted out from the otherwise empty south wall. She stared long at it. Ben joined her side, and followed her gaze.

Mara quoted from the professor's note: " 'Wash away my sins.' "

Antonio leads the limping fleet down the east coast of Africa, mapping their journey as he goes. Da Gama's command to set sail from Calicut had been hasty, a response only to his wounded pride, without consideration for the winds. When scurvy hits, the fleet lies becalmed.

The men's gums swell, so they cannot eat. Their legs turn black and enlarge, so they cannot walk. Bodies pile up on the decks of the *São Gabriel,* the *São Rafael,* and the *Berrio.* Only seven or eight men on each vessel are fit enough to serve.

The chanting from the priest's funeral masses wafts through the stagnant air. Only the splash from the bodies' sea burials interrupts the unbroken memorial hymns. The ships move through the waters as if through honey; they are so undermanned and the wind is so still.

The order comes. The *São Rafael* no longer has enough seamen to work her. She is to be burned.

Antonio, whom scurvy has hobbled but not felled, circles through the navigators' deck and the officers' quarters. Gathering his few belongings, among them da Gama's map, he works in near silence. He almost wishes for the meanness of his deceased fellow officers for company.

The *São Rafael* is anchored and readied for the fire.

Antonio loads onto the *São Rafael*'s rowboat, with its bedraggled and skeletal hodgepodge of sailors, soldiers, and the priest. Captain Paulo da Gama gets on last, carrying the figurehead of the ship, a wooden statue of the archangel Rafael, in his arms.

Antonio is happy for Father Figuerado's quiet companionship on the short trip to the *São Gabriel*. The priest's presence calms him as they approach the captain-major's vessel, where he knows he must withstand constant contact with the now-reviled da Gama. Especially since scurvy took the *São Gabriel*'s pilot.

The few survivors of the *São Rafael* climb onto the deck of the *São Gabriel*. They assemble along with its scant remaining men, and Captain da Gama hands the figurehead to his brother in a solemn ceremony.

The captain-major gives the signal to the brave sailor charged with the dangerous task. The elegant *São Rafael,* square-rigged, its wooden sides still gleaming as if new, begins to burn. As the sailor quickly rows away from the ship, the lower deck blazes with a dull orange. The flames redden and grow bold as they creep up the masts.

Antonio feels sick as he watches the *São Rafael* smolder. It reminds him of the women and children on the ship from Mecca. He glances at Father Figuerado, who nods back in understanding and begins muttering silent prayers.

The fingers of fire catch the rigging next. The flames ensnare the sails thereafter. The proud red-and-white cross of the Order of Christ emblazoned on every sail ignites.

Antonio does not want to cast his gaze upon da Gama, but he cannot stop himself. The captain-major, so impervious in the face of all the previous bloodshed, stands clutching the statue of the archangel Rafael like the security blanket of an infant. As the crosses smoke, Antonio swears he sees tears well up in the eyes of his commander.

Then da Gama turns toward him. Antonio must have been mistaken; he sees no evidence of weakness in da Gama's arrogant look. The captain-major orders him, "Take us home, Pilot Coelho."

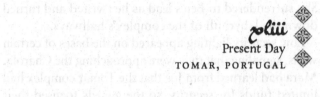

Mara's right leg cramped. She and Ben had been crouching in the far corner of a storage room, waiting for the complex to close. They had broken off from the group once the tour finished and concealed themselves in an abandoned anteroom off one of the unrestored cloisters. They'd waited for the close of the complex and nightfall.

Bit by bit, the noise of the castle and convent quieted. The buzz of visitors dulled first. The scraping and clanging of the employees stilled next. Then silence descended. Yet as a hushed calm overtook the cavernous complex, Mara's nerves became more agitated. What the hell was she doing? She was supposed to be in the business of recovering stolen artwork, not behaving like one of the thieves she pursued. And this little act of espionage had nothing to do with the stolen map, as far as she could tell.

Ben nudged Mara. They both got up. Ben's backpack had grown larger and heavier since their entry; he had grabbed some ropes and tools from a janitor's closet they'd passed before they'd secreted themselves. Both doubted that the equipment would suffice, but they wanted to try.

They stepped out into the pitch-black hallway. Ben had memorized the building layout, so she followed him as he ran his hands along the rough-hewn stone. She surrendered to Ben's lead as he twisted and turned down the labyrinth of the complex's hallways.

Low security lighting appeared on the bases of certain walls, signaling that they were approaching the Charola. Mara had learned from Joe that the Tomar complex had limited funds for security, so the guards focused their energies on the perimeter and the famous Charola, with its gilt and priceless artwork. Knowing this, Mara and Ben stayed away from the Charola as they entered the church complex. They sidled up against the nave wall opposite to it and scampered down the stairs to the vestry. No alarms sounded.

Moonbeams streamed in from the interior of the Manueline window. Along with their flashlights, the slight illumination provided Mara and Ben with just enough light to work. They knelt down next to the iron grating underneath the washbasin. Ben pulled out the tools and began trying to loosen the grillwork.

Even though Joe had e-mailed her that the nighttime guards were few, Mara left Ben to his efforts and stood watch. Each time Ben's wrench scraped against the centuries-old iron, her stomach lurched. She kept looking back at his progress, but began to think that their attempts might come to naught. After all, the iron lattice had sunk its claws into the vestry's stone and mortarwork for five hundred years—why did they think they could loosen it in a single night?

A spine-chilling, nearly human screech echoed through the vestry. She turned toward the noise. Ben held the grillwork in his hands.

He reached for his backpack, pulling out one of the

ropes. He looped it around one of the Manueline columns. As he started to wind it around his waist, she whispered, "What are you doing?"

"I'm going down. You stay here and keep watch. I might need your help getting back up."

"Ben, let me go down first."

"No way. It's too dangerous."

"Have you seen the opening? I'm pretty sure I can fit, but I don't know about you. And we don't know how tight the space will be down there."

He hesitated. She could almost see his chivalry yielding to reason. His years of experience crawling into unimaginable crevices in search of the missing Tocharian peoples told him it was the best course. "Are you sure?"

"Yes." And she was. She had made the offer instinctively, but even with a moment to consider it, she knew it made sense.

"All right." Mara put down the black bag she had slung across her, as Ben unwound the skein from his midsection. He drew close to her. She could feel his warm breath as he coiled the rope around her. His slow, slow movements revealed his reluctance.

He finished. Mara pivoted away from him and walked over to the rectangular cavity in the wall. Ben grabbed her, and pulled her close.

"You signal me the second you get scared. Do you understand me?"

"I will."

"Promise?"

"Promise."

They knelt down together on the cold, hard stone floor. He shined his flashlight into the dark opening first, and she followed with hers. No object, no structure, no bottom materialized from the pitch black.

She lowered her feet down into the opening. Taking a deep breath and making the sign of the cross, she shimmied the rest of her body down into the depths. The space felt like a rectangular shaft, sloping toward the ground. Though her body was wedged into it, she had enough space to inch downward. Bit by bit, she progressed through the passage, wondering what lurked on the other side. Then without warning the chute ended, and she fell to the floor.

"Are you okay?" Mara heard Ben call to her, risking discovery.

"I'm fine," she answered as quietly as possible as she dragged herself off the floor. Save for a few bruises, she was unhurt by the fall. She pulled the flashlight from her pocket and clicked it on.

The light shined through the years and years of dust, grime, and cobwebs. The beams revealed Manueline ropes and knots and buoys and seaweed, all crafted in stone, behind the debris. And more. The walls and the wooden cabinets and benches lining the room glowed with gilt armillary spheres, Manueline badges, and red-and-white Order of Christ crosses, while the ceiling was painted with the outlines of amorphous shapes and swaths of azure.

The flashlight reflected off the gilded paintings, providing Mara with an unexpected amount of brightness. She walked around the room, in awe of the craftsmanship and the secretiveness of this masterwork. Storage cupboards lined the walls, and an elaborately sculpted altar dominated the center. The diminutive marble sarcophagus on its surface intrigued her.

As she approached it, Mara heard Ben call to her through the opening: "Mara, what's down there?"

Her flashlight illuminated the ceiling and then the casket, revealing the room's purpose. "I think it's a map library, Ben."

Zhi returns to his cabin. The news renders him immobile. He laments Ke's sacrifice, on all that he has forgone to achieve a place on Admiral Zheng's voyage for the further glory of the Ma name. He wonders if all that he has achieved is extra taels for his family, taels that may soon cease.

After a time, he hears a knock at his door. Zhi calls out a permission to enter, but no one crosses the threshold. He rises and opens the door to find an imposing figure wearing distinctive red robes and a black hat. It is Admiral Zheng. He has come alone.

Zhi throws himself on the floor at the admiral's feet. He cannot imagine what he has done to warrant such an unprecedented visit.

"Chief Mapmaker Ma Zhi. You may rise."

Zhi tries, but his legs are so shaky, he cannot. He continues in his posture of prostration, not daring to raise his eyes in case the vision vanishes. "I am your servant, Admiral Zheng."

He hears a deep chuckle reverberate in the barrel chest of the great man. "So I understand, Ma Zhi. So I understand. Still, I would be pleased if you would rise."

Zhi stands but keeps his gaze lowered. Yet even from

his downcast view, Zhi appreciates that the two men are nearly the same height. This amazes him; he has always envisioned Admiral Zheng as a near giant.

"Look at me, Ma Zhi."

Zhi dares to look directly at his hero. To his surprise, he finds that Zheng's black eyes possess a glimmer of humor.

Admiral Zheng meets his gaze, then scans Zhi up and down. "You have the Ma look about you. In fact, you look a bit like my father."

"I am honored, Admiral Zheng." Zhi knows that he and Zheng share a distant familial connection, but to be told that he bears a physical resemblance is an undreamed compliment.

"I have been very pleased with your performance in the years since I recruited you from Kunyang."

Zhi blurts out, "Recruited me?"

"Yes, recruited you. When Emperor Yongle decided to add more eunuchs to his ranks, I sought out young relatives from my hometown for the opportunity."

"I did not know." Zhi guesses at other gifts Zheng might have granted him. "Was it you who procured the position with the Imperial Ceremonial Directorate? For me and Ma Liang?"

"Yes, Ma Zhi. I ensured that you and the other young men from Kunyang found suitable posts. I did not want you to spend your years serving the capricious whims of one of the emperor's junior concubines."

Zhi drops back down to his knees. He is stunned with the enormousness of his debt to Zheng. "I thank you, Admiral Zheng."

"Please stand, Ma Zhi. I have come to ask something of you."

"Anything you wish, Admiral."

"It is a request that will go against the very orders of our new emperor. A request that will put you in grave danger should you be discovered, one I will disavow if you are caught."

Zhi hesitates before answering. He considers what may happen to his family if he agrees and the new mandarin regime finds out, before he realizes that all the opportunities afforded to him and his family—the education, the voyage, the extra taels, the chance to elevate his parents and brothers, though it may come to naught—have come from Admiral Zheng's beneficence. Even if Zhi cannot restore the Ma standing, at least he can repay his debt to the admiral. "I serve you, Admiral Zheng. Above all others." Zhi means this pledge.

"I hoped that was the case, Ma Zhi. I would like you to gather all the maps and charts from the armada's ships. Any document showing the discoveries of the expedition. I want you to tell everyone that you are acting under orders to destroy these materials. Do you understand?"

"Yes, Admiral. I do." Zhi comprehends Zheng's request, but he cannot fathom how it places him at risk. It is precisely the type of task the new mandarin regime would praise.

"I want you to memorize the information those maps contain before submitting them for destruction in the bonfires. Can you do that?"

"Yes, Admiral."

"Then, in tribute to the late Emperor Yongle, I want

you to make a map. A map of all the lands our fleets discovered. A map of All Under Heaven. And then I want you to find a way to transport that map to the land of Marco Polo, one of the only regions not in tribute to China. I do not want the knowledge of our voyage to die with us."

Ben landed with a thud. Mara hurried over to his side and reached her hand out to help him up. He stood up, brushed himself off, and gazed around the luminous room in wonder.

"I feel like Howard Carter entering Tutankhamen's tomb," he said.

"Step back for a moment." She wanted to see if his interpretation matched hers.

Mara waited as he shined his light around the walls, the columns, the floor, the cabinets and benches, and finally the ceiling. The nebulous figures floating above them took form, and the stretches of blue gained shape.

"The ceiling forms one continuous mural—a map of the entire world. It depicts continents, seas, islands, oceans . . ." His voice grew more excited. "I see America, Australia, Antarctica, the Pacific Ocean. All painted in the late 1490s or early 1500s . . ." His voice trailed off as he studied the ceiling.

"Exactly."

"And the mural sits atop all the emblems of the Order of Christ."

They gravitated toward the altar at the same time. Ben shined his light along the Latin lettering encircling the base, which Mara could not decipher. " 'Upon this sanctified foundation our discoveries rest.' "

They examined the miniature sarcophagus. Some long-ago sculptor had draped it with marble cords, encrusted it with coral and pearls, and tied it with golden nautical knots.

Together, they lifted off its unexpectedly heavy stone lid. Setting it to the side, they shed light on the interior. A scroll rested within.

Mara reached for it.

Ben stopped her. "Should we disturb it? We might damage it."

"We haven't come this far to not learn what this room hides."

She withdrew the scroll from its chamber. Ben held his flashlight on the document as Mara unrolled it with great care. She prayed it wouldn't crumble with her touch.

With each turn of the spindles, a glorious celebration of the world emerged. Continents and oceans and islands swirled across the page in a joyous dance. Even in the darkness, vibrant colors skipped out to greet them. And the sides of the map shimmered with the graceful rhythm of Chinese calligraphy.

Ben stared at the masterpiece that unfolded before them. Before he spoke, Mara knew what words he would utter. "It's *the* map. The map I found."

"I know. But how is it possible? No one's been down here for centuries."

He paused before answering. "Wait a second. Look at the right corner. See this Order of Christ cross painted there?"

"Yes."

"On mine, there's a lotus in that corner." He shined more light on the map's right corner. "I think the cross is actually painted over a lotus. But otherwise, the two maps are identical."

All the pieces came together. "Ermanno was right. The information on the Chinese map traveled to Europe in advance of the Age of Discovery. The maker of your map must have made a copy, and it somehow made its way to Portugal."

He nodded. "So the Portuguese had the first world map all along—it gave them the edge to be the world leader in the Age of Discovery. It *is* the foundation for their discoveries."

"Precisely. But we were wrong about the *Adoration*," Mara said.

"What do you mean?"

"In the early versions of the *Adoration*, Saint Vincent didn't hold the architectural plans in his hand; he held this map. And the professor didn't promise the Order of Christ to keep this floor confidential; he vowed to keep the map secret. The original *Adoration* must have told the story of how God—through the intercession of Saint Vincent—got this world map to the Order of Christ so Portugal could disseminate Christianity and dominate trade. A story the Portuguese then concealed—by painting over the *Adoration* and building this floor, which they later hid."

"And when the professor decided to break his promise to the Order of Christ—and to God, presumably—and share this momentous secret with us, he couldn't do it directly. Maybe he's even gone into some kind of hiding. But why did he tell us at all?"

"You described the professor as a man of integrity. He must have understood that the Order's long-held secret map—which certainly he never saw—might be unleashed on the world once we found your map. In his note, he hinted that it conflicted with his personal scruples to continue keeping his vow."

"I feel terrible, Mara. As though I forced Professor Silva to do this."

Mara reached out for his hand. "Ben, please don't blame yourself. It was his choice to divulge this to us."

He squeezed her hand tight.

She continued: "He wanted us to find this floor and this map. Without him, we might've eventually found the Chinese map, but we'd never know about all this."

"So where is the map I found?"

"With Dias."

"I thought Dias didn't exist."

"Oh, he exists all right. The viscount of Tomar is Dias."

Ben stared at her. "What?"

"It makes sense, doesn't it? He's the current grand master of the Order of Christ as well as a known map collector, and his family has had the run of this place for centuries. And he's passionate about preserving Portuguese history and finding Portugal a secure place in Europe's economic future. Who else could Dias be?"

"My God, you're right."

"Come on. Let's find out what's in those cabinets. We don't have much more time down here."

Splitting up, they turned their attention to the ornate wooden cabinets lining the walls. Mara opened the door of one particularly sumptuous piece, hoping that the wood hadn't decayed over the years of neglect. The door stayed intact as she pushed it back and peered inside.

The beam from her torch revealed a heap of scrolls much like the map they'd found in the sarcophagus.

Fearful of damaging them, she nevertheless reached for one on top. She unraveled its long-curled page, and an ancient portolan chart of the African coast lay before her.

She turned to Ben, who gazed over at her just at that moment. "Maps. The cupboards are full of them."

The clatter of footsteps sounded on the floor above them. Mara and Ben froze. When the sound subsided, Ben whispered, "Get the map."

She reached for it, but her hand froze midway. If she took it, wouldn't she become just like the thieves she pursued? Yet how could she leave it here? It was the critical piece of the puzzle they needed to find Ben's map.

Mara grabbed the map, rolled it back up, and handed it to Ben. He slid it into the cylinder with the architectural plans and put it into his backpack. Though she feared getting caught, the notion of being trapped in the cavernous, musty space terrified her more. So, one by one, they hoisted themselves up the ropes.

The returning sailors receive no fanfare. There are no awards and no accolades. The new emperor Hongxi and his mandarins shower only contempt upon them. And order the bonfires.

Flames from nearly a hundred fires lick the glazed crimson walls of the Forbidden City courtyards. The many blazes turn the night sky into day, and the smell of burning scrolls permeates the air.

During evening prayers, the smoke wafts into the marble chamber reserved for Muslim worship. The acrid smell distracts Zhi from the sonorous chanting of his fellow worshippers. His mind floats like the smoke around him, and his eyes drift defiantly toward the adjoining courtyard where mandarin guards tend to the fires.

The odor reminds Zhi of his vow to Admiral Zheng. After praying, he slips away from the others. He pads down a dark hallway toward a storage room where he knows hundreds of scrolls from the voyage await burning.

No guards stand before the door. Zhi pushes it open and slithers inside. The scrolls are heaped against the walls. Kneeling down, he scans the piles for the map scrolls; he still has several critical charts to memorize—charts he had been able to gather initially but had to surrender prematurely—so he can fulfill his promise to Admiral Zheng.

The essential documents sit at the bottom of a great stack. Zhi slides out the most vital eight and tucks them under his arm. He opens the door and begins creeping down the corridor, thanking Allah for the moonless night.

Zhi rounds the bend and heads toward the chamber he's been assigned until the mandarins decide where the returning eunuchs should be placed. And bumps right into a mandarin guard.

"What do you have there, eunuch?"

Zhi keeps his head bowed in deference. "Nothing."

"Looks like scrolls," the guard says, and starts reaching under Zhi's arm.

Zhi wrenches away from the guard's grasp and starts running down the passageway. To where or to whom, he does not know, but his instinct tells him to protect the scrolls.

The guard is too fast. He grabs Zhi and shoves him into a courtyard bright with bonfires. Zhi curls his body around the scrolls to shield them from the guard's attack. An involuntary scream escapes from his mouth as he feels his ribs crack from the guard's kick.

In the far, far distance, almost as if from a dream, Zhi hears a Buddhist chant, *"Om mani padme hum."* He recognizes the mantra from Ke. She had explained that it meant "Hail to the jewel in the lotus," an invocation for compassion and enlightenment.

The deep resonant mantra is almost hypnotic, and it is the last thing he hears before he slips into unconsciousness. The clap of sandals against the marble floor awakens him. Zhi feels a hand dragging him away from the guard and opens his eyes to see a Buddhist monk taking the beating for him.

The guard stops. "I will not harm a monk," he says, then reaches behind the monk to pull Zhi away. "But I will obey my orders."

Zhi's feet drag behind him as the guard hauls him to the nearest bonfire. His laden hands burn as the guard holds them to the flames, and they involuntarily open and drop the scrolls into the fire. He has begun to despair when the monk rushes toward them again.

The guard loses his footing in the surprising assault. Zhi takes this one chance to sprint into the pitch-black night. Yet he cannot stop himself from turning his head for one last look at the courtyard. He watches helplessly as the map scrolls succumb to the conflagration.

Zhi passes the next few days in limbo. He keeps his bandaged ribs and hands carefully hidden in his robe, but awaits discovery by the mandarins for his attempt to save the scrolls, an act of treason. And a decision about his professional fate if he lives.

Time brings healing and relief. His identity as a traitor remains secret, and his practical future is decided. Zhi is reassigned to his former master in the Imperial Ceremonial Directorate. He appreciates his fortune at being placed with Master Shen. Many eunuchs have no work at all, particularly those who had served with Zheng; the unlucky ones are sent to Nanhaizi, an imperial detention camp. Zhi knows he is lucky that his family still receives his taels. For now.

He settles back into his old routine with Master Shen.

He registers communications, helps coordinate policies, and makes recommendations to his master. And, of course, he serves him tea.

In a short time, Zhi feels as though the past few long years never happened, particularly since he never sees anyone from the voyage, even Yuan—whose work wouldn't give him any reason to enter the eunuch realm. It seems as though he never traveled thousands of *li* and discovered countless new lands. His only solace is his re-union with Liang, to whom he can safely whisper tales of the armada's journeys in the darkness of the sleeping chamber.

Zhi looks for times and places to undertake the mission assigned to him by Admiral Zheng. Since he is no longer allowed to study navigation and cartography, he no longer has a reason to visit the calligraphy studio. He procures the necessary ink and scrolls through one surreptitious visit to the studio, but he cannot risk an-other trip. The walls grow eyes as the suspicious man-darin regime takes ever-firmer hold.

He informs Master Shen that the mandarin adminis-tration issues more communiqués than the eunuchs ever did, and asks for permission to work in the direc-torate office after the evening meal to ensure that he keeps up to date on logging all memoranda. Fearful of losing any footing under the new reign, Master Shen readily agrees to Zhi's suggestion.

Zhi hides his secret work in plain sight: under a pile of the latest missives on his desk in the master's office. He sets up a pyramid of scrolls to shield his project should an unexpected visitor arrive. Behind it, he works on the map.

Night after night, he paints coastlines, mountain

ranges, oceans, and continents. As the sun sets and the evening meal winds down, Zhi rushes off to see what new wonder will materialize on his map and the copy he makes by its side. As Admiral Zheng had requested and Zhi had vowed, All Under Heaven emerges.

Zhi pours steaming tea into a porcelain cup. He cradles it in his joined palms, raises it level with his chest, and walks toward Master Shen. Kneeling at his feet, Zhi offers it to him.

As Zhi waits for Master Shen to take the cup, his mind drifts. He thinks about his promise to Admiral Zheng. He wonders how he will fulfill the final part of the oath—to get the map out of China and into the land of Marco Polo, where the Chinese tribute system does not hold sway.

He absentmindedly watches a procession of Buddhists through the archway behind the master's chair. The parade of monks appears so peaceful that, for a moment, Zhi wishes he could join their ranks. He is chastising himself for thinking such a sacrilegious thought when it dawns on him: he has found a way to complete his vow to Admiral Zheng.

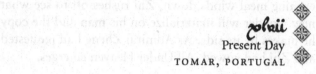
Mara emerged from the complete darkness of the shaft. In the mild glow of the moonlight, she could just make out Ben's face before he scooped her under her arms and dragged her out the final length of the passage. They fell back in a heap with the force of his efforts. For the briefest of moments, Mara lay against him. Then she jumped up to identify the source of the footsteps.

No one was there.

"Maybe it was a guard?" Mara whispered.

"Maybe."

"We need to get out of here."

"Agreed."

Coiling the ropes tightly, Mara tucked them into her bag. Ben wedged the iron grillwork back into place, though they recognized that a hard knock from an overeager tourist might dislodge it. They started up the vestry stairs, back into the nave leading to the Charola. Though they didn't have a fixed exit strategy, they headed toward the ticket office entrance, into which the Sun Gate poured. It was one of the only means of access to the Tomar complex, and Joe had informed them of a few doors located there.

As they turned the corner from the nave into the long hallway leading to the gift shop and the cloisters border- ing the ticket office, Mara saw him. The man who'd sat across from them on the train. With her Chinese friend in tow. The man must be working for the Chinese.

Mara and Ben's eyes locked, and she saw terror in his. Fearful that he might freeze up, she took the lead. She pivoted and pushed Ben back down the corridor. She didn't think the men had spotted them, but they were headed in their direction. Mara and Ben would have only a few seconds to make it down the long passage without being noticed.

So they ran. As silently as possible, they hustled down the hall and veered off to the right where Mara knew there was a staircase. She longed to fly down the steps, but she knew the noise would give them away.

When they reached the second floor, Mara thought she heard the men's footfalls above them on the staircase. Instead of descending to the first floor, she led them out into the chilly night air of the upper level of the Hostelry Cloister. If the men had indeed seen them, they would assume that Mara and Ben had headed all the way down.

Braving the floodlit perimeter of the Manueline window, they hurried straight down one side of the Hostelry Cloister and then turned right into another. Mara recalled that one of the complex's famous spiral staircases was located midway down that side. They reached it and entered. But the stairs only led up—back to the third floor.

Stymied but afraid to turn back in the direction of the footsteps, she conducted Ben onward down the Hostelry Cloister arcade. As they neared the end of the walkway, she realized she had no game plan. About to confess her failing to Ben, she felt his hand in hers and heard him whisper, "Come this way."

He led her into a warren of small rooms with inter-connecting doorways: the Attendants' Quarters. As they wove through the chambers, she realized that Ben moved with purpose; the panic hadn't taken hold of him. He steered them to another spiral staircase. Mara breathed a sigh of relief to see that this one spun downward.

As they wound round and round the dizzying conch-like swirl of the stairs, Mara prayed that they would be able to slip out unnoticed. Yet when they reached the final curl of the spiral, a security guard sat in wait at its base. The tired-looking retiree glanced up from his newspaper, startled and confused to see two errant tourists in the sleepy complex well past closing time.

Behind them, Mara heard soft footsteps approach and then backtrack. She couldn't believe that she'd prefer to rush headlong into the arms of the security guard, but it seemed the safer alternative. To retreat would mean coming face-to-face with their followers, who presumably presented more of a threat than the older gentleman in front of them.

Painting on an enormous, embarrassed grin, she clasped her hands together in prayer and walked toward him. She felt Ben's restraining hand on her shoulder, but she ignored it and kept walking. This gambit was their only chance.

"Sir, we are so sorry—"

"*Não falo inglês,*" he interrupted her.

At least he didn't reach for the phone to summon help, Mara thought to herself, or grasp for the handcuffs dangling from his waist. She and Ben mustn't look too threatening. Continuing her slow advance toward him, she began gesticulating a story. Hoping beyond all hope that her hand gestures narrated a tale of young lovers caught up in a wave of passion in a neglected castle chamber and then falling asleep after their fervor subsided, she waited for his reaction.

The guard stared blankly at her for a moment. Then, with a wag of his finger, he gave Mara and Ben a naughty smirk. Shaking his head, he jingled the ring of keys at his waist and unlocked the gate.

They were about to cross the threshold when the guard clutched Mara's arm. He motioned that he would have to search them before he could allow them to pass. Mara realized that she and Ben had no choice but to submit, so she nodded.

The guard rummaged through Mara's bag and pockets. He turned his attention to Ben, patting him down and pawing through his pockets with more zeal than he had shown with Mara. He rifled through Ben's backpack and pulled out the cylinder. Prying off the lid, he slid out the tops of the architectural plans. Mara froze with fear, and she remained immobile until the guard returned the apparently uninteresting documents to the tube and gestured for their departure.

Once they passed through the gate, Mara turned and blew the man a kiss. She grabbed Ben's hand, and they ran down the steep dusty hill toward the little town of Tomar. Mara calculated that they had several minutes of lead time on their pursuers, even if the men had a car; she presumed they wouldn't risk confronting the security guard and instead would reenter the complex and exit through the other gate.

Spying the train station in the distance, they sprinted toward it. She knew that a village like Tomar wouldn't have cabs at the ready unless a train was due to arrive.

They quickly skimmed the posted schedule and identified an incoming Lisbon train in six minutes—if only
they could hide until the cabs appeared.

To the left of the station, an eager taxi materialized
on the street corner. With glee, Mara hailed it.

They climbed in and slammed the door hard behind
them. Mara grabbed a fistful of euros from her bag and
handed them to the cabbie. Using one of her few Portuguese words, she said, *"Aeroporto."*

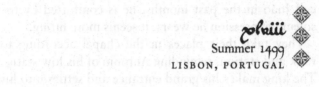

The men step onto the banks of the Tagus River one by one. While waiting for his turn, Antonio reflects on how little time the disembarkment takes compared with the boarding of the armada. Only forty-four of the original one hundred and fifty seamen—and two of the four ships—survive to bask in the triumphant return. The fact seems forgotten in the day's merriment.

The Lisboans cheer each time a new sailor reaches the riverbank. They seem not to notice the men's haggard appearance; Antonio knows they look like beggars after so long at sea, though they wear their finest garb. The people care only about sharing the victory of finding the sea route to India.

The mariners form a line behind the bishop and the knights of the Order of Christ. Antonio hears trumpets sound in the distance, heralding the arrival of King Manuel into Prince Henry the Navigator's chapel. As they proceed single file toward it, he feels a wistful glimmer of the anticipation he experienced on that innocent morning of departure over two years ago.

The men wave to the applauding multitudes, and Antonio raises his hand instinctively. But he draws it back to his side; he finds it nigh impossible to rejoice along with them. He has witnessed too much cruelty and carnage, and he knows the truth of their "discovery."

Glancing at Father Figuerado, whom he has come to call João in the past months, he is comforted by the solemn expression he wears. It seems more fitting.

They take their places in the chapel according to rank and station, reminding Antonio of his low status. The king makes his grand entrance and settles into his throne. Da Gama is summoned to the altar, and Antonio's stomach churns at the sight of the captain-major.

King Manuel stands over the kneeling da Gama. "We ordered you to make discoveries by sea. We learn that you did reach and discover India and other kingdoms bordering upon it, which carry on all the trade in spices and precious stones. We hope that with the help of God this great trade shall be diverted to the ships of our own kingdom so that henceforth all Christendom shall be able to provide itself with these spices and precious stones and that the discovery of this route will allow the spread of Christianity to heathen lands. Due to your journey, I am now King Manuel, by the grace of God not only King of Portugal and of the Algarves on this side and beyond the sea but also, in Africa, Lord of Guinea and of the Conquest and Navigation and Commerce of Ethiopia, Arabia, Persia, and India."

King Manuel's proclamation of the title Lord of India seems hasty to Antonio. He wonders how da Gama described the journey to King Manuel and whether he was honest about his visit with the Calicut king. Antonio thinks about the moment when he first laid eyes on da Gama's treasured map of the entire world, and considers whether da Gama informed the king that the armada followed a route already charted. Or whether da Gama kept the world map as his secret, his private assurance of success.

The king continues his address to da Gama. "You accomplished this unprecedented discovery at a greater sacrifice of life and treasure, and at greater peril to your own person, than suffered by those who preceded you. Desiring to recompense you for your services, we grant you the town of Sines, your birthplace, together with all the revenues, privileges, and tithes pertaining thereto. We give you, freely and irrevocably, an annuity of three hundred thousand *réis*."

The generosity of the king's bequest to da Gama stuns Antonio. The chapel audience gasps along with him. It is the largest legacy ever gifted to one of the king's mariners.

Antonio wants to rise and yell out the truth, to proclaim that though the sailors did undertake an amazing feat, da Gama is not a discoverer but only a follower of the Chinese mariners. He yearns to expose da Gama's vengeful bloodshed. But he does not. A gentleman would do so; but, he reminds himself, he is not a gentleman. So he waits for King Manuel to announce the officers' remuneration. He consoles himself for his cowardice with the notion that perhaps a good pile of *réis* will buy him a chance with Helena.

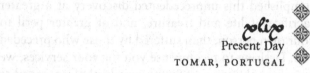

Mara hadn't really planned on ending up in the Lisbon airport when she'd directed the cabbie there. She'd just wanted to get herself and Ben to Lisbon itself, and the airport was the first place that came to mind. Yet after informing Joe about their discoveries and their pursuers, she realized that she had unwittingly made the right choice; they needed to leave the country.

After a few hours on lesser highways, the taxi flew down the A1 Oporto–Lisbon motorway. Mara and Ben kept a constant lookout for cars tailing them, but saw nothing to warrant alarm. Signs saying AEROPORTO began appearing with greater regularity, and Mara took her first deep breath since night fell at the Tomar complex. Maybe they'd evade the men and make it back to New York unscathed after all.

They pulled into the departures roundabout. Joe had booked them on the next flight from Lisbon to New York, a TAP Portugal flight leaving at seven A.M. Though the sky was still dark, the first-class gate was beginning to check in passengers.

Mara and Ben stood in line with feigned patience as the lone traveler in front of them checked in for the flight. Ever vigilant, they scanned the airport for signs of the men who'd been following them, a task made easy by its relative emptiness, but did not see anyone suspicious. The TAP Portugal attendant summoned them to the front of the queue. She took Mara's passport and credit card and started to process her ticket.

After a few seconds, the attendant excused herself. She returned to the check-in desk with a manager. Together, they reviewed the computer screen and chatted quietly in Portuguese. The holdup and the consternation on their faces made Mara uneasy.

"Is there a problem?"

The manager looked up and answered in heavily accented English while the attendant busied herself on the phone. "No, no, miss. Just a technical problem with the system. Our apologies for the delay."

Unconsciously, Mara tapped her fingers on the counter while she and Ben waited for the computer glitch to clear. Every minute in the open airport terminal was another minute when their pursuers could easily see them. She desperately wanted to get past security and into the first-class lounge, where they could better conceal themselves. And then onto the plane and to the relative safety of New York.

Ben touched her shoulder—in an effort, she assumed, to stop her annoying drumming. Though she ceased the rapping, he nudged her again. When she turned toward him, she saw his finger subtly pointing to the right of the counter.

Mara's gaze followed. The manager and attendant huddled with two security guards; all of their faces bore disquieted expressions. Since none of them had Mara and Ben in their sights at that exact moment, Mara swiveled the unattended computer screen around and read the flashing message on the screen: RISCO DA SEGURANÇA. She didn't need to speak Portuguese to comprehend that she had been flagged as a security risk.

Her passport and credit card sat on the check-in desk. She scooped them up and signaled Ben to back away. A bustling, multigenerational family pushing carts packed with taped luggage approached the adjacent coach check-in gate. Mara and Ben used the family as a shield to block the guards from seeing them as they moved away from the counter.

Fighting the impulse to run, they crept behind the family's overflowing baggage. Then, with a leisurely gait, they ducked behind a six-foot-high advertising display and rounded a corner toward the doors they'd just entered. Though Mara told herself to keep her head lowered, she reflexively looked back. The attendant, manager, and security detail were crowded around the check-in desk and scanning the room. Mara and Ben ran outside.

A yellow Hertz bus pulled into the arrivals roundabout. Without other options, Mara and Ben hopped on board the empty vehicle. She kept her eyes closed until she heard the hiss of the doors shutting and the roar of the bus's diesel engine. Then she picked up the phone to call Joe.

"What the hell is going on? I've been tagged as a security risk."

"Jesus, you're kidding."

"Why would I joke at a time like this?"

"Let me make a call. I'll get right back to you."

A minute later, her cell rang. Assuming it was Joe, she picked up immediately. "So, what's the scoop?"

"I was just going to ask you that question."

The voice did not belong to Joe. "Sam?"

"Yeah. Mara, what on earth are you up to? Your name is buzzing around all my operatives' ears."

"What are your people hearing?"

"The word is that you have the 'artifact,' and that you're in Lisbon."

"Do they know precisely where in Lisbon I am right now?"

"No, but—"

Mara hung up. She realized that surveillance ran two ways; the Chinese government might be using the operatives to listen to Sam. She didn't want her cell phone to allow the Chinese to pinpoint their location.

They waited in the hushed, vacant bus for Joe to call back. The bus's walkie-talkie came alive with the crackle of static, breaking the silence. Mara paid the noise no mind until she heard a distinctive, familiar phrase repeated again and again: *"Risco da segurança."*

The bus stopped at the next airline. Mara's heart stopped too, certain that security guards would rush in or that the faces of their pursuers would loom. Instead, an older American couple in coordinating track suits ambled on board. Mara and Ben scurried off the bus.

A cabbie was unloading suitcases onto the nearby curb as the passenger readied his payment. Mara signaled that they'd wait in the car, and the cabbie nodded. Inside, she whipped out her cell and dialed Joe. She couldn't wait another second for his return call.

"I'm going crazy here, Joe. Tell me what you've learned."

"The viscount used his clout with the Portuguese government and the European Union to have you blocked from international flights. The Chinese weren't the only ones tracking your movements, it seems," Joe said.

"So I'm trapped here in Portugal. With the viscount for company."

"Don't worry. I have a plan. Your friend know any Arabic?"

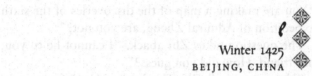

The chosen night arrives. Zhi lies in his bed, feigning sleep. He listens for the telltale signs that every eunuch in the building is slumbering, even Liang. Without moving, he opens his eyes in the dull light of the moon to confirm what his ears tell him.

Zhi runs his hand along the wooden frame of his bed. He dislodges a tightly rolled packet and slides it into the bed alongside him. He waits to make sure that the slight rustle does not waken anyone.

He lowers himself to the icy-cold floor. Crouching down, Zhi straps the packet to his back and crawls toward the door. When he reaches the courtyard, he stands, but he keeps to the shadows and dark corners of the Imperial City alleyways. He knows the lanes so well that he does not need light to guide the way.

As he approaches the Inner Court supplies building, he thinks he hears footsteps. He slows his step, then stops. The night air is silent.

He continues. Right, then left, then another right. He passes the entertainment building and the Lamaist school. Finally, the Hanjingchang, the Buddhist school, comes into view.

Zhi enters the school and begins rummaging through an armoire. He hears the slap of a shoe on the polished floor. He jumps. It is Liang.

"I know what you have been doing," Liang says. "You are making a map of the discoveries of the sixth expedition of Admiral Zheng, are you not?"

The question takes Zhi aback. "I cannot lie to you, old friend. How did you guess?"

"I know you well, Zhi. The deadened look from working with Master Shen disappeared from your eyes, and you rushed off after the evening meal to do extra work for the Imperial Ceremonial Directorate. What else could you be doing?"

"I wish you did not know."

Liang smiles. "Be assured, Zhi. I know nothing."

"Good, Liang. I could not forgive myself if my actions caused the mandarins to punish you in my stead."

Liang's voice fills with alarm. "In your stead? Where are you going?"

"I think it would be best if you were unaware, Liang. That way, when the morning comes and my bed is empty, you can say you know nothing of my whereabouts. In truth."

"If that is your request, Zhi?"

"It is."

"Then I will abide by it."

A long silence fills the room.

"I do not think I will be returning to the Imperial City, Liang."

"I do not think so either, Zhi." He hesitates. "If you make it back to Kunyang, please pay respects to my family. Tell them how I have prospered."

"I would be honored to do so."

"I feel we are always saying farewell, Zhi."

The friends embrace. "Now I must ask you to leave, Liang," Zhi says. The men bow to each other, and Zhi watches as Liang leaves the school building. He wishes he could say good-bye to Yuan as well.

Zhi finds the armoire containing the robes of the novices. He rifles through it. He slides on the cloak of a Buddhist monk and slips into the night.

The cab raced to the Hertz car rental. Inside, Mara and Ben grabbed the maps and driving directions Joe designated, then hopped into a car that Joe had reserved for them under Ben's name. They sped out onto the motorway and headed south.

They faced at least a three-hour drive to the Algarve coast before they turned east onto the A22 motorway toward the Spanish border town of Vila Real de Santo António. From there, they'd have another several hours of driving to the port city of Algeciras, Spain. Joe said that taking the ferry from Algeciras was the safest route to Morocco.

Joe wanted them out of the European Union and into a country where he could use his influence to get them on a flight to New York. His choice of Morocco had surprised Mara, but she trusted Joe implicitly. So they headed for the Tangier airport.

Mara was behind the wheel, despite Ben's protests. She needed to drive, needed the activity to distract her from her anxiety. The rhythm of the road would help her fit all the puzzle pieces together and fashion a resolution.

Mara jumped a little when Ben asked, "Assuming we make it back to New York intact with this map"—he patted his backpack, which had not left his person since Tomar—"what's our strategy?"

"I don't know yet."

"Do we know *anything* at this point?" Ben sounded frustrated.

"We know a lot, Ben. We know that the Chinese map-maker made a copy of the world map you found on the Silk Road. That copy made it to Portugal in the early 1400s, and it was used in the Order of Christ's expeditions in the Age of Discovery to help guide them on those treacherous journeys. After the order's fleets accomplished their exploration goals, its knights created an exalted place to honor the map—the first floor of the Manueline addition to the Tomar Charola—and changed the *Adoration* for some reason. Then the order decided to hide that floor—and the map along with it—for centuries."

"But the order's members knew about the map's existence over the years."

"Right. The order educated at least two of its members, the viscount and Professor Silva, about the map and then charged them with keeping that knowledge secret."

"And you think that the viscount arranged for the theft of the original Chinese map, the one I found on the Silk Road?"

"Doesn't it fit? When word of the original map spread through the cartographical underground, the viscount must have raced into action. He's so very proud and protective of Portugal, he couldn't bear to have its golden history sullied by the public revelation that the Europeans didn't discover the world but merely followed the Chinese lead. So much of Portugal's modern identity is based on its former dominance."

He nodded in agreement. "Are we going to try to get

the Chinese map back from the viscount? Do we even need to, now that we have the copy?"

"We're going to try. But first, I need some leverage with Richard."

"What do you mean?"

"He's had the two of us on some tight leash of his own design. I need to free us and gain the upper hand."

"Would some intelligence on Richard help?"

Mara stared at Ben. "Of course."

"Do you remember that I mentioned Huang has been sending me packages?"

"Yes."

"In the latest one, I learned of an investigation Huang undertook after we left."

"What kind of an investigation?"

"Huang had grown suspicious about the authenticity of the mummies initially found at the Xi'an site. He poked around and found out that the mummies were planted there. They were discovered close to the famed Tarim Basin site and moved to the Xi'an dig."

"Who would've moved them?"

"Richard."

"Why?"

"There's only one possible reason. By making it seem that the Tocharian mummies were found closer to the heart center of ancient Chinese civilization, Richard could demonstrate that the West dictated China's development."

"That proof could become a powerful political tool in his hands."

"Yes."

"Why didn't you tell me sooner?"

"I guess I thought I might use it for my own

purposes—to make sure Richard would tell me the full truth about the mummies and let me study them. The mummies really do seem to be Tocharian, even if they didn't originate near Xi'an." He grew quiet for a moment. "But I was wrong. Can you forgive me?"

Mara was hurt, but she didn't want to let him know. "I guess so, Ben. We've both been guilty of some dishonesty, haven't we?" She didn't wait for him to answer. "Do you have the documentation from Huang with you?"

"I didn't dare leave it in my hotel room."

"Good."

Mara started to wonder. If Richard was capable of forging archaeological finds to further his ideological agenda, to what other depths might he sink? She assigned Ben the task of watching the road for followers and dialed her father.

Though they believed the Chinese—and possibly others—to be in their wake, Mara and Ben made it down to the Portuguese Algarve uneventfully. They shifted onto a new highway and passed into Spain through the Vila Real de Santo António border control with only the normal customs delays, though Joe had given them no assurances that the viscount hadn't clamped down on the borders. They even traveled the final distance to Algeciras without incident.

The lack of chase only fueled Mara's anxiety as they approached the port. The other shoe must drop somewhere. She could not believe that the Chinese or the viscount would permit her and Ben to return to New York with the coveted map in their possession.

They parked the car in a lot near the ferry terminal. As soon as they left its confines, the Mediterranean Sea air assaulted them. Not with the scent of fish but with the pungent smell of smoke spewing from nearby industrial stacks. The stench reminded her of the pollution of Xi'an, but then the swish from the djellabas of traveling Moroccans and the scent of spices reminded her that they were about to enter the Arabic world.

The hordes swarming one of the world's busiest ferry ports both pleased and troubled Mara. The crowds made them less detectable should anyone be lying in wait, but they also made it harder for them to spot anyone trailing them. Her concerns notwithstanding, they had no choice but to proceed with Joe's plan. Weaving through the outstretched hands claiming to offer ferry tickets at a deep discount, they bought their tickets at the official booth and boarded a large high-speed catamaran.

The hydrofoil was packed with foreign tourists as the ticket prices far exceeded those for the slow, older ferries to Tangier. Mara and Ben settled into seats in a lounge area close to the guarded gangways, believing that proximity to security might reduce the chance of pursuit on board. Out the window, Mara saw the crests of whitecaps on the water, but she couldn't feel the chop. The catamaran glided over the rough waves with ease, delivering them into the Tangier dock smoothly and ahead of schedule.

After passing through another immigration control point without complications, Mara and Ben entered the madness of the terminal. A barrage of taxi drivers attacked them, offering the lowest prices to popular destinations. They ducked through the onslaught and gravitated toward a line of orderly, though slightly dilapidated, taxis patiently awaiting their next customers. The cabbie first in line put down his newspaper and hustled to open the door for them.

The calmness of the taxi's wait belied the mad intensity of their cabbie's driving. The narrow, ancient Tangier streets teemed with pedestrians, as there weren't any sidewalks. Traffic rules seemed nonexistent, and though they hadn't told the cabbie to rush, he propelled them along at breakneck speed. Mara and Ben sighed with relief when the car delivered them to Tangier's Ibn Batouta airport.

The chaotic airport clamored with robed travelers carrying baggage of every shape and size. Mara and Ben cut through the bedlam like a knife on their way to the Royal Air Maroc check-in counter. While they waited to be summoned to the front of the line for the flight to New York, Mara watched out for her Chinese friend and his cohort. The coast seemed clear.

The attendant waved them forward. Ben handed over his passport first. Mara held her breath until she saw the processed ticket in his hands. Joe seemed to have worked his magic, though she wouldn't feel certain until a boarding pass to New York landed in her anxious fingers. She heard the welcome buzz of the computer printing her ticket and smiled up at Ben in delight.

He grinned back, but within seconds his face fell at the sight of something over her shoulder. Mara followed his gaze.

Their Chinese pursuers were sauntering toward them. Each wore a disconcerting smile. Mara now understood why their journey from Lisbon to Tangier had been so peaceful: the men had somehow learned Mara and Ben's destination and they'd been waiting here for them, like spiders at the center of a web.

Mara had no intention of allowing herself and Ben to get tangled in it. She grabbed her ticket from the outstretched hand of the Royal Air Maroc attendant. Clutching Ben's arm, she walked purposefully toward the security line. The closer to the armed guards, and the nearer to their New York gate, the better.

The men followed. They matched their strides to

Mara and Ben's, quick steps but not so swift as to draw attention. Mara and Ben hurried into one of two parallel security lines, and a young couple quickly fell in behind them, so the men got into the line opposite theirs.

Mara kept her eyes averted, but she could feel their stares. She wondered how the men planned on separating them from the map, and what they intended to do to her and Ben.

Both groups advanced at the same rate through their lines, and by the time Mara handed her ticket and passport to the guard, she was standing right next to the Chinese man. They pretended to ignore each other as they waited for the gesture to proceed, which came first for Mara. Pressing forward, she placed her belongings on the conveyor belt, keeping tabs on Ben's progress all the while.

Ben made it to the X-ray scanner before security gave their pursuers leave to proceed. As Mara waited for Ben to finish, she watched the security guard talk on his radio while comparing a document with the Chinese man's passport. As Ben gathered his belongings off the belt and put on his shoes, a gaggle of security guards rushed to the other line and swarmed around the Chinese man. His partner backed away from the line ever so slowly. To no avail.

Ben tore Mara away from the scene. As they walked toward their gate, she dug her cell out of the bag.

"Joe, we're through security in the Tangier airport."

"Thank God."

"But our Chinese friend and his associate were not so lucky."

"I described your pursuers to some people in the

Moroccan government and suggested that their papers weren't in order. The Moroccan police needed to detain them to sort it all out."

"How did you do it?"

Joe chuckled. "I've still got a few friends in high places."

Antonio walks down the gray ramparts until he reaches the very tip of Sagres. Standing at the precipice, he looks down the near-vertical cliffs to watch the surf crashing on the rocks below. He thinks how small the Sagres waves seem to him now.

He takes a deep breath and tries to muster his courage. He is more scared to walk down the dusty streets of his hometown near Sagres and knock on her door than he was to round the tip of Africa and sail to India. For it is Helena's door on which he will knock.

But Antonio must go. He must find out if the *réis* burning his pockets are worth the sacrifices. He must discover whether Helena will have him.

So he squares his shoulders and walks away from the cliffs of Sagres and toward his town. As he nears it, he passes by the humble homes of old childhood friends and fishermen he knows. He thinks he hears his name being called from one window. Yet he does not stop. His mission is singular.

The houses grow more substantial as he approaches her lane. He recognizes the stately residences of town officials and the few gracious dwellings of merchants. Then he sees it: the whitewashed home of Helena.

Antonio walks up to the black door. He brushes the dust from his new emerald doublet and black cloak.

He smooths his hair and pats the coin bag under his cloak, as if it alone gives him license to take this act. Only then does he raise his hand to knock on the door, watching it shake as it never did mapping the route to India.

No one answers. Antonio waits long moments. As he is considering whether to tap again or perhaps leave and return later in the day, the door creaks open. Just a sliver.

He sees the eyes of Helena's maid, Sancha, peer out. They are not welcoming. She never approved of their clandestine walks, of her mistress meeting with a man whose status was no better than her own.

"I am here to call upon your mistress. Please tell her that Antonio Coehlo has returned from his voyage to India as chief pilot and mapmaker to Captain-Major Vasco da Gama."

"She is not here," Sancha answers, opening the door wide and placing her hands upon her hips.

"I will come back upon her return. When do you expect her?"

"Not for some time," she says with a certain smug pleasure.

"When will Helena come again, Sancha?" He tries to keep the impatience from his voice. He has waited this long; he can wait a few more hours, a few more days.

"She will never return as daughter to her father's house."

"What do you mean?" He wants to shake the cryptic Sancha, shake the self-satisfaction from her face and the truth from her mouth. But he does not want to ruin his chances. However small.

"Helena is mistress of her own home in Faro. Her father married her to a merchant six months after your ships sailed from the Lisbon harbor."

Antonio does not recall his last swig of ale. He does not remember rolling the dice at the game's end. He does not recollect his leaving the tavern. He retains only a single memory: of the crushing blow to his skull inflicted by the moneylender's thug after he squandered every *réis* in his possession, and more.

He opens his eyes. He lies in a tiny, whitewashed chamber, filled only with the lone cot on which he rests, a solitary chair, and a wooden cross. He struggles to sit but cannot. The pain is too great.

A monk rushes in. He looks at Antonio and says, "Oh no, I must get Prior Figuerado."

The exertion exhausts Antonio, and he falls back into a deep sleep. He awakens to see his friend João Figuerado sitting next to him. For a groggy moment, he thinks he is on board the *São Rafael*. He smiles at the priest.

"Antonio, I thank God we found you," João says, and Antonio knows he sails on the *São Rafael* no longer.

"Found me where?" he whispers, but João shushes him. The prior explains that one of his monks stumbled over Antonio in an Alfama neighborhood alleyway at dawn several mornings before while delivering foodstuffs to the poor. The monk recognized Antonio and arranged for him to be brought to the Monastery of Saint Vincent, where João was reinstated as prior after the voyage.

As soon as João mentions the Alfama, the memories of the past few months after his painful homecoming to Sagres—memories Antonio had tried to obliterate with ale—return to him. He remembers coming to Lisbon and recalls with shame his mad descent into ale and women and dice; if Helena could not wash clean his filthy *réis*, then he would squander it all in the vilest Alfama taverns he could find. Tears form in his swollen eyes.

His friend does not need to know the source of his pain to understand its depths. João says, "Stay for a while, Antonio. Let us heal your wounds."

Antonio tries to object and assume his usual swagger, but his agonizing injuries overwhelm him. He only manages to protest, "Only until I am well."

João nods. He places a cooling hand on Antonio's throbbing forehead. "We will try to provide all that you need until then."

Antonio's injuries prove to be as stubborn as he. The broken bones and gashes mend slowly. When he stands, he sways as if on a ship's deck. His distressing recollections of the voyage and Helena cling like barnacles.

Days turn into weeks, and weeks become months. Restless with the long hours sitting alone in his chamber or slowly walking the grounds, he starts attending the masses. The rhythmic Latin chanting that once annoyed begins to soothe. It starts to wear away his rough edges.

Antonio finds contentment in the monastic rituals, in the silence that pervades the halls and the refectory even during meals. He does not develop a fervent belief in Christianity; instead, he tolerates the presence of God in his days as one abides the company of a persistent and irritating but loving brother. Thread by thread,

João weaves Antonio into the fabric of life at the Monastery of Saint Vincent, and Antonio finds the peace for which they both have prayed.

Until King Manuel's knights of the Order of Christ march down the monastery's corridors.

Mara and Ben smiled at each other nervously across her office conference room. The long, glossy board-room table stretched between them. The scroll sat on the center of the otherwise bare surface like an engage-ment diamond gleaming against a backdrop of black silk.

"You're certain about this?" Ben asked.

"Absolutely," Mara answered, her conviction firm but her voice quavering with the task ahead of her. She was about to face the most daunting negotiation of her life against the most formidable players.

"All right, then. Just promise you'll call for me if you get uncomfortable."

"I promise."

Ben strolled around the table and bent down next to her chair. "I don't want anything to happen to you," he said. Reaching up to brush away a strand of hair, he touched his fingers to her cheek. Mara softened at the gesture and curved her face down so that it rested fully in his hand. A feeling of calm washed over her, though their day together in New York had left her even more confused about her feelings toward him.

The grandfather clock chimed the hour. "You'd better go, Ben."

He stood up and walked toward the conference room

door. He turned the knob, but before he opened the door he turned back and smiled.

Mara smoothed out her navy suit jacket and skirt and spread out the collar of her starched white blouse, a departure from her black traveling ensembles of the past couple of weeks. She was ready.

Joe knocked. Upon Mara's assent, he pushed open the door and withdrew. The viscount of Tomar entered.

Mara stood up and reached out her hand to shake his. His arms remained fixed at his sides, a briefcase clutched in his left hand. He had not forgiven her for summoning him. Or for her theft of his most precious belonging.

She gestured for the viscount to take the seat across from hers. He stayed immobile and silent. Until he cast his gaze upon the scroll at the table's center.

"Is that my map?" he asked.

She watched as his previously stationary right hand clenched and unclenched, almost as if it wanted to spring onto the table and seize the scroll. "Yes," she answered. "Did you bring *my* map?"

The viscount nodded and lifted up the briefcase. "Though it's hardly yours." He seethed.

"Well, I wouldn't exactly call it yours either, Mr. Dias." She couldn't repress the barbed reference, though she'd promised herself in advance that she would refrain. She stopped herself from sinking to his level, and reassumed her professional demeanor. "I asked you here for a reason. I have a proposal that may meet both of our objectives."

"I can conceive of no proposal that could meet both of our objectives." His tone was derisive.

She again signaled for him to take the chair opposite

hers, and this time, he did. "I propose an exchange of maps."

He snorted. "What good would an exchange do me? For all I know, you'd return the Chinese map to the government, so China could claim to be the first discoverer of the world. No, I don't think your proposal meets my objectives at all."

"Would it meet your objectives if I handed *your* map over to China?" Mara tapped her finger on the table, as if contemplating the possibility. "Let's see what would occur then. China would assert—with damning evidence in hand—that not only did Admiral Zheng He and his fleets circumnavigate the globe and discover the world in the early 1400s, but also imparted that knowledge to the Portuguese through the Order of Christ. China would then reveal that Portugal kept that information secret and touted the Age of Discovery as its very own. I think that revelation would cause you more problems than disclosing the fifteenth-century Chinese voyages."

He quieted. "Why are you doing this to me, Ms. Coyne? To Portugal and all the European countries that sacrificed so much in the early explorations?"

Mara saw real pain in his eyes, and it reminded her that the viscount had labored hard to reestablish Portugal on the world stage, almost like a modern-day Vasco da Gama. For a fleeting moment, she felt pity for him and his mission. "I'm not doing this to harm you. Or Portugal, or anyone else, for that matter. Portugal should be proud of its discoveries regardless; they truly were great acts of heroism. I make this proposal because I see it as the only solution that honors the intentions of the maps' creator. From the inscriptions, it seems that the Chinese mapmaker wanted *your* map to travel to

Europe so that the Chinese discoveries would be used rather than destroyed, as would have happened if the map remained in China. And the Order of Christ indeed used the Chinese's mapmaker's generosity as he desired; he wanted no glory for himself. Your order fulfilled his wishes, so I see no need to go public with your map, particularly since returning your map to Portugal—even if it remains hidden—complies with the laws to keep artifacts within the country where they are found. But I feel differently about the Chinese map."

She paused before continuing; she wanted him to fully comprehend the benefit of her proposition. "Don't forget, Viscount. This proposal would allow you to keep your map—and the Portuguese use of it—secret. As you and the Order of Christ have done for centuries."

The viscount removed a key from the inner pocket of his suit jacket. He placed his briefcase on the table and slid the key into it. The lid popped upon, and Mara jumped.

He reached deep within the interior, and Mara was not certain just what he would pull out. Yet when his hand reappeared, it held a scroll. The viscount of Tomar handed over the Chinese map. They made their trade.

In his monk's robes, Zhi is permitted to roam through the lanes of the Imperial City and into the Forbidden City; the guards do not bother him. The moment he passes under the East Flowery Gate, he hears the deep chanting of monks. He follows their voices.

A sea of monks awaits him in the smoke-scarred square in which the burned-out shell of the Hall of Preserving Harmony sits. Zhi creeps into the back of the seated group of hundreds, huddling into them for warmth. He assumes the crossed-legged pose of the praying monks and mouths the words of the strange mantra.

At dawn, the service honoring the late emperor Yongle finishes. The monks rise and form a single-file line. The procession weaves through the Forbidden City and exits through the West Flowery Gate. With clanging cymbals in the lead, they begin the long walk north to the burial place of Emperor Yongle.

Eunuchs are prohibited from leaving the imperial service without explicit, rarely granted permission. The monks render Zhi invisible to the all-seeing mandarins as he escapes from the Forbidden City to do the bidding of Admiral Zheng.

Zhi spends days in the arc-shaped area at the foot of snow-covered mountains. The monks parade up and down the frigid Spirit Way, the road leading to the late emperor's tomb. Zhi marvels at the panoply of stone animals that line the route; Emperor Yongle had commissioned the sculpting of the rare creatures as guardians to his resting place.

Zhi's time is spent in the company of the monks: eating, sleeping, meditating, and praying. He worries that his unfamiliarity with their practices will single him out as an outsider. Yet the monks are a tolerant lot, and their itinerant, wandering lifestyle anticipates the addition of new faces with different customs.

The funeral ceremonies end. The monks plan to make a pilgrimage southwest to Xi'an, the celebrated capital of thirteen past dynasties and the eastern gateway to the great trade routes. Zhi joins them, with a secret prayer to Allah that their ranks will continue to shield him from the mandarins, as he heads toward the pathway to the land of Marco Polo.

The journey to Xi'an takes so many days that Zhi loses track. The group travels by horse, cart, and camel when they come across a hospitable caravan, and by foot when they do not. In time, he sees the famed defensive walls of Xi'an, topped by pagodas, rise from the early morning mist.

The monks weave their way through the clusters of camels tethered to the city walls and around the colorful tents of the traders. They pass under one of the immense gates of the renowned city. Monks familiar with Xi'an from previous pilgrimages lead the way through the gridlike streets, which overflow with a variety of peoples Zhi has seen only on his expedition. Amid the noise of the city lanes, deafening after so long in the company of the quiet monks, Zhi hears the wafting cry of the muezzin.

The call to prayer stays with him at the monastery. As he chants mantras and *dharanis* with the monks, Zhi feels an overwhelming sense of disloyalty. To the monks who express such kindness toward him, to his long-neglected Muslim faith, and to his own family, which depends on his eunuch salary. He reminds himself that by honoring his vow to Admiral Zheng he honors his faith and his family—and that he can do so only by assuming a monk's costume.

A market assembles at the base of the monastery. Peripatetic monks spring up among the merchants offering fabrics, spices, and ceramics. The holy men set up stalls selling protective rites, divination services, and medicines. The monks in Zhi's band visit their brethren in the marketplace.

Zhi strains to hear the chatter of merchants as the monks wander in and out of the Buddhists' stalls. He is rewarded with an overheard conversation about a trader from the nation of Marco Polo. Two Arabic merchants gossip about the rare visitor from the strange northern lands who purchases spice in unprecedented quantities.

Late one evening, as the other monks sleep, Zhi sheds his monk's robe and dons a servant's one instead. He feels naked without the disguise that has served him so well. Yet he knows that a monk visiting a trader would cause too much notice.

Zhi leaves Xi'an by the gate under which he passed when he first arrived and enters the enormous field of tents surrounding the city walls. He looks for the distinctive markings he heard the merchants describe, but he cannot find the trader's tent.

He wanders among so many tents that they all begin to look the same. In despair, Zhi is wondering whether he is repeating his own path when he sees a tawny-skinned merchant exit from one of the larger tents, one with guards outside. The merchant pats his cloak contentedly, and Zhi surmises that he has stumbled upon the tent of the trader.

Two guards flanking the marquee's entry demand to know his business and remark on his poor dress. When Zhi tells them that he carries goods from the Imperial Court of China, a guard hastens into the tent. The guard emerges and pulls back the heavy fabric over the entryway so Zhi can enter.

As Zhi's eyes adjust to the lamplight, the outline of a man in peculiar dress reclining on a mound of pillows appears. And then fully materializes. In all the many *li* of his voyages, Zhi has never seen skin so pale or hair so red. He gawks until the trader breaks the spell. "Never seen a white man before, huh?" the man says, in Zhi's own tongue.

Zhi bows. "My humble apologies. I did not mean to offend."

"You do not. I am used to such stares." The trader spits out the hull of the seed on which he chews.

"Is it true that you are from the land of Marco Polo?"

"Yes." The man reaches into the bowl of seeds and pops another into his mouth. "What of it?"

"The item I come to trade must find its way there."

"If I like what you have, then I can take it there." He slows his chewing and scans Zhi. He asks, "Is it true that you have goods from the Imperial Court of China?"

"In a manner of speaking, yes."

"What do you have to trade?"

Zhi reaches under his robes to untie the packet he has carried on his back since he fled the Forbidden City. He pulls out the teak box holding his *pao*. His hands tremble as he leafs through the scrolls hidden within—the map and its copy, and his treasured painting of the lotus, his Shu—to find the proper one.

"I am here to trade a map."

The door slammed behind the viscount. Mara stood stock-still, shaking. With the Chinese map in her hand.

Slowly, so slowly, she lowered herself down into her chair. Joe and Ben rushed into the room, and Mara accepted their congratulations, always careful to protect the map from their enthusiasm.

"Nice work, Mara," Joe said with a pat on her back, and Ben echoed the compliment with a squeeze of her free arm.

"Now I just have to deal with Richard and the Chinese." She couldn't keep the quivering from her voice.

"The toughest part's over. The rest is a piece of cake," Joe reassured her.

"I hope so." She excused herself to take a quick break before the Chinese government representative arrived for their meeting. She and Joe had purposely scheduled appointments close together; they didn't want to give Richard any window of opportunity to interfere.

The click of her heels echoed as Mara walked down the long hallway to the ladies' room. She entered the mercifully empty space. She approached the sink and began patting her face with cold water.

Mara almost didn't recognize the hard, unflappable expression that materialized in the mirror. Her self-possessed countenance did not match her anxious interior, but she knew she had to play the part fully in order to make this negotiation work. So she marched back into the conference room with a confidence she didn't feel. Without a beat, she picked up the map and told Joe to bring in the Chinese official.

In walked Wang Tiankai, a Chinese Commerce Ministry representative, and Sam, flapping like an American flag in his navy pin-striped suit, white shirt, and red tie. Mara had expected Sam to accompany Wang. After all, Sam had arranged the meeting, and brokering the map's return would serve him well politically in the future. She hadn't expected, however, that her heart would inexplicably leap as she introduced Sam to Ben.

Mara composed herself as the group exchanged abbreviated bows and handshakes and made the requisite small talk about the unseasonably pleasant weather. No one mentioned the reason for their meeting, though periodically everyone's eyes lingered on the scroll in Mara's hand. She longed to present the map to Wang, but she understood that she had to bide her time.

Silence came upon them. Mara knew the moment had arrived to announce the recovery of the map and to bestow it upon the Chinese envoy. Even though Wang knew the purpose for their meeting already. She took a deep breath and said, "Wang Tiankai, it is my great honor to—"

She was interrupted by the ringing of his cell phone, in his inner jacket pocket. He reached for it and flipped open the cover. After executing a short bow, Wang excused himself from the room.

Mara stared at Sam in disbelief. He rolled his eyes and shrugged in response, but before he could explain—or criticize—Wang's actions, his BlackBerry buzzed. While he clicked on it, Ben and Mara shook their heads in wonder. Having labored so hard and risked so much to recover the map, they found it inconceivable that its recipients might delay its return for even a second.

"This makes no sense," Sam muttered.

"I'd agree with that," Mara mumbled back, making no effort to keep the disdain from her voice.

"Very funny, Mara," Sam said. "I'm referring to the e-mail I just got. The U.S. government has withdrawn the cases it filed against China with the World Trade Organization."

"You've lost me, Sam."

"You didn't read about the complaints when you were in China?"

"No. I had a pressing matter to tend to, or have you forgotten?"

"No, I haven't forgotten." Sam's patronizing tone reminded her that their parting had its upsides. "A few months ago, as a reaction to congressional pressure on trade, the U.S. administration lodged formal WTO complaints against China over trade barriers and intellectual property issues relating to imports and piracy. China issued a statement of 'deep regret,' along with a statement saying that the U.S. action will undermine cooperative relations and adversely affect bilateral trade. Obviously, these cases have made my job in Hong Kong difficult, as the Chinese see the filings as a U.S. move toward protectionism and xenophobia."

"But the U.S. administration just withdrew those cases?"

"Yes. Just now. Even though the Chinese have made none of the concessions demanded by the United States as a prerequisite to their removal."

The door opened, and Wang strode into the room. He bowed to Mara and Ben and held out his hand to shake theirs in turn.

He said, "My apologies. I have an urgent matter to attend to, so I will have to take my leave from our meeting."

Mara was desperate to deliver the map to Wang before Richard caught wind of her machinations. And derailed them. "Really, sir, there is no need to cancel the meeting. My presentation will take but a moment."

"Ms. Coyne, you do not understand. The urgent matter to which I must turn my attention demands that I call off this meeting. And that I abandon the reason for it."

Mara was confused. The link between Wang's pressing affair—presumably the WTO news—and the map evaded her. Until Wang turned to Ben and said, "You may return the map to the sponsor of your archaeological dig—Mr. Richard Tobias."

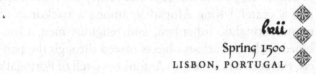
Antonio tries to ignore the presence of the knights. He skirts the newly built chapel where they work. He avoids the hallways where they reside. He fears losing the tranquillity that the monastic routines and silence bring him, but he cannot escape the visitors' din. And he cannot disregard the whispers about the wondrous altarpiece they create.

One icy morning after matins, the sky blackened with the promise of a wintry storm, he finds himself in the apse leading to the chapel. He nods to the Order of Christ knights standing guard outside the heavy wrought-iron gates. They part to let him pass: only knights, monks, and artisans may enter the sacred space. Antonio knows that, in his borrowed robes, he looks like a monk.

He pushes back the creaking gates and walks into the empty chapel, a recent commission by King Manuel as a private place of worship for the Aviz royal family. The room smells of linseed oil and hard work. He takes a seat on the heavily carved wooden pew and stares up at the nearly complete, six-paneled polyptych over the opulent marble altar.

Using masterful brushwork, the artists have painted an astonishing panoply of portraits of figures past and present. Antonio recognizes the saintly Vincent, a youthful King John, a sage Prince Henry the Navigator, and a grateful King Afonso V, among a backdrop of monks, knights, fishermen, and religious men. Combined with the curious objects placed through the panels, the portraits seem—to Antonio—to tell of Portugal's epic efforts to sail beyond the seas to spread Christianity and dominate trade. The heroic images disturb his hardwon peace.

Between the two center panels depicting Saint Vincent, a niche containing a small statue catches his attention. The sculpture looks familiar. Antonio rises from the pew and draws closer to it.

To his surprise, he knows it well. It is a wooden sculpture of the archangel Rafael, the protector of pilgrims and travelers. The very statue Antonio had watched Captain Paolo da Gama hand his brother Captain-Major Vasco da Gama the day they set the *São Rafael* aflame. The exact figure the captain-major had kept on his private altar on the long journey home to Portugal.

But the archangel Rafael no longer holds the pilgrim's staff he clasped on board the *São Rafael* and the *São Gabriel*. Antonio disobeys the monastic rules and climbs behind the altar. He is stunned to see that the archangel Rafael holds a scroll—the world map Antonio used to guide the armada to India and back again.

He recoils at the sight of the map and stumbles down the altar steps, realizing that the altarpiece forms the center of the chapel where King Manuel will secretly celebrate the Portuguese Order of Christ's discovery of the map, and will give thanks to Saint Vincent for his intercession in fulfilling Portugal's destiny. Nowhere in the painting does Antonio see portrayed the bloody means—or lies—by which Portugal executes its fate.

He cannot permit the sacrilege of the map and the sculpture and the painting on the monastery's hallowed, healing walls. An involuntary roar emerges from his throat. He grabs the bishop's crosier and charges the altarpiece, slicing it lengthwise. He reaches for the map when the knights of the Order of Christ rush in, brandishing their swords.

Antonio does not wish to fight anymore. He is tired, and he has reached his peace with his God. Just as the knights draw near, he drops the crosier. He turns and opens his arms wide to welcome their swords.

It is only the second time a blade has pierced his skin. Yet this time, the blade does not sear. It purifies.

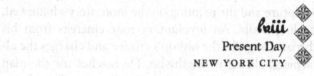

Mara flew out of the cab and into the courtyard of the Metropolitan Club. She ignored the gallant attempts by the officially outfitted doormen to escort her into its hallowed interior. Brushing past the concierge, who feebly endeavored to screen her entrance, she rushed into the dining room.

There, in his usual center table, sat Richard, flanked by two navy-suited men. She marched past the dining room's heavy velvet tapestries, its lofty murals, and the marble fireplace as she proceeded toward his table. The club's trappings of wealth, which had once so impressed her, now repulsed.

Richard watched her approach. His face showed no hint of surprise at her arrival. As she drew near, he nodded to his dining companions, who rose with reluctance. But he made no other gestures and spoke no words to her. He let her make the next move.

"I won't wait for an invitation to join you," Mara said, pulling out a chair and sitting down across from Richard. The concierge and two guards loomed, but Richard dismissed them with a wave of his hand.

"To what do I owe the pleasure?" A supercilious smile appeared on his face.

"Let's dispense with the polite banter, shall we?" She

removed two manila folders from her bag and fanned them out on the table with great deliberation.

"I would be happy to do so." His smile mutated to a sneer.

"You orchestrated the U.S. administration's withdrawal of the WTO cases against China."

"Why would I do such a thing? My positions on trade with China are well known; a tough line must be maintained."

"Unless a softening of that 'tough line' gets you back the map."

Richard's eyes narrowed, and he sat back into his chair. She shifted her gaze from him and opened the folder in front of her. Mara's audacity had left Richard unprecedentedly speechless, so she selected a piece of paper from the pile and continued. "Let me see, what does this little report say? Oh yes, it proves that your not-for-profit paid to have the mummies uncovered on Ben's excavation planted there. The bodies originated in the Tarim Basin, but your thugs dug them up and put them in false grave sites near Xi'an." She picked up another document. "And this statement lists the other digs your altruistic little group funded. All yielding questionable scientific and archaeological findings, and all advancing your unique version of history that the West dictated China's development."

Richard's prepossessing demeanor returned and, along with it, his authoritative tone. "What do you want?"

"I think you know what I want, Richard. I want to return the map Ben found on your staged archaeological site—probably the only authentic artifact discovered there—to the Chinese, as the law demands, as the map-

maker would have wanted, and as my conscience sees
fit. With your blessing."

He dropped any remnants of civility. "You are even
more naïve than I thought you were when I hired you if
you think I'm going to 'bless' the handover of the map
to the Chinese so they can use it as a symbol of their
early—and now growing—world dominance."

"You will do exactly that, or I will make these documents public."

The vestiges of his genteel façade slipped from his
face. Richard was raw and mean and ugly behind the
mask. "Mara, you are a little girl playing at a man's
game. I've weathered far worse storms than this." He
shook his head in disapproval. "Your father would be
humiliated by your behavior."

"My father?" She reached for the second manila
folder. "My father gave me these very interesting documents." Mara had learned that the rightness of her father's politics had limits.

Mara slid the folder across the vast divide to Richard.
He let it sit in front of him for a long minute before
deigning to open it. He paged through its contents.

"You're looking at a list of bank account numbers of
congressional, senatorial, and presidential candidates
and corresponding amounts wired into those accounts.
The funds come from the Committee for National Policy."

He scoffed. "The committee is permitted to make political campaign contributions. Just like any other citizen
or group."

"These wires were not campaign donations. They
were bribes."

He grabbed the documents and scanned them again.

Mara paused. "You have a choice, Richard."

He sat sphinxlike for interminable minutes. Her heart beat wildly as she awaited the verdict. Then he reached into his jacket pocket and pulled out a phone.

Zhi stumbles in the deep, worn groove of the road. His misstep jolts him from his near-sleepwalking state. He strains his eyes in the remnants of the moonlight to ensure that he has not drifted too far off the path.

The sight of marmots and mountain goats in the nearby fields reassures him. They have been Zhi's sole traveling companions for more moons than he can count. Except for the two occasions when a yak herder came into view.

Only by night does he trek the dusty trading routes. Without the camouflage of the band of monks, Zhi draws too much attention traveling alone. So he opts for the cover of night to hide him from bandits. Or worse, mandarins.

He hopes that his servant's robe belies the wealth of coins that rest in the rough leather purse around his neck. When the trader offered him gold in exchange for the map, he declined at first. Zhi felt uncomfortable taking payment for an act that honor called him to perform. Then he reminded himself that he owed a duty to his family as well and they would be without his salary of taels. So he took the trader's coins.

Zhi settles back into his pace. He thinks back on all the *li* he has traveled during the long years since he left Kunyang as an innocent youth. He wonders how his hometown will seem to him now and whether his parents and brothers will recognize him. He conjures up Shu's face in his mind and wonders what she will look like when he places the two scrolls in her hands: the map and the lotus blossom. They are his tributes to Emperor Yongle and to her, and his final apology.

Footsteps wake Zhi from his reverie. Two men emerge from the darkness: one tall and lanky, the other shorter and thickset. They make no effort to hide themselves as they advance toward him. "Look at what we have here," the taller man says.

Zhi backs away from the brigands. "Please, I beg for your mercy. I am just a poor farmer. I have nothing to offer you."

"A poor farmer? I don't think so. You escaped from the Imperial City."

He freezes and looks closer at the two men. The men are not bandits. They wear the robes of mandarin henchmen, and they have been sent to find him.

"You were hard to track. But you made the mistake of telling a trader's guards that you had goods from the Imperial Court. Those guards spread your little secret all over the markets of Xi'an."

The stockier one pushes him to the ground. As Zhi struggles to stand up, the other rips the leather cord from around his neck and tosses the pouch in the air like a ball.

"What's this? It feels heavy and sounds like coins."

"Let's take a look inside."

The stout man drags Zhi to his cohort's side. They gasp in awe at the gold glistening within the small bag.

"He must have stolen treasures from the Imperial City before he fled. And sold the goods," the tall one says to the other. The proclamation fills him with a strange relief; if the thugs are ignorant about the nature of the item he sold—the map—then the trader must have protected his secret. Or better yet, perhaps the trader has already placed the map on its route to the country of Marco Polo.

"Then our work is clear," the heavy man answers in a gruff voice. "We take the gold back to court—except our share—and leave the stinking traitor to rot on this dusty road."

"Agreed. Still, we should search him to see if he has anything else of value on him."

The men begin to wrestle Zhi to the ground when he remembers: he must conceal the copy of the map hidden in his box. It is his last chance to maintain his honor by keeping secret his work for Admiral Zheng, the man to whom he owes everything. He points to the chest. "Please let me keep my *pao*. I will not be able to go to the afterlife without it."

The two men look at each other and laugh. "You can take your worthless *pao* with you to the spirit world."

Zhi stops fighting back. He knows that resistance is futile, and the knowledge that he has protected both copies of the map comforts him. For the second time in his life, he submits to the knife.

Mara was glad they had the headlines to distract them. Ben had spread before them *The New York Times*, *The Washington Post*, and *USA Today*. Each newspaper made essentially the same proclamation, though Mara thought *The New York Times* said it best: "China Discovered the World First?"

They pored over the papers while drinking coffee at a café near Ben's neglected office at the University of Pennsylvania. The news accounts screamed with the Chinese announcement of major historical impact—that researchers had unearthed a map memorializing the naval voyages of Ming dynasty Admiral Zheng He in which he circumnavigated the globe and discovered the world. Though some skepticism persisted over the declaration, much of it fueled by challenging remarks from certain officials from the American government, the press—and the world—was taking the pronouncement seriously. Yet nowhere did they read that the famed European discoverers had carried the Chinese knowledge along with them on their voyages.

"Your negotiations reached the exact resolution you hoped for. Well done, Mara." Ben extended his coffee cup in congratulations.

"Thanks, Ben." Mara knew she should be euphoric. After all, she had orchestrated the maps' return according to her sense of moral and legal ownership. Instead, she was inexplicably unsettled. Did that stem from a certain wistfulness at parting with Ben? Or did it emanate from a deeper worry over the role her work had played in the revision of the past? As if she was some mapmaker of history. Or its thief.

"But you don't seem thrilled. Why?"

"I don't know." Tucking her hair behind her ears, she smoothed out her heather-gray sweater and skirt. At Ben's urgent request, Mara had traveled from New York to Philadelphia just two days after they'd finalized the map repatriations. Ben was tying up some loose ends at the University of Pennsylvania before returning to China for an extended period.

"You've done so much for me, Mara. Like negotiating with the Chinese to make sure that I head up the research into the map, even though it's not my area of expertise."

"Ben, it was the least I could do for you. I made you sacrifice your real discoveries—like the Charola—and made you promise to keep them secret."

"Well, I wanted to give you something. For a lot of reasons." Ben paused and reached into his familiar backpack. He pulled out a tube and slid it across the table to Mara.

"What's this?" she asked.

"Open it and find out."

After prying open the lid, she peered inside. A document lay curled within. "Let me guess. Another fifteenth-century map?" she joked.

He didn't laugh. "Unroll it. Carefully."

Mara reached in to start sliding the document out of the tube. As soon as she touched its surface, her fingers recognized the unmistakable texture of centuries-old silk paper. Paper that felt just like that of the maps. She stared at Ben, who looked so earnest and handsome in his professorial tweed jacket and worn-in jeans.

"Keep on going," he encouraged her.

She tugged the hand scroll out with great deliberation. Using the two rods at either end, she opened it section by section. A painting of a single lotus blossom materialized with each turn, a spare, mournful white flower growing from a dark pool of water. The image dominated the center of the scroll, while elegant vertical lines of calligraphy adorned the right and a single red seal appeared at the left.

The beauty of the painting captivated her. "Ben, this is breathtaking." Then she recognized the image and grew confused. "But it looks identical to the lotus blossom on the right corner of the Chinese map."

He nodded. "I know. Do you remember that I told you we found another scroll on the body of the Chinese mapmaker? A painting?"

A vague memory of his reference to another scroll, at the time unimportant, nagged at the corners of her consciousness. "Yes—"

"Well, this is that painting." He smiled.

"The body must be the mapmaker's. And this must have been for Shu."

"Yes."

"You don't mean to give this to me, do you?"

"Yes, I do."

"Ben, you can't do that. The law requires that this painting stay in China along with the map. It should be part of your research and presentations."

"Mara, you're the one who taught me that the right-ful possessor of a piece of artwork is not always dictated by the law."

She reeled, hearing her oft-repeated words used against her. "I can't conceive of any reason why I should be the rightful possessor of this painting rather than China." Rolling the painting back up, she handed it to Ben. "I really appreciate the gesture, but please, Ben, take this back to China with you."

"Remember what I told you about the symbol of the lotus?"

"Yes." She had a hazy memory of their early conversation. "That the lotus is a flower that grows from muddy water. That it's a symbol of female purity."

"It also represents a resurrection of sorts, as the water lily rises from the mire of the material world to achieve a pure, singular beauty." He stopped, as if his statement had elucidated his reason for giving her the painting.

"Yes?" Though Mara often extolled the importance of iconography in her work, she couldn't see the tie between the lotus symbolism and her ownership of the artifact.

"And it's an invitation for a union. As is the inscription beneath the lotus."

Mara began to understand.

"Don't you see?"

She did. But she shook her head, afraid of what she might say if she answered.

"You are the lotus. You are the rightful owner of the painting."

Ben rose from his chair and knelt next to Mara. He placed the scroll in her hands. "This belongs to you.

But if you really feel that you can't accept it, you'll have to fly to China and return it to me personally. Either way, I'll be pleased."

He took her face in his palms and kissed her. For the first time. So deeply and fully that, for a brief moment, she forgot about the ownership quagmire in which he had submerged her. "I hope to see you soon," he said, with a final touch on her cheek.

Mara watched as he left the restaurant, uncertain about what she would do with the treasure he'd entrusted to her. The law ordered one decision, and her desire—and possibly the mapmaker's wishes—dictated another.

With each step Ben took toward the door, her fingers curled more tightly around the scroll. Until he disappeared from sight. Leaving Mara with the painting clutched in her hands like the stem of a perfect, multi-petaled blossom.

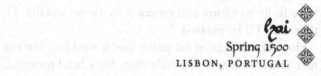

Spring 1500

LISBON, PORTUGAL

Prior João Figuerado stands at the entrance to the private chapel for the Aviz family of King Manuel. He watches as two knights from the Order of Christ hammer wooden planks over the altarpiece of *The Adoration of Saint Vincent*. João draws closer and kneels. Board by board, he says farewell to the likenesses of King Afonso V, King John II, Prince Henry the Navigator, and Saint Vincent himself.

João remains in front of the altar until one of the knights approaches him. "Prior Figuerado, forgive me, but we must ask you to leave. Our orders require us to seal up the chapel now."

"I understand, son. Might I have a moment alone here before you do?"

"Of course, Prior."

The knights gather up their tools, set them near the wrought-iron entry gates, and leave him in the little chapel. João rises and, for a final time, wanders around the marble enclave, laden with the nautical knots and oceanic motifs so beloved by King Manuel. He thinks about Antonio.

João knows that Antonio had suffered from a deep, private anger and sadness. Yet he wonders what drove him to attempt such a rash act of destruction and attempted thievery, an act that left the Order of Christ knights no choice but to kill him. An act that has led to the permanent closure of the Aviz chapel and the decision to create a new floor in the Charola at Tomar to honor the discoveries.

Tears well up in his eyes at the loss of his friend. He consoles himself only with the fact that Antonio reached some accord with Christ before his death.

"Prior?" A knight, mercifully not one responsible for Antonio's demise, interrupts his thoughts. "It is time."

João nods his assent and has begun to leave the chapel when a wrenching sound makes him turn back. One of the knights is prying the wooden sculpture of the archangel Rafael from the niche between the two center panels of *The Adoration of Saint Vincent*. João shudders. Rafael, the protector of pilgrims and travelers, had done nothing to shield Antonio from harm, even if that harm had stemmed from his own actions.

The bells of the Monastery of Saint Vincent begin to peal. Prior Figuerado takes his leave of the chapel. He is needed in the church. He must preside over the funeral of Antonio to ensure it receives the dignity it deserves. For his friend was no thief. He was, above all else, a mapmaker.

Author's Note

Not long ago, my brother Coley asked me if I'd ever heard of the Ming dynasty's Admiral Zheng He. When I answered no, he was surprised. After all, he and I had each spent considerable time in China, where the admiral is becoming legendary. Coley explained that, in the early 1400s, Zheng He had assembled a naval fleet so vast and so technologically superior that the Europeans' ships of the same time period seemed like bath toys in comparison. The presumed prowess of this armada has inspired theories that Zheng He had discovered the world decades before the famed European explorers.

I was intrigued. So, as I began to research my second book, I read about Zheng He. I learned that he was indeed a towering figure, both figuratively and literally: a Muslim, a eunuch, the closest adviser of the famous Ming dynasty emperor Yongle, and the chief admiral of an unprecedented navy. I also learned why I had never heard of this fascinating character. After the admiral returned from one of his last voyages, a new emperor assumed the Chinese throne, and with the advice of the newly reinstated mandarin court, began to order not only the prohibition of all future expeditions, but the destruction of all evidence of the seafaring missions that preceded him—on punishment of death.

I started wondering. What if the theories were true? Could Zheng He's massive fleet have discovered the world first? And, what if his achievement was lost because all documentation of those discoveries was destroyed on the whim of an imperial edict?

I threw myself into Ming dynasty China and the European Age of Discovery. As I pored over early world maps from this time period, I learned something curious, a historical mystery of sorts. Several of the very earliest European world maps—dating from the mid-1400s and beyond—showed lands and bodies of water that had not been officially "discovered" by the Europeans for decades. In 1457, thirty years before Bartolomeu Dias rounded the tip of Africa, the Genoese World Map showed the coast of Africa as navigable and connecting to the east. In 1459, the monk and cartographer Fra Mauro created a map depicting Africa as a separate continent surrounded by water with a possible route to the East Indies around its southern tip, again some thirty years before Dias's expedition and forty years before Vasco da Gama's journey to India. In 1507, the mapmaker Martin Waldseemüller produced a world chart showing America as an island continent with a mountainous western coast and an ocean stretching to Asia, even though Ferdinand Magellan did not complete his Pacific voyage for fifteen more years. These are just a few examples.

My imagination soared. Though certainly not the first to so conjecture, I wondered whether a scrap of evidence of Zheng He's voyages might have escaped the bonfires and whether that documentation might have reached the hands of the Europeans. I speculated that the surviving artifact was a Chinese map.

Thus, *The Map Thief* was born. In the book, I created a map—an early fifteenth-century Chinese chart memorializing the possible voyages of Zheng He—and set it to sail to answer the questions about the early European world maps and the Age of "Discovery."

Yet, as I struggled to solve this historical puzzle in novel form, I found that I had to play with history a bit for the purposes of fiction. For instance, I modified the dates of certain events that transpired on Vasco da Gama's voyages, transporting acts from latter journeys to his first. I heightened alleged aspects of da Gama's personality and motivations—and that of Emperor Yongle—for dramatic effect. I compressed the critical closing of China's door to the outside world: instead of occurring through imperial edicts issued over a period of decades beginning in 1424, I slammed China's door shut in one early fell swoop. I colored in the bold, yet largely empty, outlines of Zheng He's voyages with a rainbow of details and destinations, drawing on the speculations, research, and observations of many esteemed historians and historical participants—much as I did with Prince Henry's School of Navigation in Sagres. I even played with modern history, including the current nature of the Order of Christ, the existence of certain archival holdings in the National Museum of Ancient Art in Lisbon, the structure of the Monastery of Saint Vincent, and the creation of a controversial first floor of the Charola in the Templar Castle and the Convent of the Order of Christ at Tomar.

Though *The Map Thief* tries to answer a real historical

riddle via fiction, it primarily tells a story about an object's power to reveal something important about the past, as well as something private about its creator. And it poses a question about who are the rightful owners of art and history—and who are its thieves.

Acknowledgments

The Map Thief would never have set sail without the support and encouragement of many individuals. I am so grateful for my incredible agent, Laura Dail, who offered invaluable guidance and unwavering optimism. Beginning with my brilliant editor, Paul Taunton, I want to thank the extraordinary Ballantine team for their hard work and enthusiasm: Libby McGuire, Kim Hovey, Brian McLendon, Jane von Mehren, Rachel Kind, Scott Shannon, Christine Cabello, Lisa Barnes, the art department, the promotion and sales departments, and the managing editorial and production departments. And I must acknowledge the efforts of my local library in procuring obscure texts for my research and the backing of the Pittsburgh book community in general, Mary Alice Gorman and Richard Goldman in particular.

My family served as constant champions: my parents, Coleman and Jeanne Benedict; my siblings, Coley, Lauren, Courtney, Meredith, and Christopher and their families; and my in-laws, particularly my mother-in-law, Catherine, and my late father-in-law, Jim, who would have been so proud. Many friends who are like family cheered me on, including—but by no means limited to—Illana Raia, Ponny Conomos Jahn, Jamie

Levitt, the Sewickley Book Club ladies, and Patti Vescio.

I reserve my deepest, immeasurable gratitude for my husband, Jim, and our son, Jack. Without their abundant love, abiding patience, and endless inspiration, I never could have written *The Map Thief*.

Read on for an excerpt from

Brigid of Kildare

by
Heather Terrell

Published by Ballantine Books

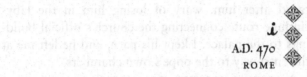

Brother,

I write you in the utmost haste, trusting in God that I will find a safe way to deliver this letter unto your hands. For this very eve, I must leave Rome for an island so far outside the bounds of civilization it has never merited the attention of our dear Republic: the land of the Gaels.

That the Lord has summoned me to this mission, I have no doubt. Yet, as dawn broke and I finished my prayers this morning, I would have sworn on the cross that the day would progress like every other.

I settled at my desk in the chambers of the papal secretary just as the sun's rays began their full celebration of God's good day. Capturing the clarity of the earliest light is as critical to my work as a scrivener for the Lord as it is to your work overseeing the family land; thus I was alone in the study. I was preparing to record the edicts emanating from a recent council meeting when I heard my name.

I turned toward the sound and, to my surprise, saw a papal page in the doorway. He said, "Brother Decius, you are to follow me to an audience in the chambers of His Holiness Pope Simplicius, bishop of Rome."

The page started off down the long and winding

corridors that lead to His Holiness's inner sanctum. I
raced after him, wary of losing him in the laby-
rinthine route connecting the church's official buildings to the palace. I kept his pace, and he left me at
the entryway to the pope's own chambers.

A crimson tapestry separated the sacred inner
sanctum from the bustle of the rest of the palace. I
approached it, and though I pulled the heavy fabric
aside with reverence and care, my fingers caught on
the pearls and rubies sewn into the silken embroidery.
In that moment of disentanglement, I know not why,
I hesitated before crossing the threshold.

My body began shaking, as it had never trembled
before. Yet I knew I could show no fear. Courage is
necessary—nay, mandated—for selection to one of
Christ's missions. And somehow I knew that this was
the purpose of my summoning.

To expel the devil's own trepidation from my heart
and soul, I steeled myself with the image, oft
described by you, of our father and mother stoic in
the face of the barbarians. If our parents could suffer
at their hands and never flinch before the final swing
of the crude battle-axe, then, I told myself, I could
take the simple step of entering the private chamber
of Saint Peter's own representative on this earth.

Peace descended upon me, almost as though our
mother and father spoke from heaven. I left the tapestry to swing in my wake and immediately knelt
before His Holiness. Or so I believed.

"Rise, Brother Decius," the order sounded out.

I readied myself to confront the intimidating phalanx of aristocratic councillors that accompany His
Holiness's every movement, which I had witnessed

during my three prior papal audiences. Yet as I rose from my deep genuflection and lifted my eyes, a single figure greeted me. I knew the man only by sight and rumor, as he would never deign to enter the secretary's study: It was Gallienus, a priest and the most senior of the pope's councillors.

I bowed my head in respect, yet could not help but note the comfortable, nearly languorous, manner in which he leaned against the empty papal throne. "Your Eminence."

"The twelfth eagle will soon fly," Gallienus said.

I did not answer at once, uncertain as to his meaning and even more unsure as to the safest response.

"Are you not familiar with the Prophecy of the Twelve Eagles, Brother Decius?" Gallienus asked.

"I am, Your Eminence." Indeed, I guess nearly every Roman citizen has heard the divination that the Republic's supremacy will last twelve centuries only, each one represented by an eagle. Even the masses must have heard it bandied about in the bars and streets of the bustling Aventine Quarter in recent times, as the Visigoths rule Rome in all but name and other hordes conquer more and more of the Roman provinces every day. Oh, but this is old, sad news to us true Romans.

"Then you know that twelve centuries of the Roman Empire's rule as foretold by the twelve eagles are nearly at an end?"

I paused before answering. I hate to speak ill of a fellow Christian, but the elite Gallienus is known for his wiles and I feared that the question was a trap. If I admitted to an awareness of the prophecy and the few years remaining on it, I could well be confessing to giving credence to pagan lore—a punishable confession, since Christianity was proclaimed the state religion almost one hundred years ago, as you know well.

I delivered a measured response. "I do, Your Eminence. Yet I also know that such prophecy is but heretical conjecture spoken by the masses."

Gallienus stared long at me, never blinking but keeping his eyes hooded in shadow such that I could not read his reaction. Then he nodded slowly and said, "That is true, Brother Decius. Still, we must be prepared."

"Of course, Your Eminence." Wary of this man, I was apprehensive of accusations that I had discounted the empire's military might with my answer. So I said, "Though the empire maintains a vast army."

"We cannot leave the fate of the Roman Christian Church to Emperor Anthemius's troops, can we, Brother Decius?"

Understanding that Gallienus' question brooked no response other than agreement, I said, "No, Your Eminence. We cannot leave the fate of the Roman Christian Church to the Roman army."

"I am glad we are of like mind, Brother Decius. Heartily glad."

I watched Gallienus saunter around the pope's chamber as if it belonged to him, pausing to touch the gilt arms of the papal throne and the intricate wall mosaic of birds in flight. As he gazed out between columns to the surging metropolis below, still crowded with marble temples and colonnaded forums dedicated to the pagan gods, despite the edict banning their worship, I waited for my mission.

"We must secure the land of the Gaels, Brother Decius," Gallienus pronounced without turning back toward me.

"The desolate isle beyond Britannia, Your Eminence?" My brother, I regretted the question the moment it slipped from my tongue. I knew, of course, where the Gaelic land lay, but I could not believe that the church would trouble itself with the unimportant, rocky outcropping on the precipice of the known world, an island so inconsequential that Rome did not bother to colonize it even in the Republic's prime. Not to mention that with Gael's lack of a central ruler, subduing its countless chieftains would have required over fifty thousand troops, which Rome could ill afford due to mounting pressures on nearly all other frontiers. But I did not want the man to think I was a fool or, worse, an insubordinate in need of punishment.

"The very same," Gallenius answered without rebuke or surprise at my response. He faced me. "Rumors are surfacing that its chieftains are uniting in power under the newly formed Christian monasteries. This news would be hailed—indeed, we always embrace new sheep in our flock—but for the reports that the Gaelic brand of Christianity is rife with heresy. We would not want Gael to unify under a Pelagian Christianity, now, would we? We must determine whether these reports bear truth."

Gallienus did not continue with any details, though, of course, I had long heard rumblings about Pelagius, the rebel monk from Britannia who had maintained that original sin does not exist and that man has free

will, a belief condemned by the church's Council of
Ephesus in 431.

"Would Bishop Patrick not be able to serve in this
regard?" The Roman Christian Church had sent
Patrick to Gael as a missionary some years before, in
an unprecedented posting. The church had never
before assigned a missionary to an uncolonized land,
but Patrick had made constant, persuasive arguments
about God calling him to convert the people who had
once enslaved him.

"Inexplicably, Bishop Patrick is too enamored with
the Gaelic people to report upon them objectively."
Gallienus then made a broad gesture toward me.

I finished for him, as he clearly wished: "You would
like me to make this appraisal, Your Eminence."

"Yes, Brother Decius. I wish you to study a particular abbey that grows in power, the Abbey of
Kildare." He paused and then asked, "Do you understand the critical importance of this work?"

"I welcome Your Eminence's wisdom." I felt the
need to remain guarded in my responses, though I
had begun to intuit his designs.

"If, in fact, the Gaelic monasteries and churches
preach heresy as charged, we must stamp out the
leaders of this profanation and replace them with
our own. Only then can we unite this disjointed,
backward land under the true Christian faith and
present it as a tribute to the emperor. To help him
bolster the empire and . . . " He left the sentence
unfinished.

"And, in turn, bolster the church, Your Eminence?" He seemed to want me to say this aloud.

"You do see, Brother Decius. I am well pleased."

And see I did, when he put it so plainly. The Roman Church stands on increasingly unsteady ground as the Roman government falters. It needs to shore itself against the barbarian onslaught by routing out all heresy. Efforts to keep the remote island fully Roman Catholic could prevent it from becoming barbarian—and create a fitting honorarium for the Roman emperor in the process.

Gallienus sidled up near me, drawing so close that, despite the early hour, I could smell his sour, wine-laden breath. "Do you wonder at your selection for this task?"

I lowered my head, away from his probing stare and his stench. "I trust in the sagacity of God, Pope Simplicius, and his learned councillors, Your Eminence."

Gallienus smiled. "Always cautious, Brother Decius. Almost as cautious as myself. It will serve you well." The smile vanished, leaving an unpleasant grimace on his lips. "We chose you not for your ardent faith or your private hatred of the barbarians, though you have both of these excellent qualities in abundance. We chose you because we need a scribe."

My dear brother, the light fades, and the horses assemble for the long journey. I have not the time to complete the description of my encounter with Gallienus or my mission to the Gaelic land, though I suspect you would reel at the notion of your pious, careful younger brother, whom you always protected as you dashed off on some adventure of your own design, heading off into the dark unknown. I pray with fervence to our Lord that He will deliver unto me the means to transport this letter to you. Until then, I will be in His hands. Pray for me, brother, as I pray for you.

Decius